THE DEVIL'S CIRCLE

Cover design by Opalworks Pte Ltd

This edition published 2011 by
Marshall Cavendish Editions
An imprint of Marshall Cavendish International
1 New Industrial Road, Singapore 536196

Other Marshall Cavendish Offices:
Marshall Cavendish International. PO Box 65829 London EC1P 1NY, UK • Marshall Cavendish Corporation. 99 White Plains Road, Tarrytown NY 10591-9001, USA • Marshall Cavendish International (Thailand) Co Ltd. 253 Asoke, 12th Flr, Sukhumvit 21 Road, Klongtoey Nua, Wattana, Bangkok 10110, Thailand • Marshall Cavendish (Malaysia) Sdn Bhd, Times Subang, Lot 46, Subang Hi-Tech Industrial Park, Batu Tiga, 40000 Shah Alam, Selangor Darul Ehsan, Malaysia.

National Library Board, Singapore Cataloguing-in-Publication Data
Woon, Walter C. M.
The devil's circle / Walter Woon. – Singapore : Marshall Cavendish Editions, 2011.
p. cm. – (The advocate's devil trilogy ; bk. III)
ISBN : 978-981-4302-98-2
1. Singapore – History – 1945-1963 – Fiction. I. Title. II. Series: The advocate's devil trilogy ; bk. III.

PR9570.S53
S823 — dc22 OCN742442518

Printed in Singapore by Fabulous Printers Pte Ltd

For my dear boys Adrian and Alex

1

FOR those of us who survived it, the War exists as a great gash in our memory. It was as if some giant hand had reached in, scooped out three and a half years of our lives and left a complete void. In the dim past was "Before the War", when life was simple and well-ordered. "After the War" was different. I had watched the DUKWs filled with troops dispensing chocolates and cigarettes roaring down Joo Chiat Road a fortnight after the atomic bombs were dropped. European faces were to be seen in the town once more. After the triumphant Victory Parade at the Padang, the Union Jack again flew proudly over the Municipal Building. The British were back and it seemed that we had come full circle. But the circle wasn't perfect. The Japanese had conquered Singapore; the British hadn't. They had celebrated their triumph, but like Caesar they heard that small voice whispering in their ears that they were but mortal. The natives knew it, happy though we were to have them back after the oppression of the Occupation. They knew that we knew. The long-accepted colonial order was never the same again. All the old certainties were gone.

We picked up our lives slowly, almost in a daze. After living so long on the edge of the sword, normality seemed strange. We were lucky of course. The Surrender spared Singapore the fate of Manila. If the Japanese had fought, there would have been precious few of us left to tell the tale. They wouldn't have given up like the British had in 1942, not as long as there was a single soldier left alive to conduct a banzai charge. General Itagaki Seishiro, the commander of the 7th Area Army in Singapore, refused at first to surrender to the British. His troops were unbeaten in the field. It took a direct order from his superior Field Marshal Count Terauchi to induce him to comply. His code of Bushido pulled him in opposite directions. He would have rather died than given in to an enemy who had not bested him on the battlefield. But the loyalty owed by a samurai to his lord was paramount. He ordered his men to lay down their arms. Even then, three hundred officers committed hara-kiri rather than give up without a fight. The Surrender saved all of us.

The firm of D'Almeida & D'Almeida had re-opened for business right after the British got back, even though the Courts were still shuttered. The British lost no time in instituting military tribunals and invalidating all pending proceedings before the Japanese courts. They invited the local Bar — those who survived — to apply to act as counsel. This we did immediately. With that formality taken care of, the d'Almeida brothers, Clarence and Cuthbert, went upcountry to settle the affairs of the Eurasian colony in Bahau. A year and half before the end of the War the Japanese thought it would be a good idea to start emptying Syonan of useless mouths. The food situation was dire and not likely to get better. Rice had disappeared and we were driven to eating tapioca morning, noon and night. So the Chinese went to Endau in Johore, where the New Syonan colony prospered. The Eurasians and Roman Catholics went to Bahau, deep in the *ulu* in Negeri Sembilan, lured by promises of Eden. The Fuji Village colony was badly conceived and worse resourced. It was miles from the railhead, in malaria-infested virgin jungle. When Archbishop Devals died the whole project fell apart. The War ended soon after, thankfully. It wasn't long before the recriminations started. Clarence and Cuthbert were called in to help sort out the mess.

They left the firm in the steady hands of my good friend George Singam, who had been made junior partner just before the Japanese took over, and the not-so-steady hands of Simon da Silva. Simon had left the practice before the War and become a journalist, but he had returned to support Clarence d'Almeida in his hour of need, or so he put it. Raja Aziz, the other partner of the firm, was dead. He was shot in Farrer Park with other officers of the Malay Regiment who had refused to forswear their allegiance to the British. Anyway, for good or ill (mostly ill), Simon was senior partner while the d'Almeida brothers were away. I was the senior legal assistant; in fact, I was the only legal assistant.

Ralph Smallwood, the other legal assistant, was yet to be demobilised. He'd returned with the vanguard of the British forces, parachuting in heroically with his Gurkhas just after the atomic bombs had been dropped, to help restore order in the vacuum that the Japanese surrender left. But Ralph wasn't sure he wanted to come back to the firm. Ralph, George and I had started off at the same time with d'Almeida. In fact, Ralph and George were exact contemporaries. Though he hadn't said it, the fact that George was a partner rankled. George was in fact related to the d'Almeidas on his mother's side, but that wasn't why he had been made a junior partner. The fact of the matter is that George was smarter than all of us and we knew it. I had accepted my lot. Ralph hadn't.

He hadn't decided whether to stay in the Colony or return to Perth, where his wife and daughter were. Ralph had married my cousin May. Baby Grace had come along just before the war. Surrounded by Mak, Ah Sum and four doting aunts, Baby Grace had been the centre of the family. She was the little sun around which all revolved. When the shooting started, May went back to nursing. She worked first with the British and then with the

Indian Army Field Hospital at Tyersall. The Japs had destroyed that in the last days before the surrender. The nurses were ordered to leave rather than trust to the tender mercies of the invaders. I gave Ralph my ticket so that he could be with his family. They had gotten out practically on the last boat from Singapore. That parting was the hardest of all for Mak to bear. We all prayed that he would bring May and the baby home now that the war was over. But he needed a job, and a job serving under George was not what he wanted.

As for the rest of the firm, we were sadly depleted in numbers. Moraiss, the Chief Clerk, was missing. He had gone up to Bahau with his whole family. They hadn't prospered. Carving out a township in the middle of the jungle wasn't the healthiest of pursuits. The land was marginal and barely suited for agriculture. Disease was rife. Food was scarce. There had been deaths in the clan. I heard that Moraiss himself came down with cerebral malaria. It was touch and go. We hadn't any news of him.

Our chief interpreter, Tan Peng Ann, died early in the Occupation, of a broken heart when his only son didn't come back from the Sook Ching operation. That left a gaping hole in the firm, as he was the one that we all depended on to translate from Chinese to English. I was in fact the only Chinese lawyer in the firm, but when it came to dialects they might as well have asked me to speak Phoenician. Tan was our constant prop. With him gone, we were deaf and mute.

D'Almeida's syce Ahmad had gone back to his kampong when the island fell and no one knew where he was now, or if he was even still alive. But there were still many old faces in the musty rooms of the firm. And Singh, the *jaga*, was there. His quiet bulk at the door was reassuring. Life could go on.

"HAVE you had a look at the obituaries today?" asked George early one morning, barging into my room without so much as a by-your-leave.

"No," I replied grumpily, "if your name's not there I'm not interested." Generally, I could only take George in small doses before breakfast.

"Well, have a look," he said, "It's our friend Lao Leong Ann. He's finally popped off." He tossed the newspaper over to me. My cousin June, who had joined us as a general do-it-all during the war, deftly caught it and scanned the page eagerly. June had decided that she would like to be a lawyer and took every opportunity to improve her education.

"So?" I responded callously. Death left me unmoved. We had seen too much in the preceding four years.

"So we shall soon have a visitation, I imagine," said George. "He died intestate. There were no children. But there will be relatives, lots of them."

"He died intestate. There were no children," said June slowly, as if trying to understand something. "Does that mean that he had no ... he had no ... no ..." Her cheeks reddened.

"He had no will," I interposed shortly.

"Oh, so that is what 'intestate' means," she said, with apparent relief.

"Why, what did you think it meant?"

"Nothing, nothing," she replied, quietly repeating to herself, "intestate ... no will."

"No will, plenty of money, a gaggle of relatives," said George, "There will be business for the courts, you mark my words."

"Consider them marked and leave me in peace," I responded, moodily flipping to the obituaries. George left me to it. The obituaries filled pages and made grim reading. Mostly, they recorded deaths that had occurred months or even years before but had only just been confirmed. Lao Leong Ann's obituary stood out, recording as it did a fresh death.

Lao Leong Ann was one of those rare people who had profited from the Occupation. He had made an indecent pile buying property left behind by those who had escaped or disappeared. I had met him in the course of my work during the War. He had moved in exalted social circles and was treated by the Japanese as a friend; as much as any Chinaman could be a friend. When the Surrender came, so did retribution. A MPAJA death squad had caught him during the interregnum before the British returned. Whether by design or not, they hadn't finished him off at once. He had lingered on in hospital since then. I couldn't truthfully say that I was sorry.

GEORGE was prescient, as he usually is. Within a week, Simon had dumped the file into my lap for action.

"Mr Lao Leong Ann's Clan Association has been in touch. There is a son," said Simon. "They want us to protect his interests."

"I thought Mr Lao had no children," said June, "He died intestate."

A look of puzzlement flitted across Simon's brow, but that soon passed. "No natural children," he explained, "but he and his late wife adopted a boy before she passed away. All nicely legal, you understand, none of this informal customary adoption business. Cuthbert d'Almeida handled all the formalities. It was after I left the firm, you see."

"So the son gets everything under the law of intestacy," I said, "what's the problem? Why drag us into it?" I wasn't particularly keen on the administration of estates. If I must deal with dead people, I'd rather have a murder any time.

"Ah, but the boy is an infant. He's five. He needs to be guided and advised. Lao Leong Ann left instructions with the Clan that they should get in touch with Cuthbert to take care of young Gim Huat should anything happen to him. He must have had a premonition, the poor fellow."

I forebore to say that the poor fellow had it coming to him and took the file resignedly. As always when I have no idea where to start, I went to George.

"The first thing we do, my son," he said, "is to have a dekko at the body in question. I'm told on good authority that they are having some sort of ceremony for the old villain at his place today. It's at 3 o'clock. We can make it if we leave now."

"What's the rush?" I asked, "He's not going anywhere."

George clicked his tongue. "Always remember that when attending a wake one should arrive dead on time and looking very grave."

2

LAO LEONG ANN did not live in ostentatious style, despite his wealth. It would have been tempting the gods to be seen to splash out too much; or, more prosaically, tempting the Japanese and the Communists. He had been moderately rich before the War, trading in this and that. It was during the Occupation that his fortune was made. He started off selling tyres and other army surplus items to the Japanese army. There were piles just lying around for the taking when the British and Australians left so precipitately. Lao had been quicker off the mark than most and got his hands on the good stuff. The Japanese were ever ready to acquire extra food, bedding, shoes and whatever. The less scrupulous ones just took what they fancied from the dead and living. But there were enough honest ones to make Lao's business profitable.

From his contacts he got the opportunity to cheaply snap up several shophouses whose owners were no longer to be found. Some were dead no doubt, but several were Chinese whose names were on the Kempeitai death-list as members of the China Relief Fund. They had gotten out before the Fall. Lao knew a good thing when he saw it. He made sure that his contacts were kept well supplied with black-market goodies and other amusements. They returned the favour by tipping him off whenever there was an opportunity to pick up a house or shop. All the conveyancing had been handled by D'Almeida & D'Almeida. Lao Leong Ann was a good client, whatever his merits as a human being may have been.

His wake was held in one of the shophouses he owned in Jim Chuan Place. The whole row was his, rented out to various tenants. They were crammed six, eight, ten to a room, one body piled above another like firewood. Whole families shared a single windowless cubicle, taking turns to lie on what passed for a bed. A single terrace unit might have had forty people in it, sharing a communal kitchen and one toilet. Not the least profitable among his other activities was the comfort house that he kept for his Japanese clients, staffed by women from Korea and China — some willing but mostly press-ganged. They had a little more room, as their trade demanded. Lao Leong Ann had lived alone with his son in the flat above his shop. Compared to his tenants and employees, his living quarters were palatial.

The first thing that assailed me when we stepped through the shophouse portal was the smell of burning joss sticks. The place was dark, hot and crowded, with small knots of people sitting around tables, drinking, smoking and playing cards and mah-jong. The air was thick with incense and tobacco smoke. A desultory wailing filled the room. It had an odd theatrical quality to it, as if the mourners hadn't quite got their hearts in it. The huge wooden coffin dominated the room. It was of expensive mahogany polished to a silken sheen, with a richly embroidered blue cover. An elaborate wooden funeral arch draped with silk curtains stood in front of the coffin. On a table laden with offerings was a photograph of the late lamented deceased, flanked by two gigantic candles in ornate bronze holders. It was apparent that no one had told Lao that you can't take it with you. Piled high in front of the offering table were intricately-made paper models of houses, cars, gold bars and other worldly paraphenalia. And not just any old house or car, but at least one mansion complete with Sikh *jaga* and what clearly was meant to be a Rolls-Royce. He evidently intended to live it up in the afterlife.

We arrived just in time for the ceremony. A priest in white robes appeared and began to chant. His acolyte punctuated the chanting by striking a little gong every now and then. The crowd fell silent at first, but as no one seemed to be paying much attention to the service they soon resumed their chatter and games, the clack of the mah-jong tiles making a counterpoint to the gong. The priest continued regardless, his monotonous voice ululating in incomprehensible tones. June nudged me in the ribs.

"There," she said, pointing, "the little boy. He must be the son."

The boy, dressed in white sackcloth, was quietly sucking his thumb and looking bewildered. He seemed rather scrawny, but then so did all of us after the privations of the previous years. Next to him sat a black and white *amah*, holding his free hand. We threaded our way between the tables towards him.

We were halfway there when a commotion started. A young woman and some rough-looking types had moved up to the boy. This evidently had not met with the approval of another group, also centred around a young woman. Her equally unsavoury entourage advanced menacingly. Then a third woman appeared, with her own group of goons. They started arguing in loud voices. The bonze continued chanting imperturbably, but the acolyte missed a couple of beats on his little gong.

Voices were raised. The three women apparently were quarrelling over the boy, who looked uncomprehendingly from one to another. He clung close to his *amah*, who shielded him with her body. Some of the more timid — or sensible — mourners decided that it was time to leave. Fists were balled. I thought I saw the glint of steel. George pushed forward to the boy, dragging me with him against my better judgment. He held up his hands.

"Ladies and gentlemen," he said, " we represent the estate of the deceased Lao Leong Ann. We've been appointed to protect the interest of Gim Huat, who is the only heir."

June had moved to take custody of the boy, daring the others to come near with her flashing eyes. The *amah* was holding him in her arms, but relinquished his hand when June put hers out to take it. I positioned myself near them, trying to look menacing but not provocative. My palms were sweating.

George was assailed from three sides by the women, all speaking at the same time. He shook his head at them. "Can't understand a word, ladies," he said, "not a word." He turned to me interrogatively. I shook my head and looked to June.

"Why you look at me?" asked June, holding the boy, "You know my Hokkien is half-past-six."

"I speak English," said a young man who materialised at June's side. He seemed to be about my age, but thin and tough. His clothes were worn and patched.

"Good," said June, "what is the problem?"

"The three woman are the boy's mother."

"What do you mean that the three women are the boy's mother?" asked George.

"They all say they are the boy's mother. She want to take him. The other one say no. Then that one also say she take the boy."

A lightbulb flashed in George's brain. "Aha, I get it," he said. "They've all realised that he'll inherit the lot. So now they all claim to be his mother." He turned to our newly-found interpreter. "Tell them that we'll take custody of the boy. They can all turn up at our office to make their claims."

A hubbub greeted this announcement. George motioned to June, "Take the kid and let's get out of here before things turn nasty." She nodded and started leading Gim Huat away. He held on to her with one grubby paw and to his *amah* with the other. People may have been unhappy, but no one made a move to stop us. Evidently, each faction thought it preferable to have Gim Huat taken away by us than by any of the others. The chanting continued, undisturbed by the worldly commotion.

WHEN we got back to the office we discovered that we had managed to pick up not only the boy but also his *amah*, who displayed a tenacious adhesive quality. Gim Huat apparently could not be physically separated from her. She held on to his hand even when he was passed around by June to me while she went off to get some food.

"You do realise that we've deprived Lao of his chief mourner," I remarked to George, looking dubiously at the boy. He didn't seem to be about to burst into tears or chew my finger off or do something unspeakable which my *dhobi* would regret, but one never knew.

"Not to worry," he rejoined, "the old reprobate isn't going to miss him. From what I could see he had mourners enough. With his kind of money he isn't going to lack for people to weep and wail at his wake. I'm sure it's all been taken care of."

This was true. If a man's passing did not evoke the proper amount of grief amongst his relatives, friends and hangers-on, professional wailers could be hired by the dozen, as befitted the rank and prestige of the dearly departed.

June returned with British Army-issue oatmeal biscuits, which she passed around. "Let's take stock," said George. "We have one child, of tender age and doubtful hygiene; one *amah*, who apparently cannot be removed from the said child except by surgery; three mothers, each of whom seems to have a gang of goons to back up her claim. It looks like it's up to the two of us to sort out this tangle, as usual."

June interjected, "What about me? You think I am here only to get biscuits or what?"

"Correction, we three," conceded George graciously. "The first thing is to find out exactly what is going on." He turned to our impromptu interpreter, who had somehow contrived to attach himself to our party when we left the wake. "And your name is ...?"

"Yeo Eng Tong," he replied shortly. ""You have work for me?" he asked. "I need work. I can do many things."

"I haven't any doubt of that," replied George. "How many dialects can you speak?"

"Hokkien, Teochew, Cantonese," he replied. "Little Malay, Japanese."

"What were you doing at Lao's house?"

"I work for Towkay Lao," he replied. George raised his eyebrows interrogatively. Eng Tong continued, a little reluctantly, "When people owe Towkay money, I collect. Sometimes I have to persuade them to pay."

I looked him over. He wasn't very large, but he was tough and taut as a spring. His arms were tanned and sinewy. He seemed to be quite the persuasive sort. I could imagine that few debtors would care to argue with Eng Tong, especially in a dark alley.

"Right," said George, "you're hired. We need an interpreter. You're it. Now, tell us what's up with this lot. Who is the boy's real mother?"

Eng Tong, it transpired, helped with old Lao's accounts but was not privy to any family secrets. As far as he knew, young Gim Huat was Lao's son. It had come as a surprise to him to discover that the boy had been adopted. It was only when Lao died that this had become an issue. He and his wife had no other living children. They adopted Gim Huat legally just before she passed away, as we already knew. Everything would go to the boy, but someone had to look after him and the estate until he came of age. This was when things got interesting. First the woman Ah Moy had appeared claiming to be his mother. She was followed in short order by another one, Ah Kwan, and then by a third, Ah Siew. Each of them was supported by a group of Lao's business associates. It wasn't entirely clear what business they and Lao were associated in. Eng Tong heard that they had secret society connections, but he knew better than to evince an unhealthy curiousity. Curiousity of this sort didn't kill only cats.

In the absence of any kin, Lao's clan association had taken care of the last rites. Normally, this would have been the prerogative of the widow and the eldest son. The three claimants didn't qualify, since Lao hadn't taken any of them as a secondary wife. The only hold that they each had was a personal one, as supposed mother to his heir. The Clan ignored this, totally irrelevant as it was to the funeral arrangements. They would in due course adjudicate on the merits of each claim; or more precisely, submit the matter to the courts when they re-opened. In the meantime each mother watched the others warily, jostling for advantage, trying to win the boy's confidence. This had gone on too long for some. Tempers were fraying. A lot of money was at stake. It was only our fortuitous appearance that had prevented the jostling from turning into something far more physical.

"So what's next?" I asked when Eng Tong had finished.

"So we get the three women here and thrash it out. Figuratively speaking, of course," said George.

3

THE meeting of the three mothers was duly called for the morrow. Simon, as senior partner *ad interim* decided that he should preside. George was to interview the elders of the Clan Association. I half suspected that Simon did not feel entirely secure about his position and needed to exert his authority over George, whose attitude towards him was subtly dismissive without being overtly offensive. Besides, Simon laboured under the delusion that his forensic skills could break the hardest case. Unfortunately, he had a mind like a bowl of spaghetti; strands kept getting tied up in knots and falling in a mess all over the place. I wasn't sanguine.

It had been decided that the boy and his *amah* should stay with us in the meantime. I don't recall having been consulted. June more or less took it as a given. We had a biggish house in Cavanagh Road, with empty rooms. May had escaped with her baby and husband. We didn't speak of Julie and her husband. The last news we had was that they were somewhere in the vicinity of Nagasaki. Even now Mak nursed the hope that by some miracle they had survived the Bomb. The end of the war was for us a very mixed blessing.

Our appearance with the child did lighten Mak's mood. It had been a long time since there had been children in the house. Gim Huat was shy and the *amah* reticent. We entrusted them to the care of our own black and white *amah*, Ah Sum. Mak and my eldest cousin Gek Neo soon had them in hand. June fussed around too, her mother-hen instincts having been thoroughly aroused. Only my youngest cousin Augusta remained unmoved. She and Julie had been very close. Since the end of the War she had retreated to her room and stayed there. The appearance of new people in the house did nothing to draw her out.

Since I was very much superfluous, I wandered out into the garden to check on the plants. Like everyone else, we had been forced to grow our own food. The ubiquitous *ubi kayu* or tapioca filled up much of the space. We also had sweet potatoes and yams, besides fruits from our mangosteen and *nangka* trees. Generally, we were well off as far as food supplies were concerned; and the neighbours muttered darkly that my job with the Japanese helped. This was a sore point with me, but d'Almeida had sworn us to secrecy about our wartime activities. It rankled nonetheless to be thought of as a collaborator, though the people that counted knew the truth. Unfortunately, the people who didn't count spread malicious tales, which grew more lurid in the re-telling. I tried not to think about it and threw myself into the work of keeping the vegetable beds in good order. Food was still scarce, and our garden provided us not only a supply for the table but also a welcome income.

The whole economy had reverted to barter. One of the first acts of the incoming military administration was to declare the Japanese currency valueless. Inflation had already made it practically worthless; especially as the Japanese seemed to have no idea about fiscal discipline. They just kept printing the notes as if there was no tomorrow; perhaps they already knew something even then. A *kati* of pork which had cost 30 cents pre-war was going for $1,500 in banana money at the end — assuming of course that any was to be had. Prices had fallen since the re-occupation, but even with food control the official cost was some 40 per cent higher than before the war. The official fixed prices were ignored by hawkers and market vendors right from the start. It was a matter of take it or leave it. Most had to leave it. Few had any savings left. Malayan notes were just coming back into circulation. Cigarettes were used as currency instead. People would price goods in cigarettes, which was fine with me. The returning soldiers were liberal with their ration of tobacco and we got a steady supply from Ralph. Since I didn't smoke, I was thankfully spared the temptation of burning the currency of the day.

We had a frugal dinner, enlivened by the company of Gim Huat. The boy had thawed out somewhat. He had hardly been let out of the house when his father was alive. Apparently, old man Lao feared that someone might kidnap him for ransom. He hired Ah Moy's lot as a sort of informal bodyguard. This information had been gradually prised out of Ah Fong, the boy's *amah*, by the combined efforts of June, Gek Neo and Ah Sum. She was more closed-mouth than an oyster and uncomfortable to be in strange surroundings. Gim Huat on the other hand bounded up and down the stairs, poking himself in all the little nooks and crannies. I looked at him with pity. He hadn't had much of a childhood, a virtual prisoner cooped up in that dank terrace house with his father. He romped around like any other five-year-old, totally unaware of the storm that was brewing around him.

MY confidence in Simon's abilities was fully justified. June gave us the gory details. She had been present at the meeting as Gim Huat's chaperone. He seemed to have taken to her. "All three say they are the mother. They showed photographs. No one could recognise him. It is hard to tell one baby from another. They called him baby names. They tried to take him. He did not want to go to any of them. Everybody was shouting at the same time. Poor Mr Simon could not make his voice heard. "

"What did poor Mr Simon expect?" said George scathingly. "That two of them would back out gracefully and toddle off home quietly?"

"We're just lucky he didn't suggest cutting the boy into thirds," I said gloomily. "Anything from the Clan?"

"No, not much," reported George, giving us a quick run-down. Ah Moy had turned up claiming to be Gim Huat's real mother. A meeting of the elders had been called, at which it transpired that there was another claimant, Ah Kwan. The elders could not come to a decision. Some were for Ah Moy but a significant group felt that Ah Kwan had the better claim. A couple of days later Ah Siew's bunch turned up. This was too much for the elders. They washed their hands of the matter. Let the civil courts decide.

"This doesn't get us anywhere," I said.

"It is worse," added June. "By the end all three were so angry they almost fought in the office. Eng Tong says that there will be trouble."

"Trouble?" asked George.

"Eng Tong says that now each gang wants to take over everything," explained June. "They are not going to share. They will fight."

"Well, too bad for old Simon," said George, "he's welcome to the whole mess and jolly good luck to him."

"Mr Simon said to tell you that you should look after Gim Huat," said June, with an impish twinkle in her eye, "since you are the one who took him here. He will send the file back."

George promptly detonated. "It will not be so bad," said June imperturbably. "He is a nice little boy. We can do it. We must get him ready for tomorrow."

"Tomorrow?" asked George, "What's going on tomorrow?"

"Tomorrow is the funeral," replied June. "He is the eldest son. He will lead the procession."

George let out a growl of untranslatable swear-words.

LAO LEONG ANN'S funeral procession stretched a quarter of a mile along the road. It was an impressive sight, with a brass band, wailing mourners, chanting priests, beating gongs and masses of hangers-on along for the spectacle. Despite petrol rationing, his elaborate wooden coffin was borne in state by a lorry decked out with a gigantic confection topped by a lion. Lao was being sent off in real style, the like of which had not been seen for the last four years. In front of it all was the little boy, walking hand-in-hand with June on one side and his *amah* on the other.

George had decided that he would keep the lorry driver company. I was consigned to keep an eye on the heir. The three mothers and their groups were engaged in a sort of slow race, each trying to get in front of the others. They elbowed the clan elders out of the way, much to the annoyance these august personages. There seemed to be an unseemly grunting and cursing just behind me, but I didn't look back. I steadfastly refused to give way and kept my eye steadily on the chief mourner and his two escorts.

The day was hot and the walk to the cemetery took forever. It was out in the far west along Jurong Road. I was fainting with thirst and fatigue by the time we got to the gravesite. Lao had a premium spot on a hillside with a view of the sea. Not a bad place for a house, actually. The priests renewed their chanting and clanging and sprinkling, while the paid mourners intensified their wailing in counterpoint. There wasn't much shade. I placed my handkerchief on my head and kept it in place by putting my hat over it; not the most elegant of funeral costumes but it kept the sun off. After what seemed a lifetime, the din reached a crescendo and they finally lowered the coffin into the grave.

We started back. I found myself among Ah Moy's group, which had managed to push its way to just behind Gim Huat. It was only after we had left the cemetery that I really looked around. I had a strange sense of *déjà vu*. It was with a shock that

I realised I had been this way before, back in '42. I'd attached myself to Dalforce, a last forlorn hope of Chinese volunteers whose job it was to keep the Japanese off the island. It was here that we had taken our positions to repel the invasion. Dalforce was decimated. I survived only because I had the good luck to have had a grenade chucked at me by someone with a grudge. The grenade killed the man next to me but I came out of it with only concussion, which got me transferred to a hospital before the balloon went up. Good thing too. The Japs overran our positions and wiped out the Chinese volunteers almost to a man. I was still thinking of grenades when I heard a metallic clang and a small oval object bounced onto the road right in front of me and Ah Moy.

"Grenade!" yelled someone. My mind went numb as I braced myself for the explosion. Without thinking, I kicked it as hard as I could. It bounced down the road and clattered to a stop. I threw myself down. The seconds went by. Nothing. Next thing I knew I was being hauled to my feet and patted on the back. June was hugging me. "So brave! You saved us!"

The hubbub was intense. A crowd had gathered round the grenade, which just lay there looking dangerously inert. George came panting up. "That was a damned stupid heroic thing to do. What were you thinking?"

"Heroic be damned," I answered shakily. I still hadn't recovered the use of my vocal chords. Some idiot started prodding the grenade with a stick. "Tell them to get away," I croaked, "and for heaven's sake stop fooling around with the damned thing. It could go off anytime."

Eng Tong, who had found his way to us, translated and the crowd melted away like magic. I saw Ah Moy being led off by her people, looking fiercely around for the other two groups, who seemed to have vanished completely.

"I didn't think it would come to this," I said when we'd gotten to a respectable distance. "Trying to kill a little boy. We're dealing with some pretty nasty types."

"Not the boy," said George grimly. "You were walking with Ah Moy's gang. That grenade landed exactly where it was supposed to. We've got a war on our hands."

4

LAW and order in the Colony were precarious at best. Most of the old Sikh police had gone over to the Japanese. When the British got back, they packed the lot off to India. The Malay policemen had made themselves scarce the moment the Japanese surrendered, not wanting to tangle with the MPAJA. They barricaded themselves in their barracks and stations and waited until the Allied troops turned up. The British had troops stationed at strategic spots all over the Peninsula, but there weren't enough of them and their main priority was to deal with the repatriation of the white former prisoners. The Japanese had been herded into holding camps, where they waited impassively to hear what their fate might be. The last thing that the authorities would bother about was a little gang war among the Chinese.

After that first attack, Ah Moy's group lay low. She had the smallest and weakest faction, and evidently thought that they would come out third best in any trial of strength. The same couldn't be said for the other two. As far as we knew, Ah Siew's gang had struck first. It started with a backyard ambush. Heads were broken, limbs were hacked. In retaliation, Molotov cocktails were thrown into her den. Blood called for blood. Each attack had to be repaid with interest, in the time-honoured tradition of vendetta. There were enough weapons lying around to fuel prolonged hostilities. Casualties started piling up with disturbing regularity. But in the general confused state of affairs, no one else took much notice, least of all the British.

"This has got to stop," said George firmly after about a week of bloodletting and a dozen casualties, "before someone gets killed."

"How?" I replied morosely. "They're not going to see sense. Life is cheap and Lao's fortune will buy a lot of lives."

"If we find the real mother," said June slowly, "will the others stop? I do not think that any of them is Gim Huat's mother. They do not care for him, only for the money."

"Why should they stop?" I responded. "After all, if it's the money they're after, they aren't likely to quietly let the real mother take the whole lot."

"No, no, June's got something there," said George. "Right now, their only claim to the fortune is through Gim Huat. If the real mother were to turn up, that would destroy any legal basis to their claims. Killing the mother won't get them the money. We'd just get a guardian appointed. They may be ruthless, but I don't think they're stupid."

"So, how do we find the mother?"

"Is her name in the files?" ventured June.

"Bright girl!" said George. "Off to the archives!"

We spent the whole afternoon going through the archives. The only one who really understood the filing system was Moraiss, and he was off in the *ulu* — assuming that he was still alive. More by divine providence than skill, we managed to track down the original adoption documents. There was a name, barely legible.

"Chan Sew Neo," read June. "Is it Ah Siew?"

"It could be anyone," I rejoined. "The name's no good without the Chinese characters. There's nothing to go on here, no address, no details."

"We'll just have to find her," said George.

"You want us to go out and find one Chinese female on

Singapore island with just a name and nothing else?" I responded. "Talk about looking for a noodle in a haystack!"

"Ah, but we do have something," said George. "According to this note here, Cuthbert went to fetch the baby."

"Cuthbert's away upcountry," I reminded him, "and by the time he gets back we'll be neck deep in bodies. It's a miracle that no one's been killed yet."

"But Cuthbert didn't go alone, did he?" responded George. "He would have been driven."

"Ahmad!"

"Yes, Ahmad. He'll be able to tell us where they picked up the goods," said George. "We'll find your noodle, just you wait."

AHMAD had been with the d'Almeidas for years. He was the faithful syce, who drove Clarence d'Almeida all over the island and the Malay states. Clarence d'Almeida had "retired" to do a little clandestine intelligence work just before the War. Cuthbert had then taken Ahmad over. When the British surrendered the shutters came down on the firm. Cuthbert told him to look out for his family. No one had seen him since. We found that people's knowledge of the private lives of others was lamentably sketchy. Most of the staff of the firm were old-timers. They had been together since heaven-knows-when. But when they left the office at five, off they went in their different directions to their separate lives. All that anyone knew of Ahmad was that he lived somewhere out west, in a kampong near the sea and next to a school. We got general directions and a description of the landmarks to look out for.

Armed with this rather meagre information, June and I set out on our journey to the west in search of the elusive Ahmad. The STC trolley buses ran to limited destinations, fanning out from Finlayson Green to Geylang, Katong and Paya Lebar. In the west only Tanjong Pagar was served. The old Chinese bus companies had yet to get back on their feet. Taxis were virtually non-existent given the fuel situation. The one useful innovation that the Japanese had introduced was the trishaw. In place of the old burly rickshaw pullers, they had cobbled a bicycle to the frame of a rickshaw. This was the only practical way to get around.

It wasn't difficult to find a trishaw rider willing to undertake the long journey out of town. Money was scarce and a man had to eat. We paid him with cigarettes and a handful of *kangkong*. The trishaw rider looked like an articulated skeleton. I cast a doubtful eye over him. He didn't look like he would make it to the foot of the hill where we lived, much less into the countryside. I said so to June. "When he cannot ride any more, you can take over," she responded unsympathetically.

We passed the old docks, looking much the worse for wear. The Japanese had bombed them mercilessly when war broke out. During the Occupation, it was the turn of the Americans. B-29 Superfortresses from India had come over during the last years of the war and unloaded their bombs on the harbour. From the ground, they were little shining specks of silver, contrails streaming through the rarified air. The Japanese fighters would scramble hoping to catch them, but the Oscars didn't have the speed to reach the Superfortresses. These raids had buoyed our spirits, even though a misplaced bomb-load meant death to the onlookers.

After an hour and a half we finally came to a lone concrete pillbox commanding a long stretch of sand. A stream met the sea at this point. A couple of hundred yards beyond it was a one-storey school building. This was the landmark that we had been looking out for.

"Stop," said June to the trishaw rider. "Go back to the stream. We get out there. You wait for us." The trishawman nodded and settled his frame comfortably. He took a cigarette and lighted it. A look of contentment suffused his face. We could take our time.

The path followed the small stream. It was sandy underfoot, bordered with nipah palms. Scrawny chickens scampered out of our way. We crossed a plank bridge to the kampong itself, a cluster of wooden huts in the usual Malay style, on stilts with attap roofs. There were no fences as such but the tapioca plants formed hedges around some of the houses, with flowering hibiscus shrubs among the coconut palms and bamboo groves.

June called out to a young Malay woman who was doing her washing on the banks of the stream. Her Malay was much better than mine. People said that I spoke with the accent of an *Orang Puteh*, which either provoked merriment or hostility depending on the audience.

"Good afternoon kak," said June politely, "we are looking for Enchik Ahmad."

The young woman ceased her work. Drying her hands, she came up. "There are many men named Ahmad in the kampong."

"Ahmad bin Johari," June continued. "the syce. He worked for a lawyer in town until the War. Then he went back to his kampong."

The woman nodded her head in affirmation. Gesturing to us to follow, she led the way through the maze of little paths. There were no road signs or house numbers. It was a postman's worst nightmare. No stranger would have had a chance of finding anyone who didn't want to be found. Small children peeped from the doorways, eyeing us curiously.

After about ten minutes, we reached a small *surau* surrounded by a hedge of hibiscus. Our guide paused in front of one of the houses next to it and called out. "Pak Chik, you have visitors." An old man emerged onto the *anjung*. He blinked at us shortsightedly.

"Enchik Ahmad," I called, "it's me, Dennis Chiang. You remember? I worked with Mr d'Almeida."

Recognition came and he beamed at us. "Tuan Dennis, *apa khabar*? It has been a long time." He invited us to come up. We thanked our guide, who left us snickering under her hand at my accent. Slipping off our shoes, we mounted the steps to his *anjung*. The house was typically Malay, raised off the ground on stilts. Underneath were neat piles of firewood. Chickens wandered around scratching for worms. Ahmad's house was comparatively larger and better built than the others. He was considered affluent, having worked for the d'Almeidas for so long. His house had had a zinc roof at one time; the remnants of it poked through the attap. During the War many people sold their zinc roofs to make money and re-thatched in the traditional way with the fronds of the nipah palm. The kitchen abutted the house at the back. This was domain of the womenfolk. They gathered there during the day ostensibly to cook, but it was the place where all the village gossip was exchanged. Kampong folk were naturally sociable. There were no locked doors. The women kept out of sight when strangers were around, so we had no inkling of how many wives or children Ahmad might have had. Guests were received in the *anjung,* sitting cross-legged on mats laid on the bare wooden planks.

When we were comfortably ensconced I made the introductions. He had never met June of course, since she had joined the firm during the War. We Babas have all sorts of words to describe relatives down to the Nth degree of affinity and consanguinity. There is a proper term for the wife of an elder second cousin once removed, and woe betide the careless Baba who forgets. The Malay language doesn't bother with such niceties. One is simply either *abang* or *adek*, depending on who is older. Anyway, to avoid a long convoluted explanation about my rather eccentric family structure, I introduced June simply as my *adek*. She frowned and nudged me in the ribs. June is actually a couple of months older, as she constantly likes to remind me. But I ignored her and proceeded to explain our errand. Ahmad listened intently. His English was as basic as my Malay, so it took a while before we were sure that he understood. At length he nodded.

"I remember Tuan Cuthbert went to fetch a baby," he said slowly, "before the *Jepun* come."

"Yes, that must have been it. Do you recall where?"

"Telok Paku," he replied, his brow creased with the effort, "where the road turns to Changi Point."

"Can you take us there?"

He nodded. "I can drive if there is a car. I cannot go so far by bicycle. I am too old and my muscles are weak."

This was an unanticipated spanner. It was six miles at least from Ahmad's kampong back to the city and maybe ten miles beyond that to Telok Paku. Our sturdy trishawman wasn't likely to take kindly to a journey of that length, whatever the price might have been. In any case, we couldn't have made it before dark. It wasn't wise to stay out late anywhere on the island. While the Japanese were in charge crime was practically unknown. You could leave your front door wide open and no one would dare take anything. Thieves literally lost their heads. The return of the British unloosed a tidal wave of crime, petty and worse. Fear had kept people's baser instincts in check; that fear had gone. The order of the day was survival, and woe to the weak.

"I know where there might be a car," said a soft voice.

Startled, I looked up. A young girl dressed in a *baju kurung* was serving us tea and *kueh*. I hadn't been paying attention. She had a *tudung* over her head, but the hair underneath was blond. And the eyes that gazed at me were sky blue.

I BLINKED. "You're English?"

"Yes, I am," she replied, hesitantly. "It's been so long since I spoke English."

"What is your name?" asked June gently.

"Margaret," she answered in a barely audible voice, hesitating as if uncertain of the words. "Margaret Barron. They used to call me Marge."

Ahmad broke in. "She is Mariam." He continued in Malay, his English having given out. This further explanation flew right over my head. June gave me a running commentary.

"Mariam is his ... how you say? His ward?"

"Ward?" I asked. "You mean he's her guardian?"

"Not guardian, *wali*. I think there is no proper word for it in English. He is her ... her protector," explained June, fumbling for the words. "Pak Chik's mother worked for her family. When the Japanese bombed, they were killed. She was a young child then. They brought her here."

Ahmad's mother worked as a washerwoman and nanny for her family. Marge and her brother knew her as Nenek. A stray bomb destroyed her house. Nenek had pulled her from the wreck, nursed her back to health and kept her all these years in the kampong. She was one of the family now, Mariam and no longer Marge. There were too many of them, these waifs of war. At least Mariam had a family who clearly cared for her. My thoughts went back to poor Gim Huat, who was a rag-doll to be fought over by the dogs. I was determined that we would find his real mother for him.

Mariam had retreated into the doorway, as befits a proper Malay girl. Ahmad beckoned and she approached shyly.

"You said something about a car?" I asked.

"Yes, there's one in the *belukar* up the hill. We ... me and the other children ... we found it when we were playing. I don't know if it'll still run though."

I turned to Ahmad for his permission to let Mariam show us the car. After a short hesitation he agreed. I told June to stay behind, but she put on her "don't-mess-with-me" face and insisted. I knew better than to argue. We set off with one of his strapping sons as company.

The path followed the lower contours of the ridge until it met a metalled road which snaked its way steeply to the summit. Mariam skipped along like a mountain goat, while I puffed my way up. June was having a bit of difficulty too. I felt furtively satisfied at that but refrained from rubbing it in. We followed the road upwards, past a couple of derelict bungalows. They looked like they had been occupied by Europeans rather than Asiatics. At one of the turns of the road there was a small flat area, overgrown with wide-leaved shrubs, the sort they use to wrap *rojak* in. Mariam pushed her way through the tangle, which gave way with surprising ease. Behind the undergrowth, covered with coconut fronds, was a red and black Morris Eight.

We stripped away the camouflage. The owners had taken great pains to keep it hidden it from prying eyes, meaning no doubt to come back for it some time. Evidently they hadn't. The Morris had seen better days; three and half years in the jungle doesn't do much for a car's resale value. We lifted the bonnet. As far as I could tell all the necessary bits were there. A quick fumble in the glove compartment produced the key. I turned it in the ignition. Not a peep interrupted the creeking of the cicadas.

"Dead," I said.

"Maybe it needs petrol?" ventured June.

I rubbed my neck. "Worth a shot. But petrol's not easy to come by. We'll give it a go tomorrow, if we can lay our hands on the stuff."

Carefully, we replaced the foliage over our new treasure, ensuring that it was not visible from the road. We covered our tracks meticulously and rearranged the vegetation to hide the traces of our visit. The idea that we were actually taking somebody's prized possession never crossed my mind. My one thought was to make sure no dishonest blackguard stole the car from us.

5

"A WHITE girl? Are you sure?" asked Simon. I had reported the result of our search for Ahmad to him as instructed. Simon liked to foster the illusion that he was in charge.

"Yes, quite sure," I said, trying to keep him focussed on the immediate problem. "We'll need petrol if we're going to carry on the search for Gim Huat's mother. You've got friends who've got cars. Can you get them to spare us a couple of gallons?"

Simon made a gesture as if brushing away something irritating. "A white girl. Does she have a name?"

"Her name's Margaret Barron. They call her Mariam now. What about the petrol?" Trying to keep Simon to the subject was like trying to trap mosquitoes with one hand.

"We should do something about it," he said.

"Yes, we should," I replied exasperatedly, "but we need petrol."

"I meant the girl. We should do something about the girl."

"Don't need to. Her family's dead. She seems quite happy and well-adjusted. We need to get on with the search for the mother."

"The mother? I thought you just said that her family's dead?" asked Simon, puzzled.

I was on the verge of throttling him. "I meant Gim Huat's mother. For that we need petrol."

"No, I haven't any petrol," said Simon absently. "Singham might be able to help. He seems to have a knack for getting things.

But we must do something about the girl."
I fled before my head exploded.

GEORGE as usual managed to tap his sources for a couple of gallons of petrol. I never asked where it came from and he never told. It was better that way. Knowing too much about George's sources of supply was apt to lead to sleepless nights and nervous glances over the shoulder. Next morning bright and early we were back to resurrect the Morris. Eager with anticipation, I turned the key and hoped for the best. Nothing. "The battery is dead, Tuan," said Ahmad. "We must push."

Push we did. There was a gentle slope from the road to the car's resting place, hardly anything when walking. But getting the thing up the slope onto the road was quite another matter. There was just me and Ahmad's son Karim. The old man had volunteered to help, but June insisted that he stop. As she put it, he was the only one who knew the way to Chan Sew Neo's place and it wouldn't have done to have him drop dead now. Besides, she said I needed the exercise.

We finally moved it the twenty yards upwards and over the ditch at the side of the road. My lungs were bursting with the effort. Karim hardly sweated. He earned his living with the *pukat tarek*, the long beach seine net that fishermen used to catch the shoals of *ikan bilis* close inshore. They pulled the heavy net through the water to scoop up the catch. His arms were sinewy and thick as an old bamboo. Hauling motorcars was nothing to him.

We positioned the Morris nose facing downhill. With Ahmad in the driver's seat, we gave it a final shove. It rolled down the slope, slowly at first and then with increasing speed. I watched with alarm as it got away from us. Then suddenly, it coughed and spluttered and the engine burst into life with a cloud of smoke.

Bringing the car to a gentle stop, Ahmad soon had the bonnet up and started tinkering with its innards. After half an hour the old Morris was purring, in a sort of wheezy, rheumatic way, like a cat with bronchitis.

Ahmad coaxed the car slowly back to town, driving at a stately pace. It felt rather grand being chauffeured through the town, though one might have wished for something a bit more impressive. The traffic was light, mostly consisting of army trucks and jeeps with the odd bus. Masses of cyclists wove in and out, but they parted like the Red Sea before Moses as we nosed our way to Battery Road.

After the initial happy reunion with his old friends in the office, Ahmad was sent off to procure more petrol for our expedition. George cast an approving eye over our acquisition. "Wait a sec," he said and disappeared upstairs. He returned shortly with a screwdriver.

"What's that for?" I asked.

"It's for you to unscrew the number plates," he answered.

It was only then that the import of what we had done struck me. I hesitated. "I'm not sure we should," I said plaintively.

"Look," said George, planting his hand firmly on my shoulder, "we can't risk someone popping up out of the blue and claiming the old warhorse now. When we're done, we'll put the plates back, but not before. Until then, use Clarence's old number plates."

"We are giving it back, right?" I persisted. "After we're done?"

"Let's be realistic about this," he replied. "If we just leave the car where it was, chances are that someone else will take it. Some of that Bahau lot are back already. You know they sold up everything when they left, so they don't have any place to live now. What do they do? They move right into any vacant house they find. The sorting out will come later. It's the same principle here. We borrow this nice little Morris, and when we're done with it we'll sort out who owns it. Or would you rather walk to Telok Paku?"

I knew he was right. The British had tried to round up all the cars that had been acquired informally during the Occupation. It was a hopeless task and they soon gave up. Whoever had a car held on to it, papers or no papers. The legalities would work their way out in due course. Reluctantly, I swopped the plates. D'Almeida used to have an antique Rolls. Like so many others, it was pressed into service for the good of the Greater Co-Prosperity Sphere. Co-prosperity of course meant that the Japanese took whatever they fancied, whenever they fancied. It was a lovely car. We never saw it again. At least the number would live on, in a more humble guise.

GEORGE insisted on coming along for the ride out to Telok Paku. Eng Tong the interpreter was in the front passenger seat, which left no place for June. She expressed her annoyance loudly, but could not gainsay the logic of the arrangement. "Besides," said George soothingly, "Gim Huat missed you. He needs a bit of cuddling."

Having mollified June somewhat, we set off. The road east was busier than the road west. We passed several gangs of Japanese POWs clearing rubble and filling in potholes. The guards were British rather than Indian, I noticed. There was a point to be made.

The road to Telok Paku took us past the mansions of the rich along Grove Road. Beyond the terrace houses of the Babas in Joo Chiat and Katong, signs of human habitation thinned out. The road was a quiet rural one, lined with coconut groves on either side. The sea was just visible to our right. We had just left the last houses behind us when Eng Tong spoke. "People are following us."

"People? What people?" asked George.

"On motorcycles. They are following. I see when they come near to us."

I turned to have a look. Two BSA motorcycles with sidecars were ten yards behind. They were faded green and had seen better times, ex-British Army I surmised. The four men in them were Chinese, not European or Indian. They didn't look like soldiers.

"Are you sure they're following us?" I queried. "They might just be going for a jaunt."

"They are Ah Siew's men," replied Eng Tong. "I know two of them. Bad men, gangsters."

I felt a frisson up my neck. "What do they want?"

"I don't propose to hang around and find out," said George. "Enchik Ahmad, full speed please."

We had been cruising along at measured pace to spare the engine. Now Ahmad put his foot down and the little Morris responded. Responded is perhaps not the right word. The engine whined and growled and the car lurched forward. There was a backfire, and then another. The old Morris managed to chug along at a slightly sprightlier pace. "We're not going to outrun them at this rate," said George, cursing under his breath.

But we didn't have to. The two motorcycles had pulled off the road suddenly and the occupants had thrown themselves down into the long grass at the side. "Funny sort of blokes," I commented, "jumping into the *lallang* like that. Whatever can have possessed them?"

George let out a sudden laugh. "It's the backfiring. They think we're shooting at them!"

Whatever it was they might have thought, they were keeping their heads down. We turned a corner and they were lost to sight. I kept an anxious lookout for any further signs of pursuit, but there was none.

"What could they have wanted?" I wondered out loud.

"The same thing we want, I imagine," responded George. "We weren't exactly discreet asking about Chan Sew Neo in town. That was a bad mistake. I should have been more careful."

"I thought you said that they wouldn't try anything."

"Well, they may not be as smart as I gave them credit for. Or perhaps they think we should be stopped from finding Gim Huat's real mother. Good thing I brought this," he said, producing a revolver from under the seat and giving it to me.

"Wherever did you get that?" I asked in alarm, pushing it away. The authorities had proscribed the carrying of weapons and demanded that all guns and ammunition be surrendered. I wasn't eager to find out how seriously they were going to enforce the prohibition.

"It's our insurance policy," he said blandly, "you take it." He lowered his voice, "You know I can't shoot for toffee and I don't trust Eng Tong. If there's going to be trouble, we aren't going to get out of it by threatening to serve a writ. Stick it in your waistband. No one will see."

Reluctantly, I complied. Eng Tong remained impassive. I kept my eye fixed on his neck, not knowing whether he heard or understood what had just occurred. It may just have been my imagination, but I fancied I saw his eyes flicker away when I looked in the rearview mirror.

WE passed Changi Prison with its sinister watch-towers flanking the gate and turned towards Telok Paku. Several side paths led off from the main road. Ahmad stopped the car and considered which one to take. I was in a sweat lest our pursuers catch up with us. At length he made his decision and we plunged down a dusty laterite road barely wide enough for one car. The going wasn't easy. The surface of the road was etched with eroded channels. At one time it seemed to have been metalled. Remains of the former surface showed here and there in broken chunks interspersed with weeds.

We drove slowly to spare the suspension. The road seemed to be leading towards the beach. There wasn't any sign of life. Then without warning a gap appeared in the tall grass and we found ourselves looking at the sea. The road ended here. "There Tuan," said Ahmad, pointing with his thumb at a cluster of wooden huts set among the coconut palms.

We got out and approached the buildings. Nothing stirred. There didn't seem to be anyone about. Chinese kampongs, unlike Malay ones, usually have a pack of mangy mongrels running around the place. The only animal life we saw was a monitor lizard, which scampered off into the undergrowth at our coming.

We reached the cluster of huts. The roofs had fallen in and the windows stared blindly. Rusty cans lay around. Weeds were growing in the door frames. It seemed as if the air itself had become completely still and lifeless. "I don't like this," I said, half to myself. I fingered the revolver under my coat and forgave George for bringing his insurance policy.

Eng Tong plucked and my sleeve and pointed. There was a partially overgrown mound near the beach. I knew immediately what it was. It was a long grave.

"This must have been one of the places where the Japs shot people," said George. "These houses don't look like they've been lived in for years."

I nodded mutely. Eng Tong was silent. I had escaped Sook Ching by the skin of my teeth. I presumed that Eng Tong must have had the same experience. We all knew that the Japanese had taken hundreds of men, young and old, to the beach that dark February after the Fall. Few had returned. The stories got around though; captives forced to dig their own graves then machine-gunned and buried. I turned away; I had no wish to see the evidence.

"Well, that's it then," said George. "The kampong folk are gone. I'd guess that the Japs cleared them out before the massacres — if they were that lucky."

6

"SO the trail's cold," I said to George dispiritedly as we tramped up the stairs to the office. "Chan Sew Neo is gone and Gim Huat hasn't a mother."

"Surely you didn't think it would be so easy?" he replied.

"No, I suppose not. But things were going so well. I thought at least we'd get a lead, not a complete dead end. Literally."

"Yes," he admitted. "I did think that we were on to something. So we still have our little problem to solve."

"Problem, Singham?" said a familiar voice. "I trust that the problems are not intractable." A silhouette appeared behind us at the foot of the stairs.

"Uncle Clarence!" exclaimed George. "I didn't know that you were back."

"I returned this morning," he replied. "There is much to be done."

"Where's Cuthbert? We need to speak to him."

D'Almeida raised an eyebrow interrogatively. "Cuthbert is still in Bahau, sorting out the various claims and counterclaims. It has been very trying. I have work for both of you."

George bit his lip. "Bad luck about Cuthbert. We need him to tell us about Lao Leong Ann's foster son."

"Walk with me," said d'Almeida shortly, indicating that we should follow him into his office. George gave a precis of the situation to date. D'Almeida listened intently but made no comment. He seemed to think it of no consequence.

There was already someone in the room when we entered. My heart sank when I saw who it was. "My dear Chiang," said the man, grasping my hand with a firm and businesslike grip, "it's good to see you. I'm glad to find you in one piece still."

I winced. "Likewise, I'm sure, Colonel," I replied unenthusiastically.

"You remember Singham," said d'Almeida. "He was involved in the Gilbert affair along with Chiang."

"How could I forget?"

George took the proffered hand. "Colonel Newman, isn't it? You look well. And with an extra pip to go with what you had before." D'Almeida inclined his head towards the door. George took the hint and excused himself.

I had made Newman's acquaintance before the War when I had a spot of bother with the law. He was with Special Branch then, chasing Communists and Japanese spies. "I've got a job for you," he said to me.

"I'm done working for you," I replied decidedly. The last time he had a job for me I ended up with front-row seats for the Japanese invasion. I wasn't about to make the same mistake again.

"Don't be so quick to refuse," he said. "Hear me out first. Mr d'Almeida thinks it's a good idea."

I looked at d'Almeida, who nodded.

Newman continued. "We've set up tribunals to try the renegades and war criminals. The trials will be starting soon. The evidence has been taken and the charges are ready. All we need is someone to defend. I thought of you."

I was shaken. "You don't want me to defend the whole lot surely?"

"No, not the whole lot, just one," he said. "We need good men to act for the defence. There haven't been many volunteers for the job, as you might imagine."

"Why me? So you can have your little show trial and claim that justice has been done?"

"Not a show trial," he rejoined. "We're deadly serious about doing justice. There'll be no kangaroo courts for the sake of vengence." He proffered a manila envelope to me. "Take the brief," he said, "it'll do you good." Reluctantly, I took it from him. He bade us good day and strode out.

"I can't do this," I said, looking again to d'Almeida. "We never act for the guilty party."

"We do not help the guilty party to evade justice," corrected d'Almeida, "but even the guilty may have some mitigating quality. It is our task to present this to the tribunal, if it exists."

"If it exists," I said bitterly. "People already think I'm a collaborator. And you want me to defend a Jap war criminal."

"It is a mistake to draw conclusions without evidence," replied d'Almeida evenly. "It might be dangerous for others to defend the Japanese at this time, given the strength of feeling against them. But you are known to the Communists as a friend. You run the least risk. It was for this reason that I recommended you to Colonel Newman."

I subsided. It was true, my contacts with the MPAJA did give me some protection. But still I hesitated. "Why can't George do it? The Commies know him too."

"I need Singham to assist me in another matter," said d'Almeida, peering at me over his horn-rimmed glasses. "I have every confidence in your abilities. As the Colonel said, it will be good for you."

That was that then. I couldn't refuse. Moodily, I opened the envelope and skimmed the file. "What became of the hand grenade?" asked d'Almeida suddenly.

Taken aback, I sputtered a little. "Grenade? What grenade?" He was always like that. He expected everyone to be as quick as he was to master a brief. I flipped through the file, hoping not seem a complete fool in front of my boss.

"The grenade that was thrown at the funeral," said d'Almeida.

"Oh, that grenade," I responded, breathing a sigh of relief. "I don't think anyone did anything about it. For all we know, it's still there in the *lallang* somewhere."

"Is Smallwood still with Force 136? Ask him to come and see me, if you please." He turned to the pile of files on his desk without further explanation. The interview was over.

THE next day I called on my client as instructed. He sat hunched over in a grimy cell in Pearl's Hill Police Station. Serves you right, I thought, then shook myself firmly. This won't do, I'm his defence counsel. Taking a deep breath, I tried to get into the proper frame of mind.

The charge was war crimes. Warrant Officer Nakamura Nagamasa of the Kempeitai stood accused of four counts of murder. He had tortured three civilians and one POW to death. The details were set out dispassionately in the particulars of the charges. In dry legalese the charge sheet chronicled the beatings, the electric shocks to the genitals, the bamboo slivers under the fingernails ... It was as much as I could bear to read it.

He seemed rather small and frail. Unshaven and dishevelled, he didn't fit the part of the beast that he was. "Let's hear what he has to say," I said to Eng Tong, who had come along as my interpreter. Nakamura had been in Formosa and spoke some Hokkien. Otherwise, we would have had to communicate in mime.

Eng Tong had no love for the Japanese, that was obvious. He was staring with unconcealed hostility at Nakamura. "What you want me to ask?"

"Name and rank, to start with. Where he's from. What unit. That sort of thing."

Eng Tong started questioning in a voice full of menace. His questions were fired in a tone more suited to an interrogator than an interviewer. Nakamura seemed to be pleading. Eng Tong raised his hand as if to strike him. Nakamura shrank back. I put my hand out to stop him. This won't do at all, I thought, we're treating him like the enemy. "Ask him nicely," I said. "We need to hear his side of the story."

"He is an evil animal," said Eng Tong with feeling.

"That may be," I replied, "but it's my job to defend him."

"What for? You defend him for what?"

"Because that's how the system works. Everyone has a right to be defended, to have his side of the story told. Even a beast."

Eng Tong calmed down a little. Still glaring at our client, he confirmed what we already knew of Nakamura. I read out the charge and particulars for Eng Tong to translate. It sickened me to do so. He had been one of the interrogators at the YMCA. His job was to obtain confessions from the poor unfortunates who came into his grasp. He was good at his job.

"Well, what's he got to say for himself?" Nakamura looked uncomprehendingly at me and then at Eng Tong.

"He say nothing, only his name and rank."

I was taken aback. "What do you mean nothing? He's accused of torturing people to death. He could hang. Does he know that?"

There was a quick exchange. Eng Tong barked questions at Nakamura, who shook his head repeatedly.

"I tell him what you say. He say nothing."

I shrugged my shoulders and packed my bag. There are easier ways to commit hara-kiri without wasting my time, I thought.

7

"HARD day?" asked George as I plopped down in the settee in his room.

"Hard case," I responded tiredly. "The man's suicidal. He's been charged with four murders — four, mark you. And what does he say? Nothing. Not a blessed word out of him."

"So what's the defence?"

"I don't know," I answered dejectedly. "Duress, I suppose. Superior orders, war is hell, that sort of thing. The judges are all serving officers. They should understand."

"They're all serving *British* officers," corrected George. "They'll understand what has to be done all right. Ten to one your man will swing."

"Cheer me up," I responded. "What's this case that d'Almeida's got you on?"

"A friend of yours, I believe," said George, "Lieutenant-Colonel Habibullah Khan."

I sat bolt upright. "Habibullah! From the Bhurtpores?"

"Yes, large as life and twice as mean, or so I'm told," said George. "They captured him in Taiping. Seems he caught a packet at Imphal and was sent back to Malaya with some of the INA wounded. He was organising replacements when the Japs surrendered. Kicked up a real fuss when they came to get him. Insisted on being shown the courtesies due to his rank and status as a prisoner-of-war."

Habibullah Khan had been a lieutenant in the Bhurtpore Regiment when I first made his acquaintance. The Bhurtpores weren't regular Indian Army but rather a State Forces battalion raised and paid for by the Rajah of Bhurtpore. They were not a happy unit. Their CO was a mad-dog English career soldier who treated his men like brutes. I'd been sent by Newman to work undercover keeping an eye on them at RAF Batu Sembilan, which they had been assigned to guard. They were right smack in the path of the Japanese landings at Kota Bahru. They mutinied and deserted without firing a shot. I barely got out of Batu Sembilan with my hide in one piece. When the Indian National Army was formed, the battalion went over practically wholesale. Habibullah had been promoted to major and given command. Evidently, his war service merited further advancement.

"What's the charge?"

"The usual," said George blandly, "waging war against the King-Emperor. Oh, and a little matter of murder — one Lieutenant-Colonel Holmes. Seems he shot the blighter."

Unpleasant memories crowded back. "Yes, I know," I said, "I was there."

George looked surprised. "This is a tale you've never told," he said.

I shrugged. "D'Almeida was there too. I can't understand why he'd agree to defend Habibullah. The man's a total renegade; went over to the Japs the first chance he got."

"Curiouser and curiouser," mused George. "There are little wheels within big wheels here. No doubt he'll tell us when he's good and ready."

We were interrupted by the irruption of June. "He has gone!"

"Gone? Who's gone?" I asked, staring blankly at her.

"Gim Huat! They have taken him. He has been kidnapped!"

"LET'S look at this calmly," said George. "What happened?"

Gim Huat and his *amah* had been lodged in May's old room, which was in a corner of the house away from the other bedrooms. Everything seemed normal at tiffin time. The boy was used to having a nap in the afternoon, so the *amah* had taken him upstairs. At tea-time, he was bouncing all over the room. The *amah* took him out into the garden. That was the last anyone saw of them.

We left immediately and searched high and low around the house. There was no sign of them. I didn't expect that there would be. We were just acting for the sake of doing something. I bitterly reproached myself for not having taken more precautions.

"I suppose that we ought to track down our three charming ladies and beard them in their lairs," said George.

This did not appeal to me in the least. "One, I have no desire to see any bearded ladies, in their lairs or elsewhere," I remonstrated. "Two, we don't even know where their lairs are; and three, even if we did I'm not about to waltz in asking whether they've got Gim Huat. We're dealing with homicidal maniacs here."

"What about Lao's house?" suggested June.

"Too obvious," George responded. "They know that's the first place we'd look. No point going there. They're not going to be so stupid as to hide him in the most obvious location."

"What do we do then?" she asked.

"What we always do when we're stumped," replied George. "We go to Uncle Clarence."

NORMALLY, most junior partners would be chary of approaching the All-Highest with minor problems like disappearing heirs. But d'Almeida was different. He throve on things like this. An appetiser for the brain was all this was.

"It could have been any of the three of them," said George after explaining the situation.

"What would they gain?" asked d'Almeida pointedly.

We thought about that for a moment. No satisfactory answer offered itself.

"None of them would gain a thing," said George slowly.

"Therefore who is left?"

"The *amah*?" I ventured.

"That would seem to be the logical conclusion. Did the *amah* have a ration card?" continued d'Almeida.

"No," I replied, "not as far as we know. She counted as part of Lao's household. He had his own sources of supply."

"The boy has to eat. She has no ration card. Where might she go to get food? You will doubtless find her there." He looked at us severely. "I need both of you to concentrate fully on the cases I have assigned to you. There is too much at stake. I cannot have you distracted all the time. Call the claimants together when you have found the boy. We will settle this matter once and for all."

D'ALMEIDA was right as usual. We found them back at Lao's shop, which was well-stocked with tinned goods and other consumables hidden away behind false walls. The house had been locked and shuttered after the funeral, but the *amah* evidently kept a pass key. She made no denial when we turned up, just pointing to the cot in the corner where Gim Huat lay curled, his thumb in his mouth. June went over and picked him up. Half asleep, he put his skinny little arms around her neck. "Why?" asked June.

The dam burst and we were inundated with a flood of tears and Cantonese. When the deluge finally abated, I turned to Eng Tong interrogatively. "She is afraid that you take the boy away," he translated succinctly. "She does not want to leave him."

"Is that all?" I asked, surprised. "Surely she said more than that?"

"What more you want me to say?" replied Eng Tong. He was not one to waste words on details. I didn't press.

"Tell her that wherever Gim Huat goes, she goes," I said. "When we find his mother, we'll make sure that she keeps her on for the boy's sake."

This reassurance was duly conveyed. The tears dried up and she smiled briefly. It was the first time I had ever seen her smile.

IT was crowded in d'Almeida's office. Gim Huat was there, together with his ever-present *amah* and June. The three would-be mothers sat in a row in front of d'Almeida, darting truculent glances at one another. We'd insisted that their respective entourages remain outside the building. Simon was deputed to keep an eye on them, a commission he accepted without great enthusiasm. He roped George in for support, much to his disgust, but d'Almeida backed Simon so there was nothing for it.

D'Almeida had asked each of the three claimants to bring along the evidence supporting her case. He listened patiently as each one presented a succession of photographs, letters, keepsakes and miscellaneous paraphenalia. Gim Huat fidgeted despite being kept supplied with sweets and biscuits. He showed no inclination to leave the protective embraces of June and the *amah*. The efforts of the mothers to coax him only made him burrow deeper.

"My dear ladies," said d'Almeida at length, "I cannot decide which of you is the lad's mother. This will have to go before the courts, when they finally re-open. I propose that each of you in turn should take care of him until that time. It will be an expensive process, and probably a long one. These matters usually are. I trust that you are well-resourced?" There was a ripple of consternation when Eng Tong translated. D'Almeida continued.

"I am certain that regardless of who the real mother is, each of you will take care of young Gim Huat admirably. The poor boy is an orphan, with nothing to his name. It is very good of you to do such a charitable thing for a destitute child." This time, there was an outburst of dismay. All three began speaking at the same time. Eng Tong looked harrassed as he tried to keep up. D'Almeida put up his hand for silence.

"What becomes of the estate of the late Mr Lao Leong Ann, you might ask? Unfortunately, it appears that Mr Lao acquired the bulk of his property illegally from the Japanese Custodian of Enemy Property. The Custodian could not by international law validly pass title under such circumstances. The true owners or their representatives will shortly be making their claims. I expect that the process of determining the true ownership of the properties in question will take some years." This was well beyond Eng Tong, who looked helplessly to June for aid.

"Mr d'Almeida says that the *Jepun* cannot sell the houses to Lao Leong Ann. The real owners will take them back," she said. Eng Tong nodded gratefully and began translating. Evidently he got through, because he was drowned out by howls of protest before he finished. D'Almeida banged on the table sternly for order and the mob subsided.

"Now," he said evenly, "who will be the first to take Gim Huat?" His eye swept from one woman to another. None of them would meet his gaze.

"I take it that none of the ladies wishes to press her claim?" he asked. Ah Siew had a face as black as a monsoonal thunderstorm. Ah Kwan looked as if she would cry. Ah Moy appeared completely stunned.

"No? Then perhaps we might bring this meeting to an end. I wish you all good day."

The three shuffled out. As they left, d'Almeida called out.

"Madam Ah Moy, may I detain you for a moment?"

Ah Moy turned in surprise to hear her name. D'Almeida indicated that she should sit. He reached into his desk drawer and presented something wrapped in brown paper to her. "Yours, I think."

She opened the packet gingerly and then suddenly dropped it. It hit the floor with a metallic clang. We all jumped back a yard. It was a grenade.

"It is empty," continued d'Almeida, fixing his basilisk gaze on her, "just a shell. There is no explosive in it. But you knew that."

Eng Tong had recovered himself sufficiently to begin translating, but d'Almeida held up his hand to stop him. "No need for that. The young lady understands perfectly, do you not?"

Ah Moy looked at him. "No need to play dumb, madam," he said. "I made inquiries with the newspapers as to the identity of the person who placed Lao Leong Ann's obituary. She was quite conversant in English according to my informant."

"Yeah, it was me," said Ah Moy. I started. She spoke like someone out of a gangster movie. I couldn't contain myself. "Wherever did you learn to speak English?"

She gave me her sardonic smile. "Shanghai. International Settlement."

D'Almeida reinserted himself into the conversation. "Why did you do it? The obituary could hardly advance your claim."

"I thought it wouldn't hurt to play the part of the widow. But they told me later it wouldn't wash, so that was money down the drain," she responded. "How'd you get on to me?"

"My former associate Mr Smallwood was kind enough to retrieve this from the scene of the attempted attack. He has a certain familiarity with such matters. He told me that the explosive had been extracted from this object. It was completely harmless. But no one else knew that. It appeared to all that someone was determined to kill you. Who would gain by such a deed? There were three factions. Madam Ah Siew's group knew they had not done it; ergo it must have been Madam Ah Kwan. Madam Ah Kwan came to the same conclusion about Madam Ah Siew. So each determined to strike first at the other 'guilty' party."

"You're very clever," said Ah Moy.

D'Almeida permitted himself the ghost of a smile. "Smallwood also told me something quite interesting about this little object. It is of American make — not British or Japanese. I am reliably informed that the OSS supplied a small group of guerillas in Malaya. Nationalist Chinese, not Communist."

"You know everything, don't you?" said Ah Moy, "Yeah, we're Kuomintang. We'd been fighting the Japs for years before you came into the picture. Now that they're done, we need to settle with the Commies. Old Lao promised to give us half his fortune for the cause. But the Reds got him first. I reckoned we could still get our hands on the dough if I played the widow, but that didn't work. The next best thing was to be the kid's mother."

"But others had the same idea."

"Got it in one. Seems we all got our brains wired the same way."

"I think you may find that it was not a pure coincidence that the others attempted the same ploy. There are hidden hands."

For the first time Ah Moy's self-assurance slipped. "Hidden hands? Who? The Reds?"

"Only you know who you may have spoken to."

"Goddamn it! The Clan elders. They're the ones we made our claim to. They must have put Kwan's lot up to it. No wonder they were so keen to decide she was the one." She added menacingly, "Or at least some of them."

"And Ah Siew?" I queried.

"Triad," she answered shortly. "Doing it on their own account.

Lao was borrowing money from those goons. I guess they wanted to cash in his marker."

"I think our business here is finished," said d'Almeida.

"Yeah, I guess so. Win some, lose some. We'll get money somewhere else. There's others who'll pay to help the cause." She got up to leave. "What's your name?" she asked me as she reached the door.

I was taken aback. "Dennis Chiang," I answered.

"See you, Dennis Chiang," she said and smiled. Then she was gone.

"So Mr d'Almeida, what do we do with Gim Huat?" asked June.

"I believe we can entrust his care to the lady," said d'Almeida, indicating the *amah*. "Lao Leong Ann created a small trust for the boy's upkeep; gold, not banana notes. Not an extravagant sum, but enough for his needs. Did I not mention that?"

"No, you didn't," I said.

"How remiss of me," replied d'Almeida with a twinkle in his eye.

A sudden thought struck me. "The *amah* Ah Fong. She wouldn't be Chan Sew Neo, would she? Gim Huat's real mother?"

D'Almeida looked severely at me over the rim of his glasses. "Life is never so neat. But though she may not be mother by blood, she is his mother in every other way that matters."

Gim Huat had gone to sleep, his thumb in his mouth, cradled in the arms of Ah Fong.

8

THE more I thought about it the less I liked it. In all the years I had been with d'Almeida, the one thing I learned was that law was about justice. As a general rule, he did not represent people he was convinced were guilty of crimes. He wasn't the sort of hired gun who would try to pull the wool over a jury's eyes for the sake of a fee. There were too many of that sort, who would do anything to win a case and rationalised it by saying that it was not for them to judge. And here I was being asked to break that cardinal rule, to represent a man whom I was sure was a beast of the most malign sort. I didn't like it at all.

I decided finally that I had to speak, whatever d'Almeida might think of me. But it was with a beating heart and sweaty palms that I knocked on the door of the Holy of Holies. "Come," said a voice from within.

"Mr d'Almeida," I started hesitantly, "it's about the Nakamura case. I can't do it." D'Almeida looked up from his books. He took off his spectacles. He started polishing them. I fidgeted uncomfortably. After an eternity he got up, walked slowly over the the large leather settee and motioned me to sit down. I did so with a churning stomach. This was the first time I had ever defied him.

"Why can't you do it?"

My mouth was dry. "It … it's against my conscience. The man is a monster."

"You have the right man? The identification in order?"

"Well, there are two witnesses who saw his photo and identified him. One's been repatriated now. The other's in hospital. They both swore affidavits. And there are the Kempeitai's own records regarding the men Nakamura was interrogating. Four of them died."

"Did they die by his hand?"

I hesitated. "No," I replied slowly, "afterwards. From the effects of the torture."

"Did he mean for them to die? Is that the point of an interrogation?"

"I suppose not," I said doubtfully, "it would be pointless to kill a subject if they wanted information."

"So we conclude that he did not intend to kill. Did he intend to cause such injury as would in the ordinary course of nature lead to death?"

"I don't know," I said, wavering, "he hasn't told me anything. But that's beside the point. He was a sadistic thug. I'm sure he enjoyed the whole process."

D'Almeida looked at me sternly. "On what do you base that assessment if he has said nothing to you?"

I fell silent. D'Almeida's tone softened. "My boy, I do not ask you to mislead the court or to get an acquittal against the justice of the case. But for justice to be done the defendant's case must be put fairly to the judges. That is our task. It may be that there are mitigating circumstances. The Japanese do not think as the Europeans do. Their military values have been formed by a different history and culture. You know them better than most. You are one of the best qualified to put the case fairly and objectively to the tribunal."

"But why?" I persisted, emotionally unconvinced though my brain told me he was right.

He looked me straight in the eye. "I said to you before that there is much at stake. Man is not by nature a law-abiding creature. When the thin bonds of custom and education are loosed, society reverts to the tyranny of the strong. During the Occupation we lost respect for the law. The Occupation has made corruption and nepotism a way of life. We have become used to caprice and arbitrariness, when an accusation is sufficient to condemn a man. Now we are free again would you have it remain so? We cannot surrender to this."

I kept silent. I knew what he wanted me to do, but I couldn't bring myself to do it. After what seemed an eternity, he spoke again. "I do not ask you to defend this man against your conscience. Think carefully about it." He took his watch out of his coat pocket. "I have an interview with my client. Singham is out. Will you come?"

He left without waiting for my answer. I followed docilely.

HABIBULLAH KHAN looked much older than when I saw him last. He seemed shrunken somehow. When he stood to greet d'Almeida I saw why. His left arm was missing from the elbow. He wore a plain khaki uniform, devoid of rank insignia. "Lieutenant-Colonel Khan?" said d'Almeida. "Allow me to introduce myself: Clarence d'Almeida, at your service. This is my associate, Mr Dennis Chiang."

Strictly speaking Habibullah was only a lieutenant, the highest rank he had attained in the Indian Army. But it was clear that he was pleased to be addressed by his Indian National Army rank of lieutenant-colonel. He grasped d'Almeida's proferred hand and shook it warmly. "Thank you, Mr d'Almeida," he said, "it's good of you to come."

I was taken aback by the voice. When I had met Habibullah, I was posing as a mute waiter in the Officers' Mess at RAF Batu Sembilan, which his battalion had been assigned to guard. Most of the time he spoke Urdu. The accent was unmistakably English, and public-school English at that. This I hadn't expected.

He was among a group of disgruntled Indian Commissioned Officers who felt slighted by the indignities piled on the unit by its Commanding Officer, Lieutenant-Colonel Holmes. These ICOs held commissions from Dehra Dun, the Indian Army equivalent of Sandhurst. They considered themselves equal to the British subalterns but the CO thought otherwise. To him they were just a bunch of pretentious *babus* trying to be what they could never be. Lieutenant-Colonel Holmes had paid with his life for the insults he had heaped on his men. That was one of the reasons we were there to defend Habibullah. He shook my hand with a firm grasp, looking me straight in the eye. It was evident that he did not recognise me at all.

"You speak English very well," I said fatuously.

"So do you," he replied, with just the faintest trace of mockery. I could have kicked myself. I had just done to him what so many people had done to me. It was unforgiveably condescending and never failed to put my back up. I mumbled an apology. "No need to apologise," he said in a matter-of-fact tone. "I was educated in England. As were you, unless I miss my guess." I nodded in acknowledgement of the common bond.

D'Almeida wasted no time in explaining the charges. The Bhurtpore Regiment had mutinied the very morning that the Japanese had landed at Kota Bahru. They had shot Colonel Holmes and left their posts. Habibullah Khan was the alleged ringleader. He was charged with the murder of Holmes or alternatively with instigating the murder. Thereafter, practically the whole battalion had surrendered to the Japanese without firing a shot. When the INA was formed, they went over *en masse*. Habibullah was promoted major and appointed to the command of the battalion, now under Japanese orders. He had seen active service not only during the capture of Singapore but also in the Burma campaign. This was the second charge, waging war against the King-Emperor. The penalty for both charges was death.

Habibullah smiled sardonically after d'Almeida's explanation. "My father was a King's Indian Orderly Officer to George V," he said. "He retired at the highest rank an Indian could attain: Subedar-Major. They gave him an OBI. For the rest of his life he was Sardar Bahadur Imran Khan, a man of honour. When he died, the Viceroy sent a letter of condolence to my mother. Now, I am a traitor to the Empire and must hang."

"Only if you are guilty," said d'Almeida. "Are you?"

"Not of murder," said Habibullah. "Holmes may have been a bounder, but I wished him no harm. Things got out of hand. He threatened to shoot me. One of the men fired first. I couldn't stop it."

"Who fired the fatal shot?"

"Who can remember after all this time? It might have been Dilawar Ali or it might have been Jagat Singh. Take your pick. They're both dead. Killed in Burma."

"Any other witnesses?"

Habibullah let out a short laugh. "Only the whole battalion. Ask them."

D'Almeida started polishing his spectacles. "I have no doubt that your men have been intensively interrogated — if they have been found. I do not believe that the prosecution will allege that you fired the fatal shot. Their case is likely to be that you were the main instigator. The penalty is the same."

"And if they don't get me for murder, they'll get me for waging war against the King-Emperor. Guilty as charged, and proud of it."

"If you are so determined to die, you may as well commit hara-kiri like the Japanese and be done with it now," said d'Almeida evenly. "You fought for an ideal, a free India, as did your compatriots.

I do not agree with your methods, nor with your choice of friends. You could take the easy way and say you were forced. Many have done so."

"That is the coward's way," said Habibullah. "I was not forced. If presented with the choice today I would do the same."

"Indeed. Will you contest the charge?" pressed d'Almeida.

"What's the point?" responded Habibullah. "The Tribunal's made up of British officers."

"British officers they may be," replied d'Almeida looking directly at Habibullah, "but they are judges and sworn to uphold the law."

Habibullah made an impatient noise. "You don't believe that rot surely? This isn't about justice. It's about making a point: that the Raj will not be challenged. I'm sure each one of them hears his master's voice loud and clear. If they haven't actually been told in so many words what verdict to bring in, they'll know what to do if they want to get on in the world."

"If I believed that," said d'Almeida solemnly, "I would not be here. There are men of honour in this world, whatever you may think. And even those who allow their judgments to be moulded by secret hopes of advancement or timid fears of retribution must justify their decisions in public for all to see. If they twist the law to please their masters, they will be judged harshly by their peers and posterity."

"Mr d'Almeida," said Habibullah, "I admire your faith in your fellow man. I have no illusions myself. But, yes, you are right. We fought and died for an ideal. I will not surrender now. I am in your hands."

WE drove back to the office in silence. D'Almeida was lost in thought and I knew better than to disturb him. When we reached the top of the stairs, I cleared my throat and summoned up my courage to speak.

"Mr d'Almeida?"

"Hmm?" he replied absently.

"I've thought about it. I'll carry on with the Nakamura case, if you still think I can handle it."

He patted my shoulder. "I had no doubt of that."

Returning to the broom cupboard that masqueraded as my office, I felt strangely torn. On one hand, I was buoyed by his confidence in me. On the other, I doubted whether I could really put my heart into defending a war criminal. Habibullah was a patriot, at least by his own lights. What justification could Nakamura possibly claim for what he had done? I didn't notice that my office was occupied until I nearly stumbled over my visitor.

"Mr Chiang?" said the woman.

"Sorry, didn't see you there," I said lamely, "What can I do for you … Mrs …?

"It's Miss Rider," she said severely. "I hear you know where my niece Marge is. I've come to take her back."

9

"IT wasn't pleasant at all," I said to Ralph, relating my encounter with Marge's aunt. "She's quite a battleaxe. Three and a half years in Changi and Sime Road don't seem to have taken the edge off. If anything, I think it's made her even more determined to take the girl back."

Ralph lounged in the chair lazily. On the rare days he had leave, he came over to the house. Mak was ever ready to ply him with delicacies and pamper him. Partly, it was her way; but there was also the hidden motive of trying to persuade him to bring May and the baby home rather than stay in Perth.

"Can she get the girl?" mused Ralph. "I mean legally, of course. The reality is something else altogether."

"Legally, I don't think she has a leg to stand on," I replied. "Marge's parents are dead. She's an orphan. The aunt doesn't inherit her like some trinket in a box. She'll have to get a court order. And the courts are still shut."

"Yes, that's true as far as I know," said Ralph, "but the authorities aren't going to like it. White girl held by Malay family. That won't go down well. The old harpy will have the MPs out there like a flash the moment she can get someone in ALFSEA HQ to give her a hearing."

"Well, for the time being that's out of the question," I answered. "I didn't tell her where Marge is, only that she's well and being cared for. You can imagine the scene she made. Imperious, that's the word. Made it absolutely clear that she wasn't about to take any lip from a native. Threatened me with hell and damnation. Lucky d'Almeida was there to sort things out. She didn't leave happy, but at least she left."

"Simon didn't have anything to say about it then?" asked Ralph.

I snorted contemptuously. "Simon's the whole reason for this mess in the first place. The idiot went and told the Missing Persons Office that we had information about Miss Margaret Barron and would any interested parties please get in touch with us. It was as much as I could do to keep from going into his office and punching him right in the snout, partner or no partner. Why couldn't he have left well alone?"

"Does Ahmad know?"

"Yes, I had to tell him. He took it badly. He may not say anything, but I can tell." I ran my hand through my hair. "It's my fault. I shouldn't have mentioned anything to Simon."

"Don't blame yourself," said Ralph soothingly. "You weren't to know. With Simon, no one knows where the depths of folly bottom out."

"The thing is, what do I do now? D'Almeida hasn't time to deal with this. I know a court order is out of the question for the time being, but can this Rider woman get the military to take Marge away? Would they?"

"Can they? The answer is yes. Who'd stop them?" said Ralph. "Would they? That's a bit more ticklish. On one hand British prestige isn't what it used to be. They've got to show that they're in charge again. A white girl brought up by natives isn't something they're ready to accept, especially if there's an aunt ready to take custody of her. From what you say she's the sort that would kick up an unholy row that they'll be able to hear all the way in Whitehall. But on the other hand relations with the Sultans and the Malays are sensitive. Confidentially, there's a plan to unify the whole of Malaya. The deal is that we won't go too hard on the collaborators if all the Sultans agree to transfer sovereignty to us. Some brigadier has been round the palaces setting out the bargain: sign up or else. You can bet that the Sultans aren't happy at being railroaded into giving equal rights to the Chinese and Indians at the point of a bayonet. The Malays already think that the British are too much on the side of the Chinese. Take the girl by force and things could turn pretty nasty if they decide to fight."

"Will it come to that?" I asked with surprise.

"It doesn't get into the papers," answered Ralph slowly, leaning forward. "There were clashes with the Chinese even before the Japs surrendered. When the Japs withdrew, the MPAJA moved in and started pushing the Malays around. There was an incident upcountry where they shot a Malay District Officer and an Indian doctor. They've been going after policemen and others who worked with the Japs — *ketua kampong, penghulu*, DOs, anyone who had anything to do with the administration. The Malays think that we haven't done enough to protect them. Now they've banded together and hit back. It's gotten very ugly in some places. It could get ugly here. All it needs is a spark."

"So will they try to take Marge?" I asked.

"Don't know," replied Ralph. "My guess is that they might try, with or without a court order. Get the girl first, apply to court later. But they can't find the girl unless you spill the beans. So your cooperation is the key to everything for them. You've really landed yourself in the frying pan this time and no mistake."

I nodded glumly. "Don't I know it. I haven't told Simon where she is. In fact, no one in the office except June knows. Maybe it would be a good idea for June to take a break and stay home for a while."

"I hear she's not in the office much these days anyway," said Ralph casually. "Seems she's got an admirer."

"June? An admirer? You can't be serious!" I was astounded. June had been one of the gang when we were little. As far as me and my friends were concerned, she was just a boy with knobs on. It wasn't easy to think of June as someone who would attract the attention of a man.

"Why not?" responded Ralph. "She's quite attractive, in her own way. Comes from a good family — male cousin excepted of course. She's not the worst catch in town."

"Who is the silly sod?" I asked.

"You mean you really didn't know," he answered. "It's that new interpreter-chappie, Yeo Eng Tong."

JUNE wasn't overly pleased to be told that she should stay away from work. Of all my cousins, she had the most unconventional upbringing. Gek Neo, the eldest, was brought up as a typical Nonya. May, the second, had become a nurse. Julie and Augusta, the two youngest, were schoolgirls when the war broke out. June by contrast had worked as companion to a formidable old Nonya before the War. During the Occupation she had joined the firm as a general dogsbody. She enjoyed the freedom that employment gave her.

She was helping Simon with a matrimonial case. It was the old story: old man meets young girl, old man dumps wife. The refinement in this case was that Wife Mark II happened to have been just shy of 16 at the time she met the old goat. This little Lolita had gone straight from infancy to adultery without breaking stride. He divorced his wife of 20 years' standing and went through a ceremony of marriage with his new paramour. Simon was trying to disentangle him from her at the behest of the first wife's children. June was enjoying herself immensely. She was getting inside information on the juiciest of scandals and was being paid to do it. Now I was asking her to give it up and go back to the shackled existence that society imposed on single girls.

"Why?" she asked petulantly. "Why must I stop because of that Miss Ruder?"

"It's Rider. You and I are the only ones in the firm who know where Marge is," I explained patiently, "not counting Ahmad of course. She doesn't know about Ahmad. So if there's to be any pressure by the authorities, we're the ones in the firing line. I don't want you involved in this business."

"What will they do? Kidnap me?" she responded scornfully.

"No, I don't think it'll come to that," I replied. "But if they wanted to get me to talk, they might threaten to hurt you or the family in some way, I don't know how. I couldn't stand that. Better that you keep your head down so they don't have that option."

She softened at this. "Okay, maybe I will not come into the office. But I can work with Eng Tong on the Lao case. We still must find Gim Huat's real mother."

I hesitated a moment. I really had nothing against Eng Tong, but somehow I didn't feel quite comfortable with the thought that he was paying court to June. "Should you be seeing so much of Eng Tong?" I ventured.

June immediately bristled again. "Who told you I was seeing Eng Tong? It was Ah Sum, right? That woman! *Ayoh, tak sudah-sudah*! She has been nagging, nagging, nagging. *Badan-nya mati, mulut tak mati*!*"

"No, it wasn't Ah Sum. As a matter of fact, it was Ralph," I answered carefully, realising what a minefield I had incautiously stumbled into. "He said that Eng Tong's sweet on you. Are you keen on him?"

---

* *Literally, her body may die but her mouth does not.*

She made a face. "I do not know. Maybe. I suppose. But it is not your *pasal* or Ralph's. Mak did not say anything. I decide for myself who I marry, if I marry. Whether Ah Sum or all of you like him or not!"

I knew better than to hold my ground under fire. "No, you're right," I said soothingly, trying to make a tactical withdrawal. "It's your life. Just don't get hurt, that's all."

"You can talk!" she retorted. "Like you are so clever about who to love!"

I winced. My own loss had left a raw wound. June was immediately contrite, "Sorry, sorry. I did not mean to remind you. My mouth is too big. Please forget it."

There wasn't anything more to say. I went back to my room, locked the door and stayed there for the rest of the afternoon.

10

I NOTICED something odd when the British came back. All of a sudden people who had quietly accepted the change in colonial masters when the Japanese took over revealed themselves to have been secretly anti-Japanese all along. They had been so good at hiding their true feelings that no one would ever have suspected their deep and abiding passion for the British and their abhorrence of all things Japanese. None of them would admit to having Japanese friends or even that there might have been some decent Japanese people.

We were all shell-shocked when the British surrendered in '42, literally and figuratively. Until then the superiority of the white race was a given. It was as much a part of the natural order as the rising of the sun in the east. I had been brought up on a steady diet of imperialist history. We were taught about Clive and Wolfe, Wellington and Nelson, the great civilising mission of Great Britain in dark Africa and the barbarous east. Little uncomfortable hiccups like losing the American colonies and massacring civilians in Amritsar had been glossed over. Until the very last day when Percival marched down Bukit Timah Road to the Ford Factory I had believed that there would be a miracle and somehow the British would turn the battle around. I wasn't the only one.

The change in management of Singapore didn't really matter to most people at first. We were willing to give the new masters a chance. The lurid stories of rape and pillage, the barbaric treatment of POWs and civilian prisoners, all these were put down to British propaganda. The Japanese soon wiped away that illusion. They extorted $50 million from the Chinese of Malaya. Family fortunes were ruined paying this "donation" towards the civilising mission of the Japanese Empire. Worse was Sook Ching, the operation to clean up Chinese opposition to the new order. I escaped with my life, barely. Many were not as lucky. Sook Ching embittered the Chinese in a way that no amount of placatory gestures would have appeased, even if the Japanese had bothered to try. Winning the hearts and minds of their new subjects was not part of their agenda.

Not unnaturally, the resistance to the Japanese was mainly Chinese-based. It was also Communist-led for the most part, although there were a few Kuomintang-affiliated groups up north near the Siamese border. Ah Moy had been a revelation to me. I hadn't realised that the Overseas-Chinese Anti-Japanese Army had a presence in Singapore. The Communist-dominated MPAJA posed as the only resistance to the occupiers. They gave short shrift to any other resistance groups when they found them. I had no doubt that Ah Moy had kept a very low profile indeed, not just for fear of the Japanese.

The sudden surrender of Japan left a void that the Communists were quick to fill. They had practically the only organised armed force in Malaya. The British pretended that the Communists were acting under orders as part of the grand Allied scheme of things, but the reality was different and everyone knew it. The small groups of Allied liason officers from Force 136 were more hostages of the MPAJA than its leaders. They were useful in getting supplies of arms and ammunition. A few were genuinely respected by their hosts; the rest were tolerated as long as they were useful.

The MPAJA had marched into the towns and villages of Malaya as the Japanese withdrew, posing as liberators. Then they started to mete out justice. The police were the first targets. So were those who had worked with the Japanese to keep the place running: district officers, *penghulu*, employees of government departments. The most savage reprisals were reserved for informers and profiteers. Popular justice was lynch-mob justice. Women who had liaisons with Japanese men were paraded through the streets naked, tortured and then murdered. Men who had worked too closely with the Japanese were dragged from their homes and subjected to all sorts of barbarities before being killed. The mere accusation of being an informer often was enough to condemn a man to a horrific death. Many personal scores were paid off during that vicious interregnum. The Japanese had been barbaric. The Communists proved that barbarism was not exclusive to one race.

In an ironic way, the British would have preferred that the Japanese had resisted their reoccupation of Malaya. They had a grand plan for the invasion and reconquest of Malaya, Operation Zipper. Operation Zipper came unzipped when the atom bombs were dropped. Reconquest would have re-established their predominance; reoccupation was such an anticlimax. They couldn't just let the MPAJA take over. The main invasion force was far from ready. It would be weeks before they could reach Malaya. So they decided that some token force had to go and plant the flag. Ralph had been one of the valiant vanguard. He told me how it had happened.

The CO of his unit had called him into his office the day after the Surrender.

"Are you doing anything in particular today, Smallwood?" asked the CO.

"No, Sir, nothing in my diary," answered Ralph innocently.

"Right-ho, get your kit packed. We're dropping you into Singapore tonight."

The next morning he and his Gurkha support team found

themselves on Farrer Park Racecourse re-taking the fortress of Singapore for the British Empire.

Like the MPAJA, the British also were out to nail the collaborators. Unlike the MPAJA, they did it legally. The started from the top, with the Malay sultans who had made their peace with the Japanese. Some, like the Sultan of Johore, were clearly white. He had put his Johore State Force at the disposal of the British during the fight for Malaya. When the British abandoned the mainland he chose to stay with his people rather than run away, and made his peace with the new imperial power. Others were grey. They said that they had no choice but to obey the new masters, but there was a suspicion that in some cases their obedience was not entirely forced. Two were black; they had been installed by the Japanese as compliant puppets. They were deposed quickly and banished. The hunt went down the line from the top to the bottom. The newspapers started baying for blood practically from the day they started publishing again. Renegades and traitors had to get their just desserts. Society demanded it. They were even going to rename Japan Street. It definitely wasn't a good time to be a friend of the Japanese.

I was acutely aware of all this as I trudged through the gates of the internment camp in Jurong. I had come to interview a Japanese friend in order to prepare the defence of a Japanese war criminal. This wasn't going to do anything for my popularity among the public.

COMMANDER HOJO YOSHISADA looked a lot older. It had only been a couple of months since I saw him last, but he had aged perceptibly. We bowed in the customary manner. I noticed though that he had added a couple of degrees to his bow and his head was lower than mine.

"Hojo-san, you are well?" I enquired.

"As well as can be expected," he replied courteously. "The British have been exemplary. I personally have no complaints. They give me much liberty. Many of my countrymen are not so fortunate. They have been made to labour in the hot sun at Tengah and are humiliated daily. Some of the British cannot forget and will not forgive the treatment that they and their comrades received. They are paying us back in our own coin. I cannot say that I blame them." He sighed. "And you, Chiang-san? You are well?"

"I also cannot complain," I responded with equal courtesy. "What news of Takeda-san?"

"He has been repatriated. The Americans need help with the occupation. His talents are in demand. He can contribute to the rehabilition of my homeland."

We sat down at the bare table in his office. Hojo and I had worked together in a department of the Syonan Tokubetusi. Our job had been to write pleasant little pieces to show the world how happy and gay everyone was under the new regime; in a word, propaganda. He was a naval officer who had lost an eye aboard the cruiser Jintsu during the Battle of the Java Sea, which gave him a vaguely Nelsonian look. Hojo had been trained in Dartmouth at a time when the Anglo-Japanese Alliance was still alive. He was a decent man. Those of us who knew him put in a good word when the British came back. It seemed to have worked. Most of his compatriots had been kept locked up in the internment camps. Hojo was allowed a degree of freedom to come and go without escort. The British needed interpreters and liaison officers. Hojo fitted the bill. He couldn't leave the camp without permission of course; but he had no reason or desire to do so. A lone Japanese wandering around the island wouldn't have lasted very long.

I explained what I had come for. "I have been tasked to defend one Warrant Officer Nakamura Nagamasa. He has been charged with war crimes, specifically murdering four people during interrogation. Do you know him?"

Hojo smiled slightly. "Why should I know him? He is *Kempei*, is he not?"

I nodded. "No reason, just asking. Anyway, I need to defend him. To do that I have to know why. Why did he act as he did? Was he ordered to do so?"

Hojo arched his eyebrows interrogatively. "Why do you ask me? Should you not be talking to him instead?"

"He won't talk. All he'll say is his rank and name. I thought you might explain it to me."

"You have cigarettes?" asked Hojo. I drew a pack out of my pocket and passed it to him. He withdrew one and lit it, savouring the aroma for a time. I waited patiently.

"You ask me why," he said at length. "Who can say? I am a naval officer. My family have been naval officers since the Meiji Restoration. Before that we were samurai, for generations stretching back long before the Gempei War. What do I know of the ways of the Kempeitai?"

I was disappointed and said so. Hojo shook his head. "You take an *ashigaru* and give him a toy sword, a *shin gunto,* and think by this to make him a samurai?" He made a scornful noise. "What does such a man know of Bushido, of the way of the warrior? He sees but he does not understand. He acts as he thinks a samurai acts, without understanding the code of the warrior and the customs of war.

"There are seven principles of Bushido: righteousness, humanity, sincerity, propriety, honour, courage and loyalty. The old samurai families understand this. But the new army is not a samurai army. An army raised from peasants, officered by peasants, remains a peasant army, for all their fine uniforms and shining medals. You met some of them, men like Tsuji, mad dogs lusting for power. They think that it is Nippon's manifest destiny to supplant the white man and rule Asia. This can only be done by conquest, by terrorising people into submission. If there is resistance, it must be crushed. If anyone fights back there must be vengence — two eyes for an eye, ten teeth for a tooth. To hold an empire by fear, that is their creed." He took a deep whiff of smoke. "The mad dogs had good teachers — Russians and Frenchmen and Germans. And even Britons. They learned the lessons of European history well; that the strong take from the weak and that there is great honour and prestige in possessing the lands of others. Now we are told that this is wrong. It is wrong to seize colonies from the Europeans. That is a war crime, a crime against humanity."

He paused momentarily. "Not all of us wanted this war," he continued. "Admiral Yamamoto did not want war. He knew that we would lose if we fought the Americans. He said so often. But he was overruled. We have paid the price. Yamamoto paid the price. The Americans shot him down in an ambush. You remember how we had to suppress the news of his assassination?"

"If you knew you would lose why did you do it?" I asked.

Hojo took a deep breath. "Duty. You do not understand the word. The duty of a samurai is to obey his lord above all. It is his duty to fight and die for the Emperor. His own life means nothing."

"Even in a war you say you did not want?" I pressed.

"Even in such a war. The Kwantung Army was responsible for getting Nippon involved in the China Incident. The civilians lost control. There was a military clique that was bent on conquest. Even senior officers could not control them. *Gekokujo* we called it; the juniors prevail over the seniors. Assassins and murderers went unpunished. The politicians were too weak or too afraid to oppose the military clique. After they assassinated Prime Minister Inukai, who can blame them? We saw where it was leading but what could we do? All was done in the name of the Emperor. We had no choice but to obey, even though it meant our destruction. When the Americans imposed their oil embargo, we were forced to fight. We could not just surrender. To surrender is to lose one's honour. To live dishonoured is far worse than to die."

I let the matter drop, not wanting to get into a long debate. "This doesn't give me anything to go on," I said. "I can't argue that because the British and the Dutch and the French have forcibly colonised Asia, the Japanese are justified in killing and torturing the very people whom they have made their subjects."

Hojo lit another cigarette. "You are right, of course. You wish to understand? Let me try to explain. Australian and British officers came into the Harbour and sank our ships. They were brave men and worthy opponents. We honoured them even as we executed them. But the Army cannot believe that such a thing can happen without help from the population. So what do they do? They turn to the Kempeitai. They order them to find the people responsible. I do not know this Nakamura. From the little you tell me, I deduce that he is not an intelligent man. To such a man, there is only one way to find out. Beat the truth out of the prisoner. Extract his fingernails and crush his genitals until he talks. That is the way of the Kempeitai."

I shuddered involuntarily. I knew exactly what he was talking about. My back still had the scars. Shaking off the evil memory, I pressed on. "Nakamura isn't being tried for that incident. Others will be in the dock soon for that, I hear. This was afterwards, early in 1944."

"The principle is the same," he responded. "The Army decides that there are too many subversive elements in the population. They fear lawlessness. Resistance must be crushed. The Kempeitai are called in to extract information."

"And what if a man like Nakamura couldn't get the information his superiors wanted? Would he be killed?" I persisted.

Hojo laughed shortly. "Killed? Of course not. No army can operate on the principle that those who fail are to be killed. He would have been disgraced. He would be dishonoured by his failure. If that failure were bad enough, he would have committed *seppuku*. To atone for his failings and redeem his honour."

"Would he have been forced to commit hara-kiri?"

"No true samurai is forced to do what honour demands. Say that an important prisoner escapes through negligence of the guards or dies in custody without giving information. The officer in charge is dishonoured. A samurai would know what to do, even if the fault was that of his subordinates. Such a dishonour can only be redeemed by *seppuku*. For one such as Nakamura, I do not know. It may be that he would have to be told what to do. You cannot ask me. He is the only one who knows. Or his superiors, if you can find them."

I pursed my lips. It wasn't much of a defence; certainly not one that I would be happy to advance as an excuse for murder. "Who would his superiors be?" I asked.

"I cannot say for sure. The 3rd Kempeitai Headquarters of the Southern Army was responsible for Malai, Syonan and Lingga. The commanding officer of the 4th Kempeitai Branch in Syonan at that time was Lieutenant-Colonel Sumida Haruzo. He would know who Nakamura's superiors were. You might perhaps ask him what you want."

"This Lieutenant-Colonel Sumida. Do you know him personally?"

"Slightly," replied Hojo dismissively. "A man of culture, but with no other redeeming qualities. The British must have him if he is still alive."

I rose to leave. "Thank you for your assistance Hojo-san," I said, bowing.

"I am pleased to have been of assistance, Chiang-san," he replied, bowing deeper. As I reached the door he spoke again. "I fear that

I have upset you, my young friend. You asked me to explain. I have done so as far as I am able. To understand is not to condone. I understand why my countrymen have done what they did in the name of patriotism. I do not condone it. I am deeply ashamed."

I never saw him again. He was repatriated early in 1946. Under different circumstances we might have become close friends.

ON the way back from Jurong I decided to drop in on Marge. Colonel Newman had provided d'Almeida with a Humber staff car, which Ahmad drove. The Morris was put at the disposal of whoever needed out-of-town transport. I enjoyed the freedom that possession of a car gave me. I took the long route by the sea. The road ran past little fishermen's kampongs set in the middle of mangrove swamps. The village folk bred prawns in the swamps and made charcoal out of the mangrove wood. Rickety plank walkways connected the huts to the road. Small crocodiles basked on the mudbanks. Once past the 7th milestone the Malay kampongs gave way to the mansions of the rich Babas, looking much the worse for wear now. Most had been taken over by the Japanese during the Occupation. They hadn't bothered to maintain them much, which was to be expected given the shortages we suffered. The grand gardens had been dug up and planted with vegetables. Despite the general dilapidation the area still retained an air of faded gentility.

I wasn't entirely sure where Ahmad's kampong was. We'd taken a trishaw from town, which was in the opposite direction. Had I missed it somehow, I asked myself. I was debating whether to turn around and retrace my road when I saw the stream and the pillbox. I might have driven right past if it hadn't been for the army truck parked by the roadside. I pulled up and got out full of foreboding.

There was a welcoming committee already at the kampong. Half a dozen British soldiers with fixed bayonets were at the small bridge crossing the stream. Beyond them was a throng of villagers, maybe thirty or forty strong. They were armed with a collection of parangs and bamboo spears. One of the soldiers stepped forward to bar my way.

"What the hell's going on?" I demanded. "Who's in charge here?"

The soldier flinched in surprise, not quite expecting to be addressed in such a manner by a native. A sergeant detached himself from the group.

"What's your bloody business 'ere then?" he demanded.

"What's your business here?" I retorted. "You've no right to block access. This is a public path."

"We 'ave our orders," replied the sergeant. "No one leaves the village."

"Well, I'm not leaving am I?" I responded, pushing my way past him. "I'm bloody well going in."

I marched right over the bridge before the astounded sergeant could react. The kampong folk looked uncertain. I was a stranger of unknown intent. There was an awkward silence as I stood facing them.

"Tuan Dennis," called a voice from the crowd.

"Karim," I responded with relief, "*apa khabar?*"

"*Khabar baik,*" he answered, giving the customary response. All is well. How ironic, I thought, with armed troops in front and a mob behind. I got the story from him with an effort, trying hard to follow his quick-fire Malay. Apparently, a British officer had appeared out of the blue and demanded to see Mariam — or Margaret, as he called her. The kampong folk demurred. Karim and his brother Roslan were called. Heated words were exchanged. Shortly afterwards the officer had returned with a platoon of troops. He tried to force his way across the bridge but found it barred by the villagers. Not wanting to break the impasse by force, he had ordered his men to surround the kampong. No one was to leave.

"How long has this been going on?" I asked.

"Since this morning," answered Karim.

"I'll see what I can do," I assured him.

As I re-crossed the bridge Karim called to me. "Tell the *Orang Puteh* that we will never give up our sister Mariam. We will fight."

11

I WAS in a really foul mood when I got back to the office. The authorities had no business stopping law-abiding folk going about their affairs. But what upset me more was the thought that somehow I had been responsible. If only I had kept my big mouth shut about Marge, none of this would have happened. I didn't know how I was going to face Ahmad. But first I was going to have it out with Simon da Silva.

"What on earth possessed you to tell the authorities where Marge was?" I stormed, bursting into his room without knocking. My dramatic entry was somewhat marred by the fact that he wasn't in. George popped his head through the connecting door.

"I gather you've heard?" he said.

"Heard? I've seen it with my own eyes," I responded heatedly. "Troops around the kampong. They won't let the folks out. How did they find the place? Only June and I knew. I haven't told anyone and June's been at home."

"We've rather underestimated our dear Simon," said George. "He's not quite as simple as we thought. He knew that she was in Ahmad's kampong. So he did what we did; asked around the office and then passed the word on."

"The blithering idiot! Does he know that there could be bloodshed? Ahmad's sons are up in arms, and I mean that literally. They're ready to fight."

George whistled. "I didn't think it was that bad."

"The question is, what do we do about it?"

"We calm down," said George, guiding me by the arm into his office. "Uncle Clarence is on it. Went off straight to see Newman the moment he heard."

George filled me in. It transpired that the old harpy Miss Rider had collared Simon on his way out of the office the previous evening and threatened him with disbarment or, worse, blackballing at his Club. He had capitulated immediately and promised to find out about Marge. He was as good as his word. The upshot was that a certain Major Ridley had appeared early that morning and asked to see Marge, with the result that I already knew.

"Ralph told me that things are a bit sensitive with the Malays right now," I said, "what with all this talk of the Sultans losing sovereignty and all. Surely this Ridley knows this?"

"I've had a word with Ralph too," continued George. "He knows the fellow. Ridley's a nasty piece of work. He was a planter upcountry and managed to get out before the Fall. He's come back to re-establish the prestige of the Empire. This is insurrection. Insurrection has to be nipped in the bud. He doesn't like it when the natives don't know their place. And keeping a white girl from her family definitely fits that description as far as he's concerned."

I was depressed. We had hoped and prayed for the return of the British for so long. Everything would be all right then. It wasn't supposed to be like this.

D'ALMEIDA returned shortly before dinnertime, with a chastened Simon in tow. He had an unexpected companion too.

"We have managed to sort things out for the time being," he said, "with the invaluable assistance of Colonel Newman."

Newman inclined his head in acknowledgment. "That damned

fool Ridley nearly set a match to the tinder," said Newman. "The word's got out among the kampongs. More armed Malays were coming to protect Margaret. This business has got them pretty riled up. We've managed to intercept them, so far without bloodshed. But that won't last."

"What did Ridley think he was up to? Surely he must have known how the Malays would react to troops coming to grab Marge," commented George.

"Ridley's the sort who thinks that the only way we can rule is with an iron fist in an iron glove. That's the way he treated his 'natives' as he calls them. And after the god-awful mess that we made in '42 people like him aren't inclined to show any weakness when faced with this kind of situation. He thinks that anything less than total subjugation of the natives would be fatal to the white man's prestige. Our right to rule depends on our power to enforce that rule."

George's brow darkened. "If he thinks that, he's going to be disillusioned quickly. Force is going to be met with force for sure."

"Exactly," replied Newman. "The more force we use, the greater the counter-force. There's a neat German word that describes it: *Teufelskreis*, a devil's circle — what you'd call a vicious circle. The more troops we send in, the larger the rebellion; so we send even more troops, which fans the flames hotter until the whole thing burns out of control. The tighter we try to hold Malaya — or India, more importantly — the quicker they will slip from our grasp. But Ridley and his sort can't see that."

"So you'll let Malaya and India go?" asked George, unable to hide the eagerness in his voice.

"Far from it," responded Newman. "I didn't fight the Communists and the Japs for a decade just to wring my hands and watch the dissolution of the British Empire helplessly. My job is to restore stability. To do that, we've got to get people used to obeying the law again. We're going to resolve this properly and within the law. Not with troops and a whiff of grapeshot."

"And how does this help Marge?" I butted in.

"We worked out a compromise," said Newman. "Miss Rider won't be pleased, but the kampong folk reckoned that they could go along with it. For the time being."

"This is where I will need your assistance again," said d'Almeida, addressing me. "It has been agreed that the issue of custody of Miss Barron should be referred to the courts as soon as possible. When that will be no one knows. In the interim, the young lady will leave the kampong and stay with a neutral party."

I winced inwardly. Every time there was a fight over some kid, we ended up doing the hosting at my place. It was like we were running a half-way house for wayward waifs.

"That neutral party will be me," continued d'Almeida. "Ahmad has agreed to it. But I have no experience looking after a young girl." He paused. "That is why I would like you to ask your Mak whether she would consent to your cousin June undertaking the task."

I was relieved and surprised at the same time. "But why don't you ask her youself?"

"If I were to ask your Mak," explained d'Almeida patiently, "she would feel obliged to agree. It is a great imposition, what I am asking. I do not wish her, or Miss June, to feel that they must accede. It would be better if the request came through you. Then they can answer frankly."

"Yes, of course, with pleasure," I answered truthfully. I was glad that we weren't going to be lumbered with Marge, having just gotten rid of Gim Huat. I even more glad that June would be put in charge. She wouldn't have Eng Tong hanging around her all day at d'Almeida's place. A sudden thought struck me. "What does Marge feel about all this?"

"I'm afraid," answered Newman solemnly, "that what Miss Margaret Barron feels is neither here nor there. This is a matter of public interest. And that means that private interests have to go by the board."

12

ALL of a sudden I felt as if I was drowning in work. Cuthbert came back from Bahau bearing cases. I started suffering from piles. Every morning I'd come in to work and the piles were there on my desk. No matter how much I did they never seemed to go down. Every settler had a legal problem of some sort; a claim, a counterclaim, a cross-claim ... it never ended. On top of everything d'Almeida seemed to think that I had agreed to help out with the Habibullah case. Then, to cap it all, came the notice that Nakamura's case had been fixed for hearing and would I please be ready in two weeks.

Truth to tell, there was little I could do to get ready. I needed someone to testify that Nakamura had been ordered to do what he did. That was his best chance to avoid the noose. But the rest of his *bunkentai* had committed mass hara-kiri the day after the Surrender. His immediate superior was dead. The only hope left was to find someone higher up to give evidence of the orders people like him would have received.

I needed to get to see Lieutenant-Colonel Sumida. As Hojo had suspected, he was in the hands of the British. Newman told me where to find him and even made arrangements for an interview. I was puzzled.

"Why are you being so good to me?" I asked. "Aren't you on the other side?"

"I am on the other side," he replied. "I want to see the war criminals brought to justice and given their just desserts."

"You could just shoot them," I said, "and save a lot of trouble." And not make me any more unpopular than I already am with my neighbours, I added silently.

"We could," he responded, "but then we'd be no better than the Kempeitai." He offered me a cigarette, which I declined. Putting away the pack, he got out his pipe, filled it and took a deep breath.

"Listen," he said, "we fought this war to wipe out a great evil. We've made the world a better place. At least I hope we have. But we can't pretend to be democrats at home and run the Empire like Fascists. Some people thought that we'd be welcomed as liberators. I don't delude myself. The Netherlands Indies declared independence just before the Japs surrendered. It's clear that they don't want the Dutch back. We've got troops over there now, trying to keep the peace. It's the same in Tonkin and Annam. Ho Chi Minh has just proclaimed the independence of the whole of Vietnam. The French will have the devil of a time retaking the place. Even here in Malaya, we've got nationalists who want to be part of the new Indonesia. And don't forget our friends the Communists; they may be our allies for the time being, but they're out to take over by fair means or foul. We need the support of people like d'Almeida and you and even Singham. We won't get it if we go around behaving like the master race."

"Very enlightened of you," I said. "But I don't get the impression that it's a widely-held view."

"No, there are those who think that the only way to hold on to the Empire is with blood and iron. But the SACSEA gave orders that there's to be no witch hunt and no suggestion of victors' justice."

"The SAC-what?" I asked. The alphabet soup of acronyms made my head spin.

"Supreme Allied Commander South-East Asia," explained Newman patiently. "Admiral Mountbatten himself. We're to deal with the renegades and war criminals in accordance with the law. I'm taking him at his word."

"Good for him and good for you," I responded.

As I left he made a parting shot. "By the way Chiang," he said, "try not to get Nakamura off if he doesn't deserve it. Justice means that the guilty should pay."

NEWMAN'S help didn't do any good. Sumida didn't want to see me. He had his own troubles. The Adjutant-General's Department was in the process of gathering evidence to prosecute Sumida and his subordinates for the Double Tenth atrocities. This had arisen out of the Anglo-Australian raid on shipping in Singapore Harbour in 1943. The Japanese were convinced that the raiders must have had local help. They didn't, but no one knew it at the time. The Kempeitai were turned loose on 10th October. A lot of innocent people were dragged in, tortured and killed. The raiders had a second go the following year and were caught. It was only then that the Japanese realised that they'd made a mistake. By then it was too late for many of the poor souls who fell into the clutches of the Kempeitai on the Double Tenth. Sumida and seven others from his unit were later convicted of responsibility for the atrocities. They were hanged in 1946.

Anyway, none of this was known to me at the time. All I had was Nakamura. A second visit to him had proven as fruitless as the first. He cringed away from us when we came to see him in prison; from Eng Tong, at any rate. If I hadn't been there, I'm sure that Eng Tong would have made him pay personally for all the atrocities inflicted by his compatriots on the Chinese people since 1931. He had a habit of firing questions in a tone of unconcealed hostility as if he were interrogating the man. The answers were always the same: he had nothing to say, no excuse to offer. It was as if he had resigned himself to death. Perhaps Hojo had been right; this was his way of expiating his sins, offering up his life in atonement for failure. Strange how a bully could turn so completely once the trappings of power were removed. Whatever may have impelled him, it gave me precious little to defend him with. If only he had shown some spark of dignity or courage like the traitor Ormonde had, I might have been able to cobble together a mitigation plea with some semblance of conviction. As it was, I was left only with pure abstract law, which would have been fine for supervisions in college but was not the stuff that tended to impress military tribunals composed of hard-nosed war veterans.

It certainly didn't impress my family. "Why do you defend this *Jepun*?" asked Gek Neo accusingly. "They are thieves and murderers. You should not be doing this."

"Because it's how the system works," I answered without much conviction. "Every man has a right to have his case put fairly and objectively to the court."

"You are right if he has a reason for what he did," she responded. "What is his reason?"

She had me there. I could think of no adequate reason to justify the torture of civilians, even in the name of wartime security. It was a good thing that there was no jury. Nakamura would have swung before I even finished my closing submissions.

ENG TONG disturbed me. Now that Ralph had pointed it out, it was obvious even to me that he was paying an awful lot of attention to June. I couldn't read June. She never spoke of him, at least not to me. But she did seem to go out of the way to spend time with him.

June continued to see Gim Huat regularly although it wasn't really necessary. In fact, we could have just let the matter go to sleep. Legally, it was straightforward. Gim Huat was Lao Leong Ann's only son. There were no other relatives. By the law of intestacy the boy would get everything. We only had to wait for the courts to start functioning again and then we could apply for letters of administration. With the three would-be mothers out of the way there could be no complications.

However, June had other ideas. It was true that she had developed a real bond with the little boy. She popped over at least once a week just to check up on him. Ostensibly, she professed to be determined to find Gim Huat's true mother. How she intended to do this was a complete mystery. Singapore was full of displaced persons. In fact, the whole of Malaya was one gigantic refugee camp. The Japanese had shipped labourers from Malaya to Siam. Prisoners and comfort women had been sent to Japan. Emigrants had left Singapore to make a new life in Endau and Bahau and Bintan. Those with relatives upcountry had left the city in the last year of the war, hoping to escape the hunger and the shortages. This whole mass of displaced humanity was on the move. The municipal records were in complete confusion. The chances of finding Chan Sew Neo were nil — assuming that she was still alive. But June wouldn't give up. She spent hours combing back copies of the *Syonan Shimbun* with Eng Tong at her side. My suspicious mind wondered whether this was the true reason for her pursuit of her quixotic quest.

The family were unanimous in their disapproval of Eng Tong as a potential suitor for June. Maybe it was social snobbery. We were after all old money, except without the money. Our family had been in the Straits for over a century. He was a *sinkhek*, a newcomer from the old country with neither family nor fortune. For June's sake I tried very hard not to let this prejudice me. She was thirty after all, way past the sell-by date for a Nonya. She affected not to care, but I had seen her with Gim Huat. She loved children. Eng Tong might be her last chance to have her own. But try as I might, there was something about him that I couldn't take to. I couldn't put my finger on it, but I felt that somehow he was dangerous. I was glad that June was moving out from our Cavanagh Road house.

I HADN'T realised how much Mak was troubled by this until she took me aside one day and said, "Boy, can you take me to visit your Uncle?"

For a moment I was stumped. "Uncle? Which Uncle? The one in Joo Chiat?"

She clicked her tongue. "*Ayoh*, you are a *gobblock*. Your Uncle, Pa."

I felt really foolish. Pa was my father's brother, who had taken me into his family when my parents died. He was an aloof man, who left my upbringing and that of my girl cousins entirely to Mak. Though I was told to call him Pa, it was clear to me that he wasn't my real father. I remembered little of him, having been packed off to England at an early age to be educated in one of those penal institutions they call public schools. He died long before I came home. It wasn't often that Mak went to visit Pa. Once a year, during the Cheng Beng Festival in spring, she would go to his tomb to clean it. Usually she went with Gek Neo, since the rest of us had given up the ancestral religion. May had been converted to Methodism at school and brought along her sister June and her half-sisters Julie and Augusta, so it was a good package deal for the missionaries. Gek Neo held out despite all blandishments, more I think from a sense of duty to Mak than any attachment to the old customs. Strictly speaking, Pa wasn't Mak's ancestor, but that little technicality didn't bother her. Someone had to do it; it should have been me, as his foster-son and the eldest male relative of my generation. But she never asked me. At least, not until now.

I borrowed the Morris for the day. We motored out to the big cemetery at Holland Road. The paths were overgrown, but Mak knew the way. Pa's tomb was on the hillside facing south. It was a large semi-circular structure faced with marble, built for more than one. He was interred there with his first wife, June's mother. His photograph was mounted in the centre. On the right was his wife's photograph. On the left there was a blank space. This was to be Mak's resting place when her time came.

The tomb itself was structurally in good shape, but the rank weeds had grown wildly around it. I cleared the undergrowth with a small scythe. We cleaned the stonework carefully. The marble was chipped in some places, but otherwise in relatively good condition. Tombs were forever; those who had the means made sure they would last. Mak laid out the offerings that she had brought: a bowl of rice, a couple of eggs, some vegetables from our garden. This was all that we could afford in those straitened times. When all was arranged, she lit her joss sticks and prostrated herself. Mak had a very personal form of syncretic religious belief. She was as happy attending novena as praying to Kuan Yin. When she was troubled, she found solace communing with my departed uncle. I moved away to give her some privacy. I felt an interloper in this conversation between husband and wife.

The graveyard was strangely calming. Europeans have a fascination with tombs and graves. Most Chinese avoid them as places of ill-fortune. Having lived in England for the better part of my life, I didn't have that superstitious dread of the dead. The birds were singing in the trees and a light breeze ruffled the leaves. It was rather peaceful. I wandered idly along the path, glancing at the graves and tombstones with macabre fascination. I couldn't read the Chinese inscriptions. I just looked at the names and dates, which were often written in Roman letters. To my surprise, on a tomb tucked away from the main path I recognised the one and only Chinese character that I knew: my surname. I scraped away the moss. There were two photos, a young man and woman. The pictures were familiar: they were my parents.

I have no real memory of my father and mother. They died when I was two. I had seen these very same photos on the spirit tablets placed on the altar in our house. But to me they were just faded pictures on an old table. I stood there in silence for a long while, wondering what they would have thought of what I'd been up to. Did they think that I had neglected my duty as a son and nephew? After half-an-hour Mak was ready. She called to me and I came over. We tidied up the place, leaving the offerings behind. "Shall we go home?" I asked.

She shook her head. "To Chinatown," she said.

Of all the districts in the city, Chinatown had recovered fastest. It was bustling again, just as before the war. The itinerant hawkers were out, selling food and heaven-knows-what from their wooden pushcarts. Families were squatting at the roadside eating, smoking and doing their ablutions. Some of the buildings were still in ruins but reconstruction was going on. Gangs of *samsui* women were clearing away the rubble, their red headdresses standing out starkly against the brown and grey stones.

Mak directed me to a little side street near the river. There was a cast-iron art nouveau pissoir here which one could smell two hundred yards down the road. She indicated that I should park there, which I did without enthusiasm, holding my nose with one hand and steering with the other. We got out and walked through the warren of narrow lanes, under the poles of washing that dripped constantly like a drizzle after a monsoon. Life was lived on the road here. There was a barber under a banyan tree, stropping his razor as his customer leaned back in the chair. Over the street a group of coolies was engaged in a card game. A letter writer plied his trade at an intersection, using an upturned crate as a desk. Mak entered a dark shophouse. It was a fortune teller's establishment.

This fortune teller employed a small parrot to make his predictions. It was a nondescript green creature which had seen better days. Its feathers were unkempt and faded. The bird was offered a cylindrical container with sticks in it. It picked one and the fortune teller squinted at it to interpret the voice of the fates. I never could summon up much confidence in a fortune cast by a bird-brain, but Mak's faith was stronger than mine. They had a consultation and money changed hands. Mak emerged with a worried look.

"This business with Eng Tong," she said, "it will end badly."

"I suppose you'd better tell June," I replied. "She won't like it."

Mak put her hand on my arm. "No, Boy, not June," she said seriously. "It will end badly for you."

13

MARGE was duly moved into d'Almeida's sprawling bungalow, with June as her chaperone and nanny. As expected, Miss Rider had kicked up an almighty fuss. Major Ridley was none too pleased either. He would far rather have sent in his troops with fixed bayonets to get her from the kampong, but since Newman outranked him he could do nothing except glower and simmer in silence. He wanted to post guards around d'Almeida's place; Newman would have none of that either. Marge would be free to come and go until a court of competent jurisdiction declared that her aunt had custody of her. Ridley agreed with bad grace. However, I noticed that whenever I came to see d'Almeida after that there was an army jeep parked near his gate, apparently with engine-trouble.

Karim insisted on taking up residence at the d'Almeida bungalow too. He couldn't overtly oppose the arrangement his father had agreed to, but it was obvious that he didn't like it one bit. D'Almeida installed him in the servants' quarters and made him *kebun*. The grounds were large and unkempt after the neglect of the war years, so Karim did have a real job. Most of the garden had been dug up and planted with vegetables and fruit trees. These had still to be tended. Fisherman that he was, gardening didn't suit Karim's temperament entirely. But he took to it with gusto, slashing enthusiatically at the long grass with a parang. It allowed him to keep an eye on Mariam and vent his frustrations at the same time.

June spent her days keeping house and watching Marge. She preferred to be called Marge and so we did, at least in private. But in public when Karim or Ahmad were around, we'd use her Malay name. The girl was just over fifteen and painfully shy. Whether this was her nature or because of the trauma she had lived through I didn't know. June has a natural flair for dealing with children, but even she had difficulty in getting Marge to open up. Marge had been barely twelve when she lost her family. When the bombs fell, the house had collapsed on her and so had her world. The broken bones had healed with time. But the spirit hadn't; not quite, not yet.

NENEK had rescued her, tended her wounds, made her part of her family. She was of course immensely grateful to Nenek, who loved her as her own until she passed away. Pak Chik Ahmad was like a father to her. He had no daughters of his own, only sons — half a dozen of them by his two wives. Slowly the nightmares receded and the memory of her former life faded. It was hard at first, learning to speak a different language, fumbling with unfamiliar clothes, coping with different customs. People were unfailingly kind. What little they had, they shared with her. She was treated like a little princess, as much as their poverty would allow. Nevertheless, deep down she felt that somehow she was being disloyal to her parents by becoming part of someone else's family.

She grew up in the kampong, brought up as a Malay girl. Initially, they kept her out of sight for fear of the Japanese. The new administration introduced a system of passes and controls. The *ketua kampong* was supposed to report any strangers. Fortunately, Pak Chik Ahmad was related to their *ketua kampong*. Nothing was said about the little white girl in their midst. Later on, she was sequestered because that was the way girls were supposed to be. There were many restrictions on girls in the conservative village society. Mixing with boys of her own age was completely out of the question. She became withdrawn and shy.

In her previous life, she had many playmates and little to do. The kampong children did play with her, but they had chores. So did she as she grew stronger. Once she turned fourteen, she was no longer treated as a child. There was water to be fetched from the well and firewood to be cut. The kitchen was the place for the women and girls. They cooked over a wood stove, simple meals of rice, vegetables, fish and on very special occasions chicken. During Ramadan the kampong folk fasted. At the end of Ramadan there was a feast. New clothes were out of the question, but she had one suit reserved for special occasions like Hari Raya Puasa.

Pak Chik Ahmad tended his vegetable plot and looked after the chickens. His sons continued their trade as fishermen. In many ways the kampong folk were better off than most others, though times were hard for all. In the last year of the war, two of Karim's half-brothers went off to Bintan to join the colony there as part of the Japanese campaign to grow more food. There were restrictions on fishing near the coast. Able-bodied men were conscripted for war work in the *Heiho*. Sentries and barbed wire appeared along the road. The old pillbox was equipped with a new machine-gun. It was whispered that the British were coming back. Everyone knew what that meant. The Japanese were not known for giving up tamely. Tension mounted daily.

Then, all of a sudden, came the news came that the Japanese had surrendered. Word went around that the Chinese Communists were coming to take over. The Malay policemen from the police station at the 7th milestone left their posts to take shelter in the kampong. The Communists were taking reprisals against policemen and other so-called collaborators. The kampong folk started arming themselves. Spears were made out of bamboo, the tips whittled down to a wicked point. Parangs were sharpened.

But the ruckus died down soon enough. The Communists did not appear after all. Neither did the British, though they heard that the *Orang Puteh* were back. Life returned to its simple rhythm. Then out of the blue, June and I came into the kampong. Pak Chik Ahmad went back to his old job. They kept the news of Aunt Dorothy from her. It was only when the soliders appeared in the kampong that she discovered that her aunt was alive and demanding to take her back to England.

WE did some digging up about Dorothy Rider to see what we were up against. I had met her sort as a schoolboy in England. A lower-middle class teacher in an upper-class public school, she would have had to constantly endure the condescension of the parents and the slights of some of the girls she taught. They looked down on her as a member of a lower social class. She resented their arrogance while at the same time aspired to join them.

Strangely enough I never felt racial prejudice in England. Social snobbery, yes, definitely. In my public school I was ostracised because I wasn't rich, not because I wasn't white. Once I left school the people I met were in general polite and considerate to strangers, if a little reserved. Some were even kind. I remember in particular Mrs MacDougall, who ran a boarding house in Wells-next-the-Sea. I stayed there for a couple of months one summer, during that long break between the end of Easter Term and the beginning of Michaelmas Term. She became quite motherly to me. I suppose that I must have had a very lean and hungry look. She took it upon herself to keep me well supplied with food, which was a mixed blessing because she wasn't a very good cook. I remember her fondly; though her scones were of stone, her heart was soft.

Out in the East it was different. Europeans were the masters. Like so many of her kind, Dorothy Rider felt that she was one of the ruling class — in Malaya, if not in England. The class barriers that had existed in England were much lower in the East. There were very few real toffs amongst the white British community. The ones who lived in Malaya clung tightly together for mutual support and company. Teachers were in short supply. Once the war broke out in Europe, it was out of the question to send the children home to be educated. Dorothy Rider found a good position in Raffles Institution, the premier school on the island. Sir Stamford Raffles had founded it in order to give the natives a decent education. Raffles was colour-blind; his successors were not. The European teachers had their own common room, separate from the Asiatics. The twain did not meet socially. That was the norm throughout Malaya. The highest position an Asiatic could aspire to in the Colonial Civil Service was that of Chief Clerk. No matter how experienced or talented an Asiatic might have been, the greenest griffin fresh off the boat from England had seniority over him. Miss Rider felt at home at last.

It didn't last though. The Japanese knocked the whole social pyramid askew when they took over. The civilians were interned first at Changi and then at Sime Road. The women were separated from the men and left to fend for themselves, something that many of them never had to do before. Although the Japanese had a well-deserved reputation for brutality against POWs, they didn't deliberately mistreat the women. The first camp commandant in Changi was a sadist, but as the tide of the war turned the succeeding commandants were more humane. A lot of the suffering was due to sheer incompetence on the part of the Japanese, who had no idea how to treat a captive civilian population of European stock. I had contacts in Sime Road during the War. They gave me a picture of what it was like. Miss Rider was one of those who stood up to the Japanese and insisted on her right to be treated as a human being. She was one of the leaders of the camp, getting things done by encouragement, cajolery and bullying. By and large, the guards respected her, perhaps even feared her a little. She was not one to put up with any guff from anyone, whether pupils, natives or prison camp guards. She came out of the ordeal in better mental shape than most.

When she learned that Marge had survived, she set her mind to reclaim the girl. There was no monetary motive, unlike in Gim Huat's case. Marge hadn't a brass farthing to her name. It was a matter of principle, pure and simple. The very idea of surrendering his sister's surviving child to the natives revolted her to the core.

IT was clear that Marge was conflicted in her feelings. She made it quite plain that she didn't want to go off with Aunt Dorothy. England was a foreign place and her memories of it were not pleasant. After nearly 10 years in the tropics, she couldn't face the cold and the drab greyness of it all. Her new life, simple though it be, was not uncongenial. She hadn't any friends in England. She didn't much care for Aunt Dorothy either. But whatever else she might have been, Dorothy Rider was a blood relative — her only one left in the world.

I don't think that Ahmad or his sons had any inkling of the way Marge felt. To them, the matter was simple. She was one of them now. Ahmad's boys were fiercely protective of their adopted sister. When Karim said they would die rather than let her be taken, I had no doubts about his seriousness. In the old days, his people had been pirates and warriors. They might be fisherfolk now, but their blood still ran hot when faced with a challenge. The *Orang Puteh* were not supermen; let them come to take Mariam if they dared. He kept glaring hostilely at the khaki-clad figures who loitered beyond d'Almeida's gate as he attacked the weeds with his *changkul*.

14

THE liberation very quickly proved to be a disappointment. People had thought that with the Japanese gone, happy days would be here again. The reality was sobering. Food prices stayed high. Rationing remained in place. There were complaints in the papers every day about profiteers and racketeers. Salaries did not keep pace with the cost of living. The BMA proved not only inefficient but venal. Corruption was rife. Whatever their shortcomings, the pre-war colonial civil servants had a sense of duty. They really believed that they were doing good for the natives. The civilians in uniform who formed the bulk of the BMA administrators knew that they were there only for a limited time. Service was not their first priority. If there was a chance to acquire something of value, it wasn't to be missed. Palms had to be greased to get things done. Otherwise, things went by the book, which meant at the pace of a crippled snail. Many of the recently-freed civilian internees complained about the slowness of the repatriation process. They felt keenly that the military had let them down in 1942 and were letting them down again.

The Communists were quick to capitalise on the general mood of discontent. The Malayan Communist Party came out of the shadows and started organising the workers. They brought the dockworkers out at the end of October. There were strikes and stoppages all over. The Societies Ordinance remained suspended, which meant that the Communist Party could operate quite legally. So could the triads. Petty crime exploded. When people are scrabbling for their existence, obedience to the law is not the first thing on their minds. The general atmosphere of lawlessness was exacerbated by an underlying tension between the Malays and the Chinese.

During the War, the Japanese had transferred the four northern Malay states to Thailand. This left the Malays as a minority in what was left of Malai. Before the War, the Sultans had been sovereign in their states, in theory at least. The Japanese supplanted the Sultans and ruled through governors. As the writing on the wall got plainer towards the end, they began to give some thought to the future of Malai. There was even a suggestion that it should become part of a new Japanese-dominated China, given that there was an actual majority of Chinese. None of this made the Malays feel any more secure. When the War ended, the predominantly-Chinese MPAJA antagonised the Malays with their arrogance and indiscriminate brutality during the interregnum after the Japanese surrender. The MPAJA had marched like conquering heroes in the victory parade at the Padang. The British passed out gongs to the resistance fighters and treated them as allies. What with the plans for the Malayan Union, the Malays feared that they were about to be sold-out by the British. They took matters into their own hands. The violent extremist fringe hit back at the Chinese, whether Communist or not. At the beginning of November came news of the massacre of 35 Chinese civilians upcountry at a place called Padang Lebar. The British were either unwilling or unable to clamp down effectively. Relations between the races stood on a knife-edge.

The Indians in Malaya were also agitated at almost precisely the same time by the commencement of the trial of three senior officers of the Indian National Army at the Red Fort in Delhi. Major-

General Shah Nawaz, Colonel Prem Saghal and Colonel Gurbaksh Singh Dhillon had been officers of the Indian Army and fought in Malaya. They were captured by the Japanese when Singapore fell and subsequently joined the Indian National Army, rising to senior positions. Like Habibullah, they had been in the thick of the fighting in Burma. Unlike Habibullah, they were captured and repatriated to India to stand trial. The charge was treason: or more technically, waging war against the King-Emperor. A whole galaxy of legal stars had volunteered to defend them, with Pandit Jawarhalal Nehru first among them. The trial created a sensation in India. The Congress Party took up the banner. There was mass agitation in the cities and mutiny in the Indian Navy. In Malaya, the English language newspapers kept reporting to a bare minimum, but word of mouth spread the news much more effectively. Many of the Japanese-Indian Fifth Columnists or Jifs, as the British called them, were local boys recruited in Malaya. The all-woman Rani of Jhansi Regiment was raised right here in Singapore. Feelings ran high.

There was only one thing that everyone — European, Malay, Chinese and Indian — could agree on: that the Japanese were the main villains of the piece and should be punished to the limit of the law and beyond. I found myself right in the line of fire because of Nakamura. He was one of the first of the war criminals to be brought to book. The British and Australians were assiduously putting together the evidence to try those responsible for the atrocities against Allied POWs and civilians. They were also going after the perpetrators of the Sook Ching massacres and the Double Tenth atrocities. That took a lot more time as there were many more victims and defendants. Nakamura's case was neat and straightforward. Four dead victims, two witnesses, one survivor of the Kempeitai unit responsible; a nice open-and-shut case as the curtain-raiser for the big show later on.

ACTUALLY, Nakamura was going to be part of a double-bill. The Police Courts in South Bridge Road had been opened for the tribunals hearing criminal and other cases, as the Supreme Court remained closed. Nakamura was to be tried there. Since the place was already set up with the necessary security, the authorities must have thought that it would be more efficient to have the preliminary hearing for Habibullah's court-martial there too. D'Almeida wasn't ready for a full trial yet. George had been tasked with rounding up witnesses for the defence, a job that taxed his contacts to the maximum. We were trying to locate members of his unit, the Bhurtpores. This was no easy task, as most of the Jifs had been shipped to Burma as the INA's contribution to the liberation of the motherland. There a large number of them died of disease or wounds. The lucky few who survived the fighting and the rigours of the Burmese jungle surrendered to the British. They were sent back to India to await their fate. Finding any of Habibullah's men still in Malaya would have been like striking the lottery. The court-martial would just take Habibullah's plea and decide on a date for the substantive hearing. Nakamura, on the other hand, was slated to go on as scheduled. I hadn't the excuse that we were waiting to locate our witnesses; there were none for the defence.

The day before the hearing I received an unexpected parcel from Hojo. It came by messenger and was brought to me by George. "Something from your friend Hojo, all nicely gift-wrapped," he said, handing me the brown-paper package tied up with a ribbon. The Japanese have a fine sense of aesthetics. Even with plain paper scrounged from his office and a piece of worn ribbon, Hojo had managed to make the parcel look elegant.

I opened the note that came with the present. "Chiang-san," it read, "you asked me to explain how my countrymen think. I enclose three documents that may assist you. The first is the Imperial Rescript to the Military Forces issued by the Emperor

Meiji in 1902. The second are instructions to Military Forces. The third is an extract from the Army Training Regulations. I have made a humble attempt to translate the relevant passages for you.

I also send you a small token as a mark of my esteem. I know you to be an upright man, and I commend you for undertaking the task of defending my countryman. I beg your pardon for the humbleness of the gift. The officer who owned it did not use it at all and he has no need of it now. It is my earnest hope that you will find some use for it."

I unwrapped the parcel carefully. Given the care with which it had been wrapped, I felt that it was the least I could do. The first fold revealed the three documents that Hojo referred to. Underneath was a bundle wrapped in tissue paper. "What is it?" asked George curiously.

"It's a *yukata*," I said, holding up the garment, "a summer kimono." It was of light cotton, with a simple pattern of stripes. It was clearly not the most expensive or well-made of its kind, but I was touched by the gesture nonetheless. He could have traded it for food or even sold it instead.

"Very nice," remarked George. "What are you going to do with it?"

"Don't know," I replied doubtfully, "I wouldn't be caught dead wearing such a thing. My bottom would feel exposed."

"Correction," responded George, "you'd be dead if anyone caught you wearing that. It's not wise to look too Japanese nowadays."

Maniam the office boy interrupted us. "Letter for you, Sir."

"Another one?" I asked. "Who from?"

"Chinese man give it to Singh the *jaga* for you," he replied.

This missive wasn't as carefully prepared as Hojo's. There was no envelope, just a folded square of paper. I unfolded it. It was written in Chinese, in red ink. I called Eng Tong to come in and translate for me.

"It say that you are a Japanese running-dog and will die," he read laconically, as if announcing the day's weather.

"Oh, wonderful," I responded, "just what I need to make my day. Nakamura won't talk even though it's his neck practically in the noose. If by some miracle he gets off, I'm in line to get the chop."

"You're not thinking of chucking it in, are you?" asked George.

I was sorely tempted, but I answered, "No, I suppose I can't back out now. And certainly not in the face of threats."

"Why don't you give the yuki-thingy to Nakamura, since you don't want it?" suggested George. "He might be touched enough by the gesture to open up. We need his cooperation."

"We do?" I asked, surprised. "Since when?"

"Since we have to defend Habibullah. I've drawn a blank locating old Bhurtpores. You can't just wander round the island calling for them like trying to find stray goats. But if there were any deserters picked up in Malaya, the Kempeitai would have gotten hold of them. I'm hoping that Nakamura might give us a lead."

NAKAMURA had been transferred from his holding cell in Pearl's Hill Police Station to the lock-up under the Police Courts in anticipation of his trial. The move was done surreptitiously under the cover of darkness, to avoid any unpleasantness with the crowds who might have been inclined to hang him first and have the hearing later. The Courts building was surrounded with barbed wire. Though the trial was to be held in public, access was restricted to ensure security. For this I was mightily thankful. It was clear to me that some people couldn't distinguish between the defendant and the defendant's counsel.

Habibullah too was in the lock-up. He had been held in Selarang Barracks, a long way from town. The British were not happy to have to admit that so many of their loyal Indian sepoys had gone over to the other side. Keeping him with petty criminals was out of the question. So was putting him into a POW camp, since that would have meant recognising his status as a POW and not a renegade. Selarang was about as far as they could get and still have him on the island. He would be out of sight and out of mind there. But it was too far to transport him just for a morning's hearing, so as a temporary expedient he was lodged in the cell next to Nakamura. This suited us fine, as d'Almeida wanted me along to interview Habibullah. It was my job to take notes and generally jog his memory about details, since I had been in the vicinity when Lieutenant-Colonel Holmes was killed. If nothing else, I could poke holes in any false story.

D'ALMEIDA, Eng Tong and I were dropped off in front of the Courts by Ahmad. There was a little trouble with the guard commander, who eyed us suspiciously. He was a tawny-haired freckle-faced young corporal from a county regiment, wearing a jungle-green uniform that was still unfaded. From his pallor I surmised that he hadn't been in the tropics for long. He wasn't used to English-speaking Asiatics claiming to be lawyers. He examined our papers minutely. Finally deciding that to give use the benefit of the doubt, he signaled to his men to let us through.

Once in the Courts, however, it was different. They knew d'Almeida there. Every few steps he was stopped by a clerk or peon, who shook his hand warmly and said how nice it was to see him back there again after so many years. Down in the cells, the warder greeted him like an old friend — which he was. D'Almeida had made it a point to keep in touch with his contacts during the war years. Many had benefitted from his generosity, since the big garden in his bungalow produced more than enough food for his simple needs. The warder Amin was one of them.

Nakamura didn't seem particularly overjoyed to see us. He stared at us phlegmatically when we were let into his cell. Perhaps the presence of d'Almeida had a sobering effect on Eng Tong. He was more subdued than usual in announcing us. At least it didn't sound as though we had come to beat the truth out of Nakamura. "Tell him that this is for him," I instructed Eng Tong, handing Hojo's package to him.

Nakamura's eyes widened in surprise. He hadn't expected kindness. It was alien to his mind that prisoners were to be treated with any consideration. He opened the paper gingerly, as though afraid of what it might contain. Drawing out the *yukata*, he held it up uncertainly.

"Go on," I urged with gestures, "put it on."

He took off his shirt, which was stained and frankly stank. Evidently, he hadn't washed for a long, long time. Slowly and hesitantly he put on the *yukata*. With his right hand clutching one edge as if paralysed, he tremblingly folded the other edge over with his left hand. He fumbled with the knot of his sash, as though his fingers were crippled. He was a pitiable specimen of humanity, but far from provoking sympathy in me I only felt revulsion. Again, the thought of giving up the case and leaving him to his fate flashed across my mind. D'Almeida watched this performance attentively with narrowed eyes. Abruptly, he went to the door of the cell and called for the warder. "May I have a cup of tea, Enchik Amin?" He asked politely. Amin looked surprised, but being used to d'Almeida and grateful for small favours he went off to get the requested tea.

Meanwhile, Eng Tong had commenced questioning Nakamura as d'Almeida had instructed. Did he know anything of deserters from the INA? Were such deserters held by the Kempeitai? If not, who would have had responsibility for them? Nakamura proved no more forthcoming in this than in the matter of his own defence. He pleaded ignorance of anything to do with the INA or its deserters. He did not know which army unit was in charge of picking up the strays. I seethed with frustration. He could not justify our help to him by being even the least bit helpful to us.

Amin returned with d'Almeida's tea in an enamel mug. D'Almeida handed it to Nakamura with both hands. "Drink," he said in Japanese.

Nakamura accepted the proffered mug, bowing. He cupped his hands gingerly around the hot container. D'Almeida indicated that he should drink up. He did as he was instructed. "Ask if he has anything more to tell us," instructed d'Almeida. "What does he say to the charges against him?"

Eng Tong translated. Again there was that shaking of the head that I had become so used to. "He say nothing to the charge," reported Eng Tong. D'Almeida nodded and indicated that we should leave. The warder let us out. D'Almeida told me to proceed to Habibullah's cell first while he had a quiet word with Amin. Eng Tong was dismissed. To my surprise, as I turned towards Habibullah's cell, he plucked at my sleeve.

"I want to talk to you," he said. "I come to the house tonight, can or not?"

"Talk to me? Can't we do it now? I'm awfully busy tonight. The case is coming on for hearing tomorrow morning and I've got to get ready."

He shook his head emphatically. "No, cannot talk here."

I sighed with resignation. He evidently had something on his mind that wouldn't wait. The last thing I needed was for him to walk off the job in a huff. "All right, if you must. Seven o'clock, and don't be late."

THE night before a case is always the worst. I have gigantic butterflies in the stomach no matter how many times I may have done it before. A lot of it is fear of appearing foolish in public. It would have helped a lot to have had a client who might invoke the sympathy of the judges. The trouble with being the low man on the totem-pole is that you never get to choose your cases. D'Almeida had the luxury of being able to say no to a potential client. He had reached the happy position in his professional career where clients felt priviliged to have him defend them. Besides, he was independently wealthy and didn't really need the business. Even after the depredations of the War, he still retained a comparative affluence. All this meant that he could choose to do only the cases he believed in.

I had no such choice. True, he had said that he would not force me to do the case if my conscience would not let me. But whatever my conscience might have said, I didn't want to appear a quitter in the eyes of my boss — not after he had expressed his faith in my ability. It would have been too much like desertion in the face of the enemy.

It was hard trying to put together a defence for Nakamura. It would have been so much easier to have just have spun a fairy tale out of hot air and imagination. D'Almeida would have none of that. He insisted that we put the client's case fairly to the judges; and it had to be the client's story, not something some sharp lawyer had cooked up for him. Given Nakamura's lack of cooperation, there was little I could say. Nor did the law books provide much help. I was in uncharted waters without a compass.

Engrossed as I was preparing myself for the impending doom of my client, I'd completely forgotten that Eng Tong was coming over until Gek Neo appeared at the door of my room to announce him. "That man Yeo Eng Tong from your office has come to visit you," she said. "He is waiting downstairs."

The interruption did not please me, but I felt that I had to humour him. It wasn't for the sake of politeness; I needed his active assistance and I didn't want to antagonise him. I hurriedly shut my notebook and trotted down the stairs to the sitting room. Eng Tong was standing in the verandah, looking out into the garden. I was mildly surprised to see that he had on a proper shirt and well-pressed pants, held up with a pair of braces. His hair had been slicked back and lay neatly plastered to his head instead of sticking up all over the place like an unruly thicket of bamboo. He turned when he heard me. Before I had time to ask what he wanted, he blurted out: "I want to marry your sister. You give me permission?"

15

THE tribunal trying Nakamura consisted of three officers, a lieutenant-colonel of Indian Army as President, a British major and an Australian captain from the Australian Army Legal Corps. Lieutenant-Colonel Watkins, the President, had an impressive string of letters to his name, including MA (Cantab) and KC. The prosecuting counsel was a barrister of the Middle Temple, who held the rank of major in the 17/21 Lancers and the grand appellation of Assistant Judge Advocate-General, HQ ALFSEA. I hadn't met him before, but he seemed to be a decent enough fellow. He came over to introduce himself and shake hands like a gentleman. Beatty was his name. We exchanged a few pleasantries before the court convened, talking inconsequentially about the impending monsoon and how humid it had become. Major Beatty was assisted by a young British second-lieutenant of the North Anglian Yeomanry, who sat morosely at the counsel's table sifting through the documents. He looked up briefly when I came over to introduce myself and smiled wanly. I didn't catch his mumbled name.

I was alone.

Eng Tong should have been there with me, but he hadn't shown up. I wasn't surprised. It had been hard explaining to him that I couldn't give permission for June to marry him. At first he thought that I was refusing outright and started to become agitated. However, I finally got through to him the fact that firstly, I wasn't her elder brother and secondly, even if I was she wouldn't listen to me. June, I said, had a mind of her own and had to make her own decisions about his proposal. It took him a while to grasp that. This was foreign to his world view. He thought that the landed gentry (meaning us) kept the old customs. As far as he was concerned, I was paterfamilias in default of any other male relatives. If anyone had a say about June's marriage, it should have been me.

I suppose that I should have given him credit for trying to do things the proper way. We were a society in transition. Mak's generation took it for granted that marriages were to be arranged. Hers certainly was. It had been a deal made between my uncle, whose wife had recently died without bearing him a son, and Mak's father, who wanted to see his daughter married off. There was no talk of love, affection or even of liking. In those days, a girl was considered fortunate if her husband was a good provider and came from a respectable family. If he was faithful, that was a bonus. Uncle proved to be a good husband by the conventional criteria. She looked after him and he took care of her needs. When he died, Mak made sure that the customary offerings were made to his soul at the necessary times. Though there was no open display of emotion, by any reasonable definition of the word theirs was a loving relationship.

When it came to getting her step-daughters and daughters married off, Mak laboured under the grave disadvantage of not having any money. She had tried for years to find a suitable boy for Gek Neo, but without success — mostly because Gek Neo insisted, in that self-sacrificing way of firstborns, that she would not marry until all the girls were out of school. To top it all, we were poor but genteel. Gentility counted for little. It was hard to find a good Baba husband from a respectable family without a proper dowry. Then May cut the matrimonial queue and *potong jalan*, as we called it, by accepting Ralph's proposal. Ralph was Eurasian, though he looked completely European. He didn't care about the dowry. He was my friend and came to the house occasionally. There was a mutual attraction, but both of them were shy to the point of muteness. Being dumb in both senses of the word, neither would make any move. June intervened. She egged Ralph on and he finally screwed up the courage to actually ask her out. If it hadn't been for June they would have missed one another completely, like two sheep that pass in the night.

Then during the War Julie *potong jalan* in front of June herself. She had to fall for and marry a priest. They got sent back to Nagasaki, with all the tragic results that followed. With such a family history, there was no way that June would have even thought about being hitched to someone by arrangement. Ralph had said that she was attractive. I couldn't see it myself, since I had known her in her mud-covered, tree-climbing, knee-scraping days. He must have been right though, because she didn't lack for suitors. There had been a steady stream of men, introduced by Mak with the active collaboration of Ah Sum. June knew how to behave and played the part of dumb blond perfectly, although she wasn't blond and was far from dumb. Her intellectual blondness was merely protective colouration. June was in fact the smartest of my girl cousins. But she hid it well, instinctively knowing that men in general did not care for cleverness in a wife, just domesticity. She had nicknames for all of them, some of which I remember: *Si-Gemok*, Fatty; *Si-Kurus*, the Thin Man; *Si-Botak*, Baldy; *Si-Jangut*, Beardy; and my personal favourite, *Si-Bengkok*, the Crooked Man. None of them met her exacting standards. With the insouciance of youth she had cavalierly dismissed them one after another. "Plenty of fish in the sea," she said. Unfortunately, as the years progressed fewer and fewer of the fish swam into her *kelong*. Eng Tong was the first one in a long time.

Nobody really knew what June thought about Eng Tong as a suitor; she kept closed-mouthed on that score. Gek Neo had warned June that he was a *samseng*. Ah Sum was equally voluble in her opposition. June can be as ornery as an old mule when nagged. The fact that others expressed their clear disapproval of him merely hardened her resolve. As far as she was concerned, it was no one else's *pasal*. Mak hadn't said anything out loud, but the impression I got was that she didn't think Eng Tong would be a suitable match for June.

Now there he was, standing right in front of me asking for June's hand in marriage. I had neither the energy nor the inclination to argue with Eng Tong his merits as a mate. So I did what any reasonable coward would have done under the circumstances: I called Mak and fled upstairs to finish my legal submissions. Mak has a delicate way of broaching sensitive subjects, a talent that is invaluable in running a complicated household. She spent some time talking to Eng Tong and eventually persuaded him that nothing could be done that night. I gather that he wasn't overjoyed, but finally agreed that June would have to make the decision. He wanted to go and see her there and then, but was dissuaded by the prospect of disturbing the great d'Almeida in his den at dinner. He left and that was the last I saw of him.

GEORGE had made sympathetic noises and given me his lucky rabbit's foot. Though I appreciated the gesture, I didn't set much store by it as a good-luck charm; after all, look what happened to the rabbit. The butterflies in my stomach were having a merry dance when, to my surprise, d'Almeida appeared. He walked over to Major Beatty and introduced himself. Beatty looked completely astounded. He hadn't expected to be faced with such an opponent. His assistant started burrowing even deeper among the papers. D'Almeida came over and sat himself down behind me.

"Are you taking over?" I asked, hope springing in my breast.

"No," he replied, "I shall just observe. It is your case."

Hope died a pathetic death. The butterflies redoubled their frenzy.

The President and members of the tribunal trooped in and took their places. The charges were read and prisoner was asked whether he admitted to them. Nakamura looked completely lost. He was dressed in an ill-fitting uniform that had obviously been scrounged for the occasion. He glanced uncomfortably around the courtroom. The interpreter prompted him again. He shook his head. "The prisoner pleads not guilty to the charges," announced the interpreter.

Major Beatty was a good speaker and set out the facts clearly, presenting the documents and records in a logical manner. I heard that he took silk when he went back to England. Nakamura was a member of the second *bunkentai* of the Singapore branch Kempeitai. His unit was commanded by a Lieutenant Saito, now deceased. He was based at Kempeitai headquarters in the YMCA at Stamford Road. In early 1944 there was an upswing in resistance activity on Singapore island. Stocks of rubber were sabotaged. A bomb was detonated at the Capitol Cinema. Seventh Area Army Headquarters demanded that the outrages be stopped. The Kempeitai were called in. Informers said that the saboteurs were being coordinated by radio. The ringleaders were to be found in the prisoner-of-war camp at Changi and the Sime Road internment camp for civilians. The camps were raided. A dozen unfortunates were brought to the YMCA for interrogation.

The prisoners were kept in underground cages, barely as big as a dog-kennel. There was only a small grille on the door, through which food could be passed. High up on the wall was a tiny window, with a sliver of blue sky showing. The prisoners were crammed together so tightly that they could not lie down on the bare floor. There was no bedding. The lights were kept on all the time, night and day. The only way that they could keep track of the passing of time was to watch the changing of the light through their little window. The food they got was just enough to keep them alive so that they could continue to be interrogated. Water was not provided. There was one pedestal toilet. They got their water from that. The daily routine was monotonously similar. At 8 am the guards would come and get them. They would be taken to a bigger room and made to sit bolt upright in a row on the floor. Talking was not allowed. They were not even permitted to move except to go to the lavatory. Any infraction was punished with a severe beating. After the day's interrogation, they were taken back to their cage at 10 pm. This continued for a week; more for some.

The Kempeitai's own records showed that Warrant Officer Nakamura was the chief interrogator. Four of the persons in his charge died. This fact was uncontradicted and incontrovertible. It came from the official records kept by the Kempeitai. They didn't die by his hand; not in the sense that he had beaten them to death on the spot. Death came later, when they were brought back to the cage bruised and bloodied and left without medical care. There was no direct evidence of how Nakamura had conducted his interrogation of the victims, since all of them were dead. So were the other members of his unit who might have given evidence. Major Beatty, to his credit, admitted that no one had actually seen Nakamura torturing any of the deceased. But he did have two witnesses who survived the hospitality of the Kempeitai.

The first was a Mr David Howard, who had been a manager with the Straits Steamship Company before the war. He had been interned first in Changi Camp and then later in Sime Road. Howard was a trained electrical engineer, which was possibly why he had been picked out for interrogation. Beatty took him through his evidence-in-chief competently. Howard, like the others, had been held at the YMCA. He was taken into the interrogation room every day for eight days. As the prisoners sat waiting for their turn, a clerk with a file would come in and indicate who was to go for questioning. The guards then seized the poor wretch and bundled him into the interrogation room. The room was bare, except for a wooden chair and table. There would have been at least one interpreter and sometimes another relief interrogator at each session.

The session started slowly, even politely. They simply wanted to know who his outside contact was, they said. All he had to do was just name a few names. Even one name would be enough. Howard answered that he wasn't part of any plot and couldn't name the conspirators even if he wanted to. He was slapped. After a while, the slaps turned to punches. When he again denied having any contacts, he was made to kneel on sharp pieces of wood. The interrogators would kick the wood so that it cut into his flesh. He was flogged with leather belts and burned on the forehead with cigarettes. When he collapsed, a lighted paper was put in his hands to test whether he was playing possum. Every day, they took him to the edge of death and then stopped. He was returned to the cage barely able to walk or speak. The following day, the process was repeated. Somehow, he managed to survive. Four of those in the cage with him did not. His injuries were light compared to theirs.

Then came the moment I had been dreading. Beatty finished his examination-in-chief and passed Howard over to me for questioning. I glanced at d'Almeida, who muttered quietly, "Ask how the witness recognised the prisoner." I stood up to cross-examine, my throat completely dry.

"Mr Howard," I said in a voice rather higher-pitched than I would have liked, "look carefully at the accused. Do you recognise him?"

Howard was middle-aged and balding. He gave the impression of having once been fat, but now the skin hung off his bones. He squinted at Nakamura. "Yes," he said, "he was there. He was one of them."

I was seized by a sudden inspiration. "Do you habitually wear spectacles?"

"Yes," he replied warily. "But I can see without them, if that's what you're getting at. I lost my glasses during the torture. They never replaced them."

This was more information than I wanted. But having started, I felt I had to persist. "Without your spectacles now, how can you be so sure that the accused was one of those who were there when you were tortured?"

Major Beatty rose. "Is my learned friend suggesting that the accused was not present when the tortures were inflicted on the witness?"

"No, not exactly," I answered lamely, "but I'm raising the possibility."

Beatty sat down with a slight smile. I felt my ears redden. He knew I was grasping at straws. "How did you identify the accused?" I asked with a hint of desperation.

Howard looked surprised. I repeated my question. "There was this officer from the BMA," he said. "He brought a folder of photographs and asked if I recognised any of them. I picked out three or four, I can't remember exactly."

I thought I saw an opening and pounced. "Three or four? Including the accused? I put it to you that you weren't sure about the identification, which is why you chose so many."

Howard responded with some irritation, "No, I'm sure he was one of them. I was told that the others were dead. That's why he's the only one in the dock. He was there in the YMCA. I'm certain of it." I hate it when witnesses refuse to cooperate by folding. I had reached the end of the line and looked at d'Almeida for guidance. He merely nodded. I sat down despondently.

Beatty had no further witnesses present. The other eyewitness, one Alfred Granger, had been repatriated to England. Granger couldn't even walk when they took him out of Sime Road Camp. Immediately after the return of the British, some of the internees took the initiative to record statements about the ill-treatment they had been subjected to. Granger was one of them. His evidence was contained in an affidavit. "Does my learned friend object to the introduction of the evidence?" asked Beatty.

I briefly toyed with the idea of objecting, but discarded it almost immediately. There was no point being difficult for the sake of being difficult. The tribunal was already against my client and this sort of niggling technical defence wouldn't have endeared me to them. "No, Sir," I said, addressing the tribunal, "but I merely point out that there will be no opportunity to cross-examine the deponent."

"We will bear that in mind," responded Lieutenant-Colonel Watkins shortly. I had the distinct impression that he was not impressed with the defence.

Granger's evidence was more of the same. He had been subjected to much more severe torture than Howard. The interrogators had put bamboo slivers under his nails. They also suspended him from the ceiling and applied electric shocks to his genitals. He had to be carried back to the cage in a rattan chair. They continued to torture him for another four days. It was a miracle that he was still alive. He too had identified Nakamura from photographs. Apparently the same officer from ALFSEA HQ had shown him their folder and he had picked Nakamura out. It was all very discouraging.

Fortunately, the tribunal ended my torment by adjourning for lunch. I turned to speak to d'Almeida, but he was already at the door of the courtroom. "Mr d'Almeida," I called after him, "have you any instructions for me?"

"Yes," he called back over his shoulder. "Stall until I return."

16

"IS your client serious?" asked Lieutenant-Colonel Watkins, staring crossly at me. "After all that this tribunal has heard, you are telling us that he will not give evidence or even make an unsworn statement from the dock?"

I had trouble swallowing. My vocal chords seemed to have dried up completely. I forced the words out of my mouth. "Yes, Sir. He has been advised of his rights. He elects to remain silent."

Major Beatty had taken the better part of two hours after the lunch recess to wind up his case with formal witnesses. Now it was my turn to present the defence. Only there was no defence to present. I had just informed them that Nakamura would not be saying anything. Watkins conferred with his colleagues on the bench. After a moment, he resumed glowering at me. "What do you propose to do, Mr Chiang?"

"If it please you, Mr President and honourable members of the tribunal, I would like to make a submission on behalf of the accused."

Watkins put down his pencil and leaned back in his chair. He rested his arms on the armrests, placing his fingertips together. His moustache twitched. He fixed me with his basilisk glare. "Proceed."

Not very hopefully, I began. "We have to appreciate that the accused comes from a very different background and culture. The Japanese have developed in isolation from Europe for a millenium.

It is only in the last century that they have had a sustained contact with the nations of the West. Their values are not the same as those of a European soldier. They a place a different importance on life. For them, duty is more important than life, loyalty is required above all. I ask this tribunal to bear this difference in mind when judging the culpability of Warrant Officer Nakamura. He should not be judged as though he were British, or even as you would judge a German soldier."

I could see from the faces of the tribunal that I wasn't making any impact.

"Gentlemen, you have before you three documents which set out the framework within which the Japanese Army functions. The first is the Imperial Rescript issued by the Emperor Meiji in 1902. It is considered to be a sacred document setting out the guiding principles for the Japanese soldier. Remember, to the Japanese, the Emperor is a god. The second document is a set of instructions issued by the Japanese War Ministry to amplify the Imperial Rescript. The third is the Military Training Instructions of the Japanese Army.

"I read to you what these documents say: *The essence of military discipline is obedience. Therefore, it is necessary that the officers and men of the whole army should form a habit or a second nature of sacrificing their lives for their Emperor and country, obeying their superiors implicitly and executing their superiors' orders faithfully. For the cultivation of military discipline it is necessary, first, to seek absolute obedience and, next, to make officers and men fully understand the significance and inviolable dignity of the Supreme Command, so that they will sacrifice their lives willingly for their Emperor and country at the order of their superiors. Subordinates must obey immediately the orders of the superior, irrespective of their nature. Such orders are irresistible.*

"The duty of the military is to sacrifice their lives for their Emperor and country. It is a tradition inherited from the time of the old samurai.

A samurai's loyalty to his lord is more important than his own life. Remember the old saying: life is as light and negligible as a feather; loyalty is as heavy and lofty as a mountain."

Eyebrows were raised. I pressed on regardless.

"These are not the King's Regulations. They embody a wholly different philosophy of war. To obey is the soldier's prime duty. It is a duty owed to the Emperor, who is not just his sovereign but his god. There is no question of refusing to obey an order from a superior officer. Warrant Officer Nakamura was not the one who gave the orders; those orders emanated from the Headquarters of the 7th Area Army and were transmitted down the chain of command. Headquarters demanded an end to the sabotage. Their information was that the POWs and civilian internees were involved. Nakamura's unit was ordered to investigate. His OC Lieutenant Saito set the tone. He had no choice but to comply. It was his duty as a soldier."

The honourable members of the tribunal sat immobile as granite statues, not betraying any reaction at all. I felt vaguely disturbed. It wasn't because I knew I would lose and I hate losing; it was the knowledge that if by some miracle I won, it would have been with arguments that I didn't myself believe.

THE tribunal only took half an hour to deliberate. For all I know, they may have made up their minds in the first five minutes and spent the rest of the time having tea and biscuits. The three members of the tribunal trooped back in grim-faced. Beatty's final submissions had been masterful. He drew the threads together and built up an unanswerable case. I had no illusions about what the verdict would be. Nakamura was commanded to stand. He got up uncomprehendingly, with all the animation and intelligence of a scarecrow with straw for brains.

"Nakamura Nagamasa," pronounced Lieutenant-Colonel Watkins solemnly, "having considered all the evidence presented, it is the conclusion of this tribunal that you were an instrument in a campaign of torture designed not to elicit military information but to cow and terrorise the population of this unhappy island. You are a professional bully with no sensibility or finer feelings whatsoever. You must die because you were a willing tool and willing tools of an inhuman, murderous purpose must be destroyed. It is the verdict of this tribunal that you are guilty as charged and that you be sentenced ..."

Watkins never got to finish his sentence. There was a bustle and commotion at the rear of the courtroom and d'Almeida burst in. Breathlessly, he spoke as he rushed to the front, "You cannot sentence this man to death!"

Completely taken aback, all Watkins could manage to blurt out was, "Why the devil not?"

"Because," said d'Almeida, recovering his customary composure, "this man is not Warrant Officer Nakamura Nagamasa."

17

"WHAT put you on to him?" I asked d'Almeida. We were back in the office. George had joined us after tidying up Habibullah's preliminary hearing.

"It was the *yukata*," answered d'Almeida. "He folded it left over right, as you or I would with a shirt. But that is not the Japanese way. Only corpses are dressed with the *yukata* or kimono folded left over right."

"Well," chipped in George, "it was a stroke of genius to get his fingerprints on the tin mug. That was the clincher."

"You might have told me," I said reproachfully, "and saved me from making a fool of myself."

"I could not be absolutely certain," d'Almeida responded. "It could have been that Nakamura – or Lim Tay Lin as I should properly call him – was symbolically indicating that he was a dead man. It was only after the identification evidence was presented that I was sure."

"You certainly cut it very fine," I said.

"It was not my intention to be quite so dramatic," replied d'Almeida. "Although I had asked for the fingerprints to be identified when I got them, I only obtained confirmation myself during the luncheon recess. Mr Newman was most helpful in procuring the assistance of Special Branch. But it took more time than I had desired or planned for."

D'Almeida's precipitate entrance had thrown the proceedings in an uproar. To the great credit of the President, he had not ordered the redcaps to bung him into the cells on the spot but heard him out instead. D'Almeida produced the nominal roll of Nakamura's *bunkentai*, which he had obtained from Newman's contacts. Among the members of the unit was one Lim Tay Lin, a native of Formosa. He was a clerk, employed because he spoke Hokkien as well as Japanese. The fingerprints lifted from the enamel mug that d'Almeida had given him to drink from matched those found in the Kempeitai's own personnel records.

Major Beatty was a perfect gentleman. He did not object to allowing the defence to be re-opened. This time d'Almeida took charge, with the great indulgence of the tribunal and my infinite gratitude. 'Nakamura' was put on the witness stand and confronted with the evidence. He readily admitted that he was indeed Lim Tay Lin. Apparently, when news came of the surrender, Lieutenant Saito told his men that they should all commit *seppuku*. The whole *bunkentai* got roaring drunk on sake and beer, except for Lim, who had no desire to join his ancestors just yet. He went and hid himself in the lavatory until it was all over. His problem was what to do next. MPAJA death squads were hauling collaborators out onto the streets and brutally killing them after unspeakable tortures. He knew what his fate would be if they got their hands on him. The Communists reserved special treatment for renegade Chinese who had worked for the hated invaders. He decided that it would be far safer to get sent to a POW camp. So he took over the identity of Warrant Officer Nakamura, who was about his height and build. The trick worked. The British and Indian soldiers couldn't tell a Formosan from a Japanese. He was put in the Jurong Camp like the rest of the Japanese garrison.

Things started coming unglued when an officer from ALFSEA arrived demanding to see Nakamura. He was arrested and brought to the Pearl's Hill Police Barracks. No one thought to check his identity. Who would be crazy enough to pretend to be a member of the universally-loathed Kempeitai? Later, he was told that he, Nakamura, was to be charged with war crimes. He didn't know what that meant, but it seemed that prison was a better bet than being let out onto the streets and left to the tender mercies of the Communists.

That was when we came into the picture. Eng Tong discovered right away that Lim wasn't Nakamura and wasn't even Japanese. When Lim told him that he was from Formosa, Eng Tong had nearly beaten him up. It was only my intervention that had prevented it. Then Eng Tong told him that it was vital that he should keep up the act, no matter what the pressure. It was his only hope, said Eng Tong. Otherwise, the British would hand him over to the MPAJA. As a Japanese, he would be tried and sent to jail but that would be all, Eng Tong assured him. So it was that he went quietly like a brainless lamb to the slaughter. If it hadn't been for d'Almeida's intervention, he would have been hanged for someone else's crimes. Who would have believed him if after the sentence had been pronounced he had protested that he wasn't really Nakamura?

Faced with the new evidence, the tribunal had no choice but to acquit. Lim was discharged, still looking completely bewildered. He immediately sought sanctuary with us when it was made clear to him that he was free to go. Freedom was the last thing on his mind.

"But what of the identification evidence?" pressed George. "Didn't two witnesses identify him?"

"Yes, indeed," replied d'Almeida, "but never underestimate the fallibility of human memory. An officer came to each of the witnesses more than a year after the event with a folder of photographs. The Legal Department of HQ ALFSEA had some of those photographs taken in the POW camps. Others were from the Kempeitai files. The investigating officer asked each witness whether he recognised anyone. Both recognised Lim, amongst others, but of course they did not know his name. According to the POW records he was Warrant Officer Nakamura. Nakamura was listed as the chief interrogator. The case against him seemed perfectly clear."

"But Howard was pretty positive that Lim was there," I pointed out.

"Indeed so," said d'Almeida, "but not in the interrogation room. He was the clerk who kept the records and picked out the detainees to be interrogated in turn. It was an easy mistake to make. After all, Mr Howard had been told that the authorities were going to bring the torturers to book. He was given photographs and recognised Lim as one of the men who was present at the YMCA. What could be more natural than that he should connect Lim in his mind with the torturers? He honestly believed that Lim was one of the torturers, because his mind had been subtly predisposed to think so."

"All I can say is that Lim's jolly lucky," commented George. "What's to become of him now?"

"He will be handed over to the Chinese authorities in Formosa," replied d'Almeida. "They will decide what is to be done."

"And Eng Tong?" I added. "He deliberately tried to get Lim killed. We can't let him get away with that."

"What would you have us do?" asked d'Almeida. "He was not a sworn interpreter, so there is no oath-breaking. It cannot be attempted murder, because the act of killing would have been done by the British. I doubt that the legal authorities would expend resources to prosecute Yeo, even if an appropriate charge could be laid. They understand the depth of feeling against the Japanese and their collaborators. If they catch him, they would just let him go."

"What do you mean, 'if they catch him'?"

"Yeo has absconded," replied d'Almeida simply. "We do not know where he is."

18

"CONGRATULATIONS on your win," said Ralph when we met the next day.

"Don't congratulate me," I responded morosely. "I lost the case. Nakamura was tried and found guilty. The client got off because he wasn't Nakamura. Justice was done, but not with my help."

"Cheer up," said Ralph, "no more war criminals, only renegades left for you to defend."

There was no respite for me after the disposal of the Nakamura case. D'Almeida handed me the Habibullah file with instructions to get everything from the accused — his whole life story from the start of the war to the very end. George had already taken his statement, but d'Almeida was a stickler for detail. "One never knows what might be relevant," he always said.

I asked for the rest of the day off, which d'Almeida was kind enough to give. I had to make sure that everything was secure at home. Eng Tong's absence bothered me. He doubtless thought that I had ruined his chances with June. Now his plot to have Lim hanged had been laid bare. I didn't know what mischief he might be up to. On top of that, I could imagine how the mob would react. They would be baying for blood. All they would see is that 'Nakamura' had gotten off. You can't count on hotheads to read the papers carefully; in the febrile atmosphere of the time, the word would go round that I had got the torturer off with clever legal tricks and devices.

Ironically, we had been safer during the Occupation. The fact that I worked for the Japanese gave me a certain protection from casual crime. My contacts with the Communists provided me cover from that angle. No one would have dared to molest us for fear of one or the other. Now that the British were back, our protection had disappeared. The house was wide open to intruders. Anyone could come in over the fence or even through the gate, which we did not lock. Baba houses were designed to be airy, not secure.

June at least was safe. Staying with d'Almeida, it would be difficult for Eng Tong to get at her. Between Karim in the house and Ridley's men in front of the gate, June was about as secure as anyone could be without actually being in prison. I dropped by to see how she was doing. I also needed to enlist her help with Habibullah, at George's suggestion. Taking down a life story is a two-person job. June was the only one free to help. Apart from keeping an eye on Marge and helping Simon with his cases, June was still watching over Gim Huat.

"He is quite happy now," she reported with satisfaction. "To see him laugh warms the muscles of my heart."

"You mean cockles," I corrected, "it warms the cockles of your heart."

Her brow creased. "Why cockles? Aren't cockles *see-hum*?"

"Yes, I suppose they are," I replied, "but that's the expression."

"But why *see-hum*? They are shellfish. What have *see-hum* got to do with the heart?" she persisted.

"I honestly don't know," I responded, getting a trifle exasperated, "I can't be responsible for all the strange quirks of the English language."

"I think my version makes more sense," said June decidedly. "Muscles of the heart, not cockles."

"Cockles, muscles, alive alive-oh," George interrupted. "Children, we really must focus now. It's less than a month until the trial and we've an awful lot to do. June, you'll have to pitch in."

"No can do," answered June. "Mr Simon has given me a lot of work to do. And there is Marge. She does not like it when I leave her alone. When Towkay goes out there is no one in the house. She is scared to be here by herself. It is a big old house. She thinks there are *hantu*."

"*Hantu* in my house?" said a soft voice. It was d'Almeida. He had a disconcerting ability to move around noiselessly and startle people by materialising suddenly behind them. No *hantu* in its right mind would have stuck around.

June reddened. "No, Mr d'Almeida, Sir, I did not mean ..."

"I can assure you that there is no one here that I haven't invited," he responded with mock severity. June, who wasn't used to him, took it as a reprimand and subsided. He softened his tone, "There is nothing to be afraid of, my dear." She gave him an uncertain half-smile.

George explained the situation shortly to him. "Bring young Miss Barron along with you," he instructed. "Let her take the notes. It will be good for her. She should not be shut up here like a prisoner. For you, June, I have a special task."

June was overwhelmed and mute for once. She had never done any work for d'Almeida personally. "This case that you are helping Mr da Silva on," he continued, "have you done any research on marriage and divorce in the Malay States and the Colony?" She nodded her head, still unable to bring herself to speak in his presence. "Good," he went on, "I want a summary of the law pertaining to marriage."

When he had gone she turned to me. "What to do?" she asked plaintively. "Where to start?"

"Do what the King of Hearts suggested," I said, "begin at the beginning, go on until you reach the end, then stop."

She threw a cushion at me. "Ayoh, don't joke. Help-lah!"

I took pity on her. "Start with the Christian Marriage Ordinance. There's also a Civil Marriage Ordinance I think, but it may not be in force yet. Oh, and don't forget, the Muslims have their own Shariah law. The books are in the firm's library. I'd have a look there if I were you."

June acknowledged my aid gratefully and retreated to find a sheaf of paper and a new pencil. Meanwhile, I took Marge in hand and briefed her on what was necessary. She was apprehensive at first, but the prospect of getting out of the house was appealing. After a short pause for reflection she agreed.

Ahmad had no objections, but Karim remonstrated. He didn't like letting Marge out of his sight. To allow her to wander into a British camp was for him the height of folly. He made his opposition clear. I stood my ground firmly, invoking the orders of the All-Highest. Karim had to agree, albeit with bad grace. So it was all arranged. But he made it quite clear that he was holding me personally responsible for Marge's safe return. To emphasise the point, he stroked the sharp edge of his parang with his fingers.

THE British were surprisingly open about access to their prisoner. I suppose that there was no reason not to be. He wasn't going anywhere, not on an island full of British troops surrounded by a sea controlled by the Royal Navy. The Red Fort trials in India were stirring up dangerous passions. If there had been any suggestion that Habibullah was not being treated fairly, those passions could have spilled over to Malaya. As it was, the British no longer took for granted the loyalty of the Indian Army in Malaya. The War was over. The *jawans* wanted to go home to their families. Instead, some of them had been deployed to the Netherlands East Indies to fight the Indonesian nationalists. Mountbatten didn't want to risk British lives to reinstall the Dutch colonialists; the Indians were asking why theirs should be risked instead. The Dutch had not been model colonial masters. They had exploited the East Indies mercilessly and brutally. Now they needed the wealth of the Indies to get back on their feet after the devastation of the War. The average Indian *jawan* didn't see why he should die to help rebuild Rotterdam.

I found that I got on quite well with Habibullah and rather liked him. This was a surprise to me, since my initial impression of him — formed when I worked under cover at Batu Sembilan — was that he was a trouble-maker. I didn't tell him about our earlier encounters, though. D'Almeida had persuaded the British authorities to let Habibullah stay under house arrest in one of the flats that had formerly been occupied by married NCOs. It had two bedrooms and a small living room. We conducted the interviews there. It was so much more civilised than the lockup under the Police Courts. Marge proved surprisingly adept at taking notes. Relieved of the necessity of copying everything down, I concentrated on the task of learning all I could about our client.

HABIBULLAH'S father Imran Khan was the brother of the *wazir,* or chief minister, of Bhurtpore. Habibullah's family were *wazirs* by hereditary right and practical political necessity. The Hindu Rajahs kept the peace among their Muslim subjects by making sure that they were supported by people like the Khans. The British had placed the present Rajah's grandfather on the throne, having deposed his brother for being insufficiently enamoured of the Queen-Empress. Since then, the Rajahs had been great supporters of the British Raj. At the end of the day, they knew that if their subjects grew too restive their throne rested ultimately on the bayonets of the Indian Army.

Imran Khan joined the Indian Army and rose to the highest rank possible for a native: Subedar-Major in Wilde's Rifles, a Frontier Force regiment that saw constant action on the North-west Frontier. A Pathan himself, he fought to keep the *pax britannica* among people of a kindred race; not for love of the King-Emperor but for the honour of the Regiment and of his family. For his services, Subedar-Major Imran Khan became a King's Indian Orderly Officer to George V and travelled to England. He brought along his eldest son, Habibullah Khan. Habibullah was enrolled in a minor public school at the expense of the Rajah. After six years, he returned to India planning to join the Indian Army, as his father and his grandfather before him. Only this time, the Indian Army was in transition.

After the Great War, Britain had promised self-government to India at some unspecified future date as a reward for the sacrifices of the Indian Army in Europe and the Middle East. Indian soldiers had borne the brunt of the fighting that had taken General Allenby all the way from Egypt to Jerusalem and Damascus. The Jodhpur Lancers had made the last great mounted cavalry charge in history to capture the fortified port of Haifa; a deed that had been promptly forgotten by the British and Australians, who chose to celebrate the less significant action by the Australian Light Horse at Beersheba. The Indian Army had won with blood the gratitude of Great Britain and gained the prospect of autonomy for India. Something had to be done to adapt the Army to fulfil that promise.

It was decided that some regiments would be 'Indianised' and eventually officered by Indians rather than British officers. The idea was that Indian officers would be posted in at the bottom and by a gradual process of attrition replace the British officers.

The whole process would take, say, 40 years. This leisurely pace of reform would ensure the minimum disruption to entrenched interests. But opposition there was, even at this glacial pace. The plan was scaled back. Only a few regiments would be converted to start with. The Rajah offered to let his Bhurtpore Regiment participate in the grand experiment. The Bhurtpore Regiment was not formally part of the Indian Army. Rather, it was a field service unit paid for by the Rajah personally and placed at the disposal of the Commander-in-Chief. Legally, the Rajah was a sovereign prince bound by treaty to the Empire. For the British, it was politically advantageous have the active support of the princely states in the creation of the new Indian Army. For the Rajah, it was a matter of shrewd political calculation; if there was to be a new Indian Army, better that it should be officered by men well-disposed towards him rather than by rabble-rousing nationalists. The British graciously accepted the Rajah's generous offer.

So it came to pass that Habibullah Khan was sent off to the Indian Military Academy at Dehra Dun to be trained as an officer. This was India's equivalent of Sandhurst. Some Indians had in fact been commissioned at Sandhurst, obtaining the same commission as British officers. But there were too few of these King's Commissioned Officers. The process was horribly expensive, suitable candidates were thin on the ground and those who went found the climate and customs of the country tough to adapt to. Many dropped out. Dehra Dun was the answer. The officers who graduated from Dehra Dun were the cream of the crop. They got a real commission, as second-lieutenants rather than *jemadars*. They were posted first to a British battalion and subsequently to an Indian battalion, where they replaced the British company commanders. The Indian Commissioned Officers from Dehra Dun were destined for high command in the new Indianised Indian Army. In theory, they were the equal of the British officers. In theory.

The reality had proven quite different. The Bhurtpore Regiment was not like most of the battalions raised by the princely states. These tended to be officered by Indians of indifferent quality, not products of either Sandhurst or Dehra Dun. The Rajah of Bhurtpore had the means to hire British officers on secondment from the Indian Army, courtesy of the gold-mines that nature had blessed his little parched patch of hill country with. The Bhurtpore Regiment was run and organised exactly like any other battalion of the regular Indian Army, with British company commanders supported by Indian *jemadars* and subedars. In this milieu, Second-Lieutenant Habibullah Khan found himself very much an outsider. Some of the older Viceroy's Commission Officers resented the newcomers. They were *jemadars* and subedars who had risen from the ranks and could go no higher. The VCOs knew that they were inferior in status to British officers, no matter how junior. They accepted that as part of the order of the universe. They were used to deferring to white sahibs. An Indian lieutenant or captain was a different matter altogether. Many found it difficult to defer to a brown sahib.

The British officers of the Bhurtpores looked upon him as a jumped-up *babu* with ideas above his station. They cold-shouldered him socially. Their wives were worse; whenever an Indian got into the swimming pool at the officers' club, the women would pointedly get out. His Pathan blood ran hot at the discrimination and petty humiliations he faced. He felt he was their equal; their better in many ways, as the type of white who became an officer in the State Forces was not usually a man of great education or distinction. This made their arrogance and that of their low-bred wives that much harder to tolerate. Indian soldiers saluted even the most junior British officer as a matter of course; no British soldier ever voluntarily saluted an Indian officer, of whatever rank.

There were several other young Indian Commissioned Officers officers who felt equally frustrated and chafed at the constant slights. They knew that the whites who officered the Bhurtpore Regiment were not first-rate. The malcontents gathered together in the Mess, where the natives were kept apart from the whites. Habibullah became their leader. He had a natural aura of authority. A circle of discontented, angry men formed around him. They began to wonder out loud why they should be serving the British. India, they said, should be ruled by Indians for the benefit of Indians. The British had promised self-government. They were not taking any meaningful steps to make good on that. It was clear that the promises were empty.

It was in this frame of mind that the Bhurtpores were posted to Malaya and stationed at RAF Batu Sembilan to protect the airfield. This was where I joined them, at the behest of Colonel Newman, to observe and report. At that time, it was known by British intelligence that the Bhurtpores were not a happy unit. The suspicion was that Japanese agents were subverting the troops. D'Almeida and I were tasked to find out how far the rot had gone. Newman placed d'Almeida as an accounts clerk in the unit. I became a mute waiter in the officers' club. We didn't find any evidence of Japanese subversion. The agitation was homegrown, by Indians inside and outside the ranks striving towards a free India.

There was simmering discontent too among the rank and file, who did not care about politics. Most of that had to do with the personality of the new CO, Lieutenant-Colonel Holmes. By this time, all the British company commanders had resigned or been re-assigned. The only one left was the second-in-command, Major Leslie, an ineffectual though not unpleasant man. Holmes had been transferred from a regular Indian Army unit after a scandal and given command of the Bhurtpores. It was meant as a reprimand. He felt it a professional disgrace and took it out on the men. He insulted them. He humiliated them. He punished them for every minor infraction. He treated them as scum. It was clear that the CO despised his unit. The men reciprocated with sullen hostility.

Things came to a head when Habibullah was framed by two corrupt senior Indian officers who had been selling off the unit's supplies. It was an open secret that the two, Major Naidu and Captain Prithvi Singh, were involved in embezzlement on a grand scale. Naidu, the senior Indian officer, was a distant relative of the Rajah. Bhurtpore, like so many of the princely states, functioned on the basis of kleptocracy. Naidu, being royal (albeit barely), did not see a distinction between public and private property. He had no qualms about helping himself. Prithvi Singh was a thoroughly bad piece of goods. Where the Rajah disinterred him from only heaven knew. He was the battalion adjutant. Between them they had a nice little racket going, skimming the rations, drawing allowances for non-existent pensioners, making the troops do with sub-standard bedding and equipment. They had confederates on the outside, but no one knew exactly whom. The border country between the Malay states and Siam was infested with smugglers and assorted cut-throats, both private and official.

But there was a code of silence among the Indians and the British officers were kept in the dark. The second-in-command, Major Leslie, had served in the battalion since he was a subaltern. He owed his promotion to that singular lack of drive that keeps a mediocrity in place until more talented men have left. Leslie may have been ineffectual, but he was honest. As for the CO, no one doubted that he wasn't involved. To have been involved would have meant fraternising with the natives, and that wasn't on. That tacit agreement of silence broke down one night when Naidu had argued with Habibullah. Hot words were exchanged, knives were drawn. Although a fight was averted, Habibullah had threatened to blow the whistle on both Naidu and Prithvi Singh. To stop him, they planted subversive materials in Habibullah's sleeping quarters. He had been arrested and marched off to the guardhouse. When his company heard this, they had effectively gone on strike. So had the other Mussulman company. The Rajput companies followed in short order. Holmes had gone beserk when he heard about the mutiny. He marched right over and threatened to shoot Habibullah as the putative ringleader. This was too much for the troops. Their pent-up hatred for the CO exploded. One of the men shot Lieutenant-Colonel Holmes dead.

I hadn't been a witness to the actual shooting, but I met Dave Blake, a young Australian RAAF corporal, who had. He had the bad luck to have been at the wrong place at the wrong time and was captured by the mutineers, but managed to slip away in the general confusion. He confirmed what Habibullah had told us, that the shooting was done by one of the men and not by him. That was the very day that the Japanese landed at Kota Bahru. We got out by the skin of our teeth, Corporal Blake, me and a couple of others. We had an eventful journey getting back to Singapore. When the island fell, Blake went off to try his luck finding a boat. I had no further information on what had become of him.

Habibullah was a little surprised at the amount of information we had about his activities at Batu Sembilan. However, he didn't remark on it further. By this time he had heard of d'Almeida's formidable reputation and his unparallelled network of friends and acquaintances. He also knew of George's deep involvement in the Indian Independence League; in fact, it was that connection that brought the case to D'Almeida & D'Almeida in the first place. Habibullah filled in the blanks, fleshing out the tale after d'Almeida and I had quit Batu Sembilan.

19

THE death of Lieutenant-Colonel Holmes was the Rubicon. Habibullah knew that there was no going back after that. They knew of the Japanese landings at Kota Bahru. The sounds of artillery could be heard clearly even at Batu Sembilan. The British and Australian airmen had bolted in unseemly panic before the Bhurtpores mutinied, stampeding at the rumour that the Japanese were coming. The antipathy that Habibullah felt towards the British turned to disgust when he witnessed it. This was the master race that claimed the divine right to rule India. But he had no time to indulge in reflection on the iniquity of the Raj. The immediate problem was what to do. To ask his men to defend the airfield was completely out of the question. They had broken the link that bound them to the King-Emperor. They had no loyalty to the Rajah of Bhurtpore, even though he was their paymaster. Their only loyalty was to the Regiment. Men would have fought and died for the honour of the Regiment, but that too was gone. They were masterless warriors, adrift in a foreign land, embroiled in a war not of their making, for a cause that they did not believe in.

The men looked to him for leadership. Although he was not the most senior officer, the mantle of command had fallen naturally on his shoulders. Habibullah was in a dilemma. From all accounts, 8th Indian Brigade was putting up a good fight, but it was hard-pressed. His sense of honour and loyalty impelled him to go to their aid. But he knew that he could not ask it of his men. With a heavy heart, he gave the order to disperse. The men should make their way as best they could to the Siamese border and there surrender themselves. There was no choice. If the British caught them, would be summarily shot as deserters and mutineers. This way most would survive. At some point, perhaps, they might find they way home. It was the death warrant of the Regiment. The 1st Battalion of the Bhurtpore Regiment would cease to exist. Even if the Rajah raised a new unit, none would bear its name ever again.

Habibullah himself resolved to remain at the camp and take what was coming. It was the only thing he could do to salvage the Regiment's honour, a personal sacrifice to expiate the sins of the many. He was under no illusions as to his fate. The British were not the sort to forgive a mutineer. Since the Great Rebellion of 1857, their nightmare was an uprising among the sepoys. To prevent such a thing, the Indian Army had been deprived of field artillery. Every brigade had one British battalion to two Indian. Indian battalions were segregated by race and religion, recruited only from certain martial races and kept separate from the civil population, so that they would not find common cause to rise up against their masters. Even so, the 5th Light Infantry had mutinied in Singapore in 1915. The mutiny had been put down, ironically with the help of sailors from Imperial Japanese Navy ships that had fortuitously been in port. No mercy had been shown to the ringleaders. They were shot in front of Outram Road Gaol. Habibullah expected no better.

Some of the men hesitated. His orderly Nisar Ahmad insisted on remaining. There was an almost feudal tie between an officer and his orderly. Habibullah did not insist that Nisar Ahmad go. But for the rest, he saw no need for them to risk their lives for his sake. There was nothing that they could do. He didn't intend to put up a fight, whether it was the British or the Japanese who came for him. He ordered them to head for the border. Military discipline re-asserted itself. The men left as ordered. When they had gone, the thought crossed his mind that there was one way out: shoot himself. But the thought was gone almost as soon as it surfaced. To commit suicide was not the way of the warrior. His code of honour demanded that he should face whatever punishment the British might choose to mete out, and face it unflinchingly.

THAT night, he spent a strangely peaceful time in his quarters. Nisar Ahmad prepared his food, a simple meal of rice and lentils. For the first time in many months, he had leisure to read and relax. The stifling poisonous atmosphere created by Holmes was gone. It was only then that he realised how much tension he had been under, not only because of Holmes but also on account of that crooked pair Naidu and Prithvi Singh. For months, he had lived with the knowledge of their thievery, constrained to silence by the need to preserve the honour of the regiment, watching with impotent rage while they pulled the wool over the eyes of the egregious Major Leslie. If Holmes had been a more sympathetic CO, he would not have hesitated. But Holmes was a maniac, and he had no desire to carry tales to such a man. His public school education restrained him. There was nothing worse than a sneak. The other Indian officers took their cue from him. He could not very well ask them to do something that he would not do himself. His only regret was the effect that this would have on his mother. The old lady should not have to bear such a disgrace in her last years. But there was nothing for it. Habibullah decided to compose a letter, to be sent to his mother upon his death.

There was a commotion while he was writing. Shots were heard from the direction of the Operations Block. This is it, he thought to himself. Buckling on his revolver, he sallied out to meet his captors, followed by the faithful Nisar Ahmad. A few

Bhurtpores still remained in the camp, clustering in small groups near the fence. The airfield was still burning from the air raid earlier in the day. The smouldering fires gave enough light to see by. He looked around. There was no one on the road beyond the fence. Gathering a few men, he investigated the administration buildings. In a room in C Block they found traces of fresh blood. There was a strange contraption, which looked like a typewriter but contained what seemed to be parts of a radio. It had been smashed. He detailed the men to search the surrounding area, but they found nothing. Looters, he guessed and put it out of his mind. It didn't matter anyway. They just had to wait for either the British or the Japanese to show up.

The following morning, Habibullah woke with a start. He was used to being awakened at the crack of dawn by Nisar Ahmad with a mug of *char*. His first groggy thought was that he had overslept. Then it all came back to him. Nisar Ahmad was there. He had let Habibullah sleep in. There were no regimental duties to do. The customary mug of *char* was procured, together with a fresh chappati and dhal. Habibullah was not fastidious about what he ate. Food to him was a necessary distraction. He left the matter entirely to his orderly.

At mid-morning came another commotion. This time it was caused by a group of Chinese, who appeared at the gate with a lorry. They drove it right into the camp without even stopping. They knew exactly what they were after. The lorry was parked at the Officers' Club. To Habibullah's surprise, the men went into the derelict servants' quarters behind and emerged with boxes and bags. It was then that he realised where Naidu and Prithvi Singh had been hiding all the stores that they had stolen from the regiment. Evidently, these men were the ones whom they had been dealing with. Now that the soldiers were gone, there was nothing to stop them helping themselves to the loot.

Some went to the armoury and broke it open. One of his men came running up breathlessly. "Sahib," he said, "the Chinese bandits are stealing the guns and ammunition. Shall we stop them?"

Habibullah strode out to the armoury, where some of his men stood around indecisively. They automatically stiffened to attention when they saw him. The Chinese ceased their activity and looked nervously at him.

"Who is in charge here?" he demanded loudly, not really expecting an answer.

A young man detached himself from the group. "I am the headman," he said. Though the accent was strange, the English was tolerably good.

"Where are the Japanese?"

"They are near Kota Bahru town. They will come here soon. Will you fight them or not? The *Orang Puteh* have run away," he answered.

"No, we will not fight them," replied Habibullah. "My men are gone. You should go too."

The young man said, "We will go, but we must have guns and bullets. The *Jepun* will come and kill us. We must fight here as our brothers fight them in China. Give us the guns."

Habibullah nodded. He had heard of the blood feud between the Chinese and the Japanese. Word of the Rape of Nanking had penetrated even to the wilds of Bhurtpore. He had no use for the weapons. The Chinese would need them. Let them take what they wanted. He gave the order to his men to help load up the lorry. They hesitated at first, not able to comprehend this breach of all that had been drilled into them about custody of weapons. He repeated his order. The sepoys obeyed and moved towards the armoury. The Chinese recoiled, thinking that the sepoys were reclaiming the weapons. Then they understood and broke out in smiles. The lorry was filled and despatched. The Chinese remained behind, methodically emptying the armoury. A second lorry appeared after half an hour. This too was filled. Habibullah left the men to it. As he returned to his quarters, he noticed that the Chinese were systematically looting the Operations Block, carting away lamps and furniture and even the filing cabinets.

BY late afternoon, the camp had been stripped bare. The word had gone round that the garrison had decamped. The Chinese had taken what they wanted. People came from the nearby kampongs to pick over the leavings. There were still some scavengers among the buildings when the Japanese finally arrived. They scuttled away immediately, clutching their bundles of loot.

The Japanese came on bicycles. He eyed them curiously. They were short, much as British propaganda had portrayed them, but without the buck-teeth and squint-eyes. Comically, their rifles seemed taller than they were. But there was no mistaking their determination or ability as fighting troops. They dismounted quickly and spread out, searching the buildings methodically. Habibullah watched them with professional interest. It was odd to see modern troops led by officers with swords. There was a flag-bearer and a bugler. Their uniforms were loose-fitting khaki. On their legs they wore puttees, a fashion that the British and Indian Armies had abandoned two decades previously. Instead of boots, they had curious split-toed shoes. They moved very fast, with a fluid grace that elicited admiration. This was a discplined, experienced army, not a horde of slant-eyed myopic monkeys as the British believed. Knots of sepoys emerged with their hands up. The Japanese rounded them up and hustled them towards the gate.

A staff car pulled up in the middle of the parade square. Habibullah decided that it was opportune to emerge. He stepped out into the sunlight, his back ramrod straight, and marched over to the car. A Japanese officer got out, his long scabbard clutched in his white-gloved hands. He wore a white open-necked shirt under his coat. His riding boots were polished to perfection. Evidently, he had come prepared to accept the surrender of the base from the commanding officer. Habibullah saluted, removed his pistol and handed it over, butt first. The officer returned the salute and accepted his token of surrender. Then, to his surprise, an Indian emerged from the car.

"Lieutenant Habibullah Khan of the 1st Bhurtpores," said the Indian, "I have waited a long time for this pleasure."

20

MAJOR FUJIWARA IWAICHI had a big job for a man who did not speak Hindustani and only had a smattering of English: subvert the Indian Army. He commanded Fujiwara Kikan, a unit whose objective it was to bring the Indians over to the Japanese side when war should come. The Japanese had cast their eyes on the Southern Ocean for many years. To get at the riches of the Netherlands East Indies, they had first to overcome the French in Indochina and the British in Malaya. The French and Dutch were taken care of by the Germans. The only real obstacle to their conquest of the East Indies was the British. Contrary to what all of us were taught in school, the British were not universally beloved by their subject peoples. Rash Behari Bose had tried to assassinate the Viceroy, Lord Hardinge. He failed and fled into exile, eventually finding his way to Tokyo. From Tokyo Rash Behari Bose carried on his agitation against the British Raj under the banner of the Indian Independence League. He was useful to the Japanese. They preached that the European colonial powers had no place in Asia. Asia belonged to Asiatics. The natural leader of such an Asia was, of course, Japan, which had proven her ability to match the Europeans by annihilating the Russian fleet at Tsushima a generation previously. Through Rash Behari Bose the Japanese made contact with one Pritam Singh, who had founded the Independence League of India in Bangkok. In autumn 1941 Major Fujiwara travelled incognito to Bangkok to meet Pritam Singh and set up the infrastructure for undermining the Indian Army when the shooting finally started. Fujiwara Kikan would be in the vanguard of the coming war.

Among the network of agents that Fujiwara established was one VR Narayanan, a trader who lived in Kota Bahru and had extensive contacts among the shady people who made a living by moving goods over the porous border. Narayanan was a patriot by conviction, not a simple mercenary as so many agents were. He really believed in the ideal of *Azad Hind*, Free India. Fujiwara also believed in a free India in an Asian Asia. It was a crusade to rid Asia of the parasitical European colonialists.

Narayanan was the one directing the subversion of the Bhurtpores in Batu Sembilan. Special Branch was on to him, which is why d'Almeida and I were sent to that god-forsaken hole in the first place. To be precise, Special Branch in the form of Colonel Newman knew that there was someone in Kota Bahru engaged in cloak-and-dagger work for the Japanese, but didn't know exactly whom. D'Almeida rumbled Narayanan within the first month of his stay. Special Branch bided its time, hoping to round up the whole network at one fell swoop. But it wasn't Narayanan who was responsible for the awful state of morale among the troops. He just tried to take advantage of it. Most of his propaganda efforts fell on barren ground. Neither the sepoys nor their officers were interested in politics. It was another matter when the Japanese attacked Kota Bahru. Word soon got to him of the mutiny. When the advanced elements of Major-General Takumi's 56th Infantry Regiment broke through 8th Indian Brigade's lines, Narayanan was there to welcome them with a plan to completely undermine the Indian units that formed the backbone of the defence.

HABIBULLAH had been treated with every courtesy by his captors. The Japanese major who accepted his surrender could speak no English. He left the talking to Narayanan, who was the Indian man in the staff car. Narayanan introduced himself to Habibullah, explaining how he knew his name and background. He described the activities of Fujiwara Kikan. He sketched out his plans to get the Indian troops to lay down their arms and defect. Habibullah found this distasteful. He was a soldier and instinctively recoiled at this kind of stab-in-the-back warfare. Narayanan however persisted.

"Do you remember what is written on the walls of the Military Academy at Dehra Dun? Let me quote: '*The safety, honour and welfare of your country come first, always and every time. The honour, welfare and comfort of the men you command come next. Your own ease, comfort and safety come last, always and every time.*' I ask you, Lieutenant Habibullah Khan, what is your country?"

Habibullah hesitated. Narayanan pressed home his advantage. "Is it England that is your country? The England that feted General Dyer when he massacred innocent men, women and children in the Jallianwala Bagh? Or is it India? India must have *purna swaraj*, full independence. The Britishers do not have the right to enslave our people."

"What do you want me to do?" asked Habibullah cautiously, still unwilling to commit himself.

"Look after the welfare and safety of your men," replied Narayanan. "If they are caught by the Britishers, they will be shot as traitors. You have a duty to gather them and place them under the protection of Japan. And to help any others of our compatriots who wish to claim that protection."

"You haven't answered my question," persisted Habibullah, "what exactly do you expect me to do?"

"Nothing at present," responded Narayanan soothingly, "but at some point in the near future we will need someone to be in charge of the Indian prisoners-of-war, from the Bhurtpores as well as other regiments. We cannot let their white officers lead them astray."

It was not an unreasonable thing to ask. Habibullah agreed. The die was irretrievably cast.

IN the following days, the stragglers from the Bhurtpores were rounded up. Those who had made it to the Siamese border were interned and then handed back over to Japanese. They were gathered together in a camp outside Kota Bahru. The Indians were segregated from the white prisoners. Habibullah was appointed to command them. By and large they were treated well. Habibullah was more or less free to come and go as he pleased. The Japanese, efficient though they might have been at the art of war, proved to be hopelessly incompetent when it came to logistics. Their own men could subsist on nothing but rice. They expected their prisoners to do the same. They had absolutely no idea of the dietary requirements of Muslim and Hindu troops. Fortunately, Narayanan was there to intercede and organise. The men got ghee and dhal and flour to make chappatis. The British were not so fortunate. They got nothing but rice, and precious little of that. To the Japanese, they were nothing. They had forfeited their honour by surrendering. It was a matter of total indifference to them what became of such despicable creatures.

Major-General Takumi's troops had better things to do than look after POWs. They were pressing Brigadier Key's men hard, pushing them back to the railhead at Kuala Krai. Despite the pressure, 8th Indian Brigade maintained its cohesion. The same could not be said of the RAF groundcrew. The vital northern airfields were precipitately abandoned as what remained of the fighter and bomber squadrons were pulled back to the south. Signs of their panicked flight were everywhere. They left without even bothering to destroy vital stores to deny them to the enemy. The Japanese had full command of the air. Fresh troops came from the north — the 5th Division and the rest of the 18th Division, which had landed in Singora and Patani. They swung over to the west coast, slicing through the thin screen in front of them. The rapidity of the Japanese advance left a vacuum in its wake. Lieutenant-General Yamashita Tomoyuki, the commander of the invading 25th Army, was loth to tie up combat troops to garrison the line of communications. Second echelon units were landed, including Koreans and Formosans, to hold the rear areas. The Koreans and Formosans kept the civil population in line and formed a reserve in case of counterattack. Behind the fighting troops came the 2nd Field Kempeitai. They had a simple way of dealing with lawlessness; a few judicious beheadings and looting ceased completely.

The Japanese decided that the Indian POWs should be put to good use. Habibullah's men were tasked with maintaining order in the towns and kampongs behind the front line. They were unarmed except for truncheons and the odd *lathi*. The second-line Japanese units and the Kempeitai were in charge of the POW camps. The Indians manned the roadblocks and patrolled the streets to enforce the curfew. Most of the population kept indoors, bewildered by the speed of the conquest and cowed by the ruthlessness of the Kempeitai. The second-line units did not have the discipline of the frontline soldiers. They swaggered around taking whatever they fancied and generally behaving in a loutish fashion. They were in charge now and no one was allowed to forget it. Anyone who had the temerity to pass a sentry without showing sufficient respect was peremptorily summoned back, slapped and roughed up. Administration of summary justice was done with the arbitrariness of the playground bully. Before the invasion, Yamashita had issued his troops with a document enjoining them to treat the "liberated" population with kindness. Obviously, few of his troops had bothered to read it.

DESPITE the oppression, there was resistance to the Japanese. The Chinese population was hostile. Ever since the Marco Polo Bridge incident in 1937, the Chinese in Malaya had been implacably anti-Japanese. They had organised a boycott of Japanese goods in retaliation for Japanese aggression in China. They contributed money towards the defence of the homeland. When the Japanese invaded, some of the Chinese took to the jungle, armed with weapons left behind by the British. They hit back at the invader, pinprick attacks on isolated sentries, sabotage of a bridge here and there. The Japanese reacted with characteristic ferocity. The Kempeitai took savage reprisals on suspected guerrilla supporters. Whole families were massacred as a lesson to others. In a special act of defiance, the guerrillas tore down the *Hinomaru* from one of the public buildings in a town and raised the Nationalist Chinese flag in its place. The reaction was brutal. All the Chinese in town were driven out and their houses destroyed. They were left to starve at the jungle fringe. Despite their professed aim to unite Asia to resist white colonialism, the Japanese displayed a special barbarity in dealing with the Chinese. The years of fighting in China had brutalised them. They could not understand why the Chinese would not accept their leadership of Asia, which was to them the most natural thing in the world.

Habibullah tried to keep his men out of the fight. This was a matter between the Chinese and the Japanese. He sympathised with the Chinese, who were clearly the underdogs. He had done his bit to help them by letting them take the weapons and ammunition from Batu Sembilan. He didn't want any of his men killed by either side. It appeared that his early act of generosity had been noted. The guerrillas left the Indians alone. When they sabotaged the roads and bridges, they avoided those manned by the Indians, who were easily recognisable by their turbans. The guerrillas concentrated on the targets guarded by the Formosans especially. For them, special treatment was arranged. After a couple of guards had been horribly mutilated, the Formosans kept close together and only ventured out in large armed groups.

In the middle of December Narayanan left them. He had other business to attend to. Word came that the 5th Division had punched through the Jitra Line, which was supposed to hold for six months. The trickle of Indian prisoners turned into a torrent. Fujiwara Kikan had been very active. Their biggest coup was to persuade the 1/14 Punjabis to surrender. The gaping hole left in the line was quickly exploited. Northern Malaya was lost. Penang fell on 14 December. In a clear breach of faith, the British stealthily evacuated the white population, leaving the Asiatics behind to fend for themselves. Japanese propaganda had a field day. More damaging from the military point of view, in their panic the retreating British left all sorts of small boats undamaged. *Chachiru kyuyo* the Japanese called them, "Churchill rations". If it hadn't been for the food, ammunition, weapons and transport that the retreating British left behind, the Japanese advance would have ground to a halt waiting for their unsteady supply lines to catch up. They used the boats and bicycles to good effect, constantly outflanking the defensive lines that were hurriedly thrown up. The long retreat took its toll on the morale of all the troops, British as well as Indian. The siren song of *Azad Hind* found more ready listeners.

Though Narayanan had left, the subtle pressure on Habibullah continued. A Sergeant Sato Kenji appeared on the scene. "Call me Ken," he had told Habibullah on their first meeting, speaking in a broad American accent. Ken Sato was a Nisei, a second-generation Japanese-American born in Hawaii. He had lived on Oahu until the death of his father. His mother had then taken him back to the old country when he was 13, to stay with his paternal grandparents in Sendai. It was a lucky break he said; his uncles, aunts and cousins who lived in California had been rounded up the moment war was declared and put into concentration camps. The Americans hadn't interned the German-Americans or Italian-Americans, only Japanese-Americans. Sato had been conscripted and assigned in due course to Fujiwara Kikan. He was genuinely friendly and outgoing, in a most un-Japanese fashion. He too had bought the ideal that Asia should be for Asians. Japan was the natural leader, but a free India would be an indispensable partner. He tried to talk Habibullah round. It all sounded so reasonable.

Yet Habibullah held back. He had a frontier code of honour, which prized loyalty over all other virtues save courage. Holmes had betrayed that loyalty by his contempt for the regiment, displayed in public for all to see. His killing was justified, for he had forfeited his honour as a leader. But to actually descend to urging other Indians to break their oaths of fealty was something Habibullah could not bring himself to do. There was something distasteful about skulking around trying to get soldiers to sell out their regiments. If they themselves came to the realisation that they were serving a base cause and quit, then so be it. But if they chose to remain true to their salt he respected them for it, mistaken though they be. The politics of pan-Asianism held no interest for him. His task was to keep his men safe. He did not intend to fail them.

BY early January the Japanese were poised in front of the British Army line at Slim River. Fujiwara Kikan was in the forefront. Units that stayed together provided slim pickings. Those were the ones with strong regimental traditions and officers who knew and cared for their men. The battalions that had emergency-commissioned officers fared much worse. The officers were newly posted-in, inexperienced in the ways of the Indian Army and unfamiliar with their men. Experienced NCOs and VCOs had been stripped out to man the new units raised for service in the Middle East. The *jawans* had no confidence in their new leaders. It takes time and considerable effort to earn the respect of the rank and file; a white skin alone is not enough. When these units saw the British break, their morale shook even when they were not in direct contact with the enemy. Panic was contagious. The sight of men streaming back from the frontlines was too much for the inexperienced young *jawans*, lost in a strange land, surrounded by jungle instead of the rugged dry hills that they were used to. When Fujiwara's newly-recruited Indians appeared with their siren song of *purna swaraj*, the shaky Indian units started fraying. A few men would leave a forward picket. Then the whole platoon would go. If the British officers weren't paying attention, in the blink of an eye a company-sized hole would appear in the line and the Japanese would come pouring through.

The tales grew in the telling. It was part of the Japanese propaganda war to magnify the scale of the defections. The seeds of distrust were sown and soon began to sprout. British troops looked nervously at their flanks, fearing at any moment to be betrayed by the Indians. The Indians were at first hurt and then outraged at the slurs on their honour. The prophecies of betrayal became self-fulfilling. Incidents of friendly fire between British and Indian troops exacerbated the tense situation. These happen in any war. But in the climate of mutual suspicion, a few mis-aimed shots became sparks for the tinder. The British began to suspect the loyalty of all Indians, military or civilian.

THEY were just north of the Slim River line when Habibullah was interrupted at breakfast by the sudden appearance of Lieutenant Bhajan Singh, an officer of the 1/14 Punjabis who had been captured at Jitra. "You'd better come and see this," he said breathlessly.

Habibullah didn't have a high opinion of Bhajan. He had met the man a couple of times before, when their troops were engaged in policing the Japanese lines of communication. His impression was that Bhajan was too much of an opportunist. The senior Indian officer of the 1/14 Punjabis was a Captain Mohan Singh. Mohan Singh was an idealist and disillusioned with the British. The 1/14 Punjabis had been overrun by Japanese tanks at Jitra. After wandering for a couple of days in the jungles and swamps of Kedah, he had been picked up by an enemy patrol. In the POW camp the Japanese separated the white officers from Indian officers and *jawans.* He discovered that his men were treated with respect rather than the brutality that they had been led to expect. Fujiwara Kikan brought him round with the promise of a free India in a free Asia. That promise resonated with Mohan Singh. He got on with Major Fujiwara. The two were the same age; like all career soldiers, they swapped war stories and commiserated with one another. Mohan Singh was impressed by the Major's apparently sincere desire for a partnership with India. He promised to raise an army to fight for *Azad Hind*. He began helping Fujiwara recruit among the Indian POWs. One of those recruits was Bhajan Singh. Bhajan was not a patriot in any sense of the word. He saw which way the wind was blowing and trimmed his sails accordingly.

Reluctantly, Habibullah rose from his uncompleted breakfast. Nisar Ahmad, his orderly, hurriedly cleared the dishes and followed him. They got into a Morris 15-cwt lorry that had been assigned to the Indians. It was *Chachiru kyoyu* and still bore its previous unit's markings. The driver wore his Indian Army khaki uniform but without insignia. Those who had been recruited by Fujiwara Kikan were identified by white armbands emblazoned with an "F" in red. They were kept behind the frontlines in reserve. When an Indian unit was encountered they went into action, infiltrating between the pickets and persuading the frightened *jawans* that there was a better way. When persuasion did not work they resorted to trickery, spreading false orders to withdraw. They added confusion to disorganisation in a miasma of distrust.

Habibullah had asked where they were going, but Bhajan had only responded with a non-committal "You'll see." He didn't press. The road was well metalled and flanked by rubber estates on both sides. The Japanese appeared to have complete air superiority. No attempt was made to hide from aerial attack; whatever aircraft remained to the British had been pulled back to defend Singapore. After about five miles they turned off onto an estate road. This was of packed earth but well tended. Perak was one of the more prosperous Malay states. The backbone of the Malayan economy was tin-mining and rubber cultivation. The tin and rubber business was dominated by the Chinese and Europeans. The mines and estates, worked by Indian and Chinese coolies, produced the sinews of war for the British Empire. Now they would do the same for the Japanese Empire.

They pulled to a stop and got out. Bhajan led the way between the rows of rubber trees, standing in straight lines like guardsmen on parade. They came to a clearing by a stream. There were huts here, built of simple wooden planks and thatched with attap. These were the coolie lines. The rubber trees were tapped early every morning by an army of uneducated Indian peasants, literally scratching a living from the trees. Habibullah smelt them before he saw them. He was familiar with the stench of death. By the stream was a line of bodies, men and women, at least fifty of them. Their faces were contorted in pain and fear. The flies swarmed around their bloated corpses. Habibullah looked on without emotion. Dead civilians were nothing new to him, not in this war. He had seen them too many times before, the handiwork of the Kempeitai up north. He glanced interrogatively at Bhajan.

"Why are you showing me this?" asked Habibullah impatiently in Punjabi. "I have seen what the Japanese do to civilians. So they butcher Indians as well as Chinese. What is that to me that you should bring me to this place?"

Bhajan motioned to his men, who brought out a coolie. The man was dark-skinned, Dravidian rather than Aryan. He was trembling uncontrollably. His shoulder was bandaged, as was his side. He had apparently been shot and bayonetted. "Ask him who did this," said Bhajan, "he speaks some Hindustani."

The coolie did not wait to be asked. "It was not the Japanese, sahib," he replied in a voice choked with pain. "It was the white sahibs. They kill us all."

21

PARIT BATANG was a turning point on Habibullah Khan's road. The revelation that the massacre of the coolies had been perpetrated by British troops cut whatever residual bonds of loyalty that remained. In their headlong retreat, the British blamed the Indians for the loss of northern Malaya. It was so much easier to believe that the treachery of the Indians and not the incompetence of their own troops was responsible for the debacle. Officially, of course, the line was that the Indian troops were fighting magnificently with their customary courage alongside the British — which was entirely true. But privately, officers and men muttered about the disloyalty of the sepoys. They were unreliable and apt to go over to the enemy at the slightest pretext. The civilians were no better. Despite being British subjects, the businessmen and professionals supported the Indian Independence League with money while the coolies led the Japanese by hidden paths around the frontline defences. The Indians were rotten through-and-through, subverted by politicians calling for Indian independence at a time when the Empire was in peril. Watch your back, the men said; they won't have any scruples about stabbing you. If there's a choice between a snake and an Indian, shoot the Indian.

At Parit Batang the anger boiled over. The North Anglian Yeomanry were territorials, not regulars. The battalion was raised from the tenants of the Duke of Norfolk during the dark days after

Dunkirk, equipped with whatever equipment could be scraped together after the British Expeditionary Force had been rescued from France. They had trained for desert warfare, expecting to be sent to join the 8th Army fighting Rommel in Libya. Instead, with no warning, they had been shipped off to the Far East and pitched straight into battle against fanatical slant-eyed hordes who fought like maniacs and took few prisoners. The air cover they had been promised was non-existent, destroyed by the enemy in the first week of hostilities. The Royal Navy's contribution to the defence of Malaya, the battleship HMS Prince of Wales and the battlecruiser HMS Repulse, were lying at the bottom of the South China Sea. Since the fall of the Jitra Line they had been in constant retreat. Every time they took a stand, the line was compromised. The Japanese miraculously appeared in their flanks and rear, passing through the impassable jungle like wraiths. It was clear that they had help from the locals. The little yellow men must have been led through secret paths by the black and brown natives, all of whom were not to be trusted.

Then three companies of the North Anglians were annihilated at Parit Batang in a ferocious Japanese attack. The Japs appeared from nowhere, screaming, blowing bugles and waving flags. They were everywhere, in the flanks and rear as well. The Indian units guarding their flank dissolved too; the North Anglians believed that most of the *jawans* had just gone over to the enemy. The survivors stumbled back through the rubber estates, harried by the Japs, not knowing where the next ambush would be, bitter at their betrayal. They came upon the Tamil coolies at the Parit Batang estate, small evil-looking creatures, black as sin with mouths stained red with betel-nut juice. An officer questioned them regarding the whereabouts of the Japanese. No one would give any information. They said they knew nothing but it was plain that they were working with the enemy; no human could get through the trackless jungle without help. Beatings did not loosen any tongues. Then a couple of the coolies tried to make a break for it. They were shot in the back. One thing led to another and soon the whole group was running for the jungle. Someone gave the order to open fire. The troops kept firing until they ran out of ammunition. They bayonetted the ones who were still twitching.

Habibullah was inclined to be sceptical at first. This man Siva, the sole surviving witness, could have been put up to it by the Japanese — or by Bhajan Singh for that matter. But the evidence was plain to see. Nisar Ahmad poked around the stream. He came back with a handful of .303 cartridge casings, the same sort of ammunition used by the British Lee-Enfield rifles and Bren guns. The ground was littered with them. The Japanese Arisaka rifles fired a 7.7 mm cartridge, quite different in appearance. Siva was a Tamil whose native language was incomprehensible to Habibullah and Bhajan Singh. He was of a completely different race, being a dark-skinned Dravidian from the south. Even if he had been able to write, the Tamil script was totally different from that used in the north. The only thing he shared in common with them was that the British ruled his homeland. Siva could speak only a few words of Hindustani, just barely enough to get his story across. It was enough for Habibullah. He ordered Nisar Ahmad to tend to Siva and stormed off, his heart burning within him. He was white with anger, shaking with barely-controlled fury. "Where are the dogs who have done this?" he demanded. "We must hunt them down and kill them all."

The Japanese Army broke through the Slim River line on 7 January and went on to take Kuala Lumpur, the capital of the Federated Malay States, on 11 January. This was a symbolic moment. All the Indian POWs were congregated together, nearly five thousand of them. Fujiwara and Mohan Singh announced that they had formed an Indian army to free India. The kernel had been created after Jitra. They invited the POWs to join them in fleshing out that army. The Bhurtpores, who had followed in the wake of the Japanese all the way from Kelantan, responded enthusiastically. General Mohan Singh offered Habibullah command of a new provisional battalion formed around the Bhurtpores. He accepted. He was now Major Habibullah Khan of the Indian National Army.

"I HAD no idea," said Marge, evidently shaken. "We were never told any of this. Aunt Dorothy did say that the Indians were traitors, bad men all of them, that they had betrayed the Empire. I heard her talking to Father. And I believed it all, every word."

"You are not to blame, child," said Habibullah gently. "You are not the only one who believes that the Britishers can do no wrong and that all they do is for the good of the poor ignorant natives."

"I'm sorry, sorry for all the things they ... we ... did to you," she said softly. She put her hand in his and he patted it.

He had taken to her, recognising a fellow soul in anguish perhaps. I noticed that he was more relaxed when she was around. With me he was always on guard. We took short breaks in between our sessions, more for me than him. It was hard going as he would reply to my prodding questions in the most economical fashion. By chance, I found that he would tell her things that he told no one else. Stepping out to stretch, I overheard them talking. She too seemed to open up more when she was alone with him. It was good to see her smile, something that she seldom did around any of us. Once, I even heard her giggle like a schoolgirl. June was surprised and pleased at the change when Marge came back every night. She had been afraid that the experience of interviewing Habibullah would prove too depressing. Quite the contrary; she had blossomed. I decided that I would leave them to it as much as I could, keeping just within earshot but out of sight. My absence was clearly welcome. Habibullah asked her about her life. She hesitated at first, but slowly her story came out.

MARGE had spent her early childhood in England. To her it was a grey, drab place. The terrace house they lived in was the colour of soot. A few bedraggled plants tried valiantly to brighten up the small square of earth they called a garden; when autumn came, they gave up the struggle. Money was short. Some of the houses along their street were boarded up. She remembered her father being away a lot.

Beyond her street lay a forest of cranes and the smell of the sea. There were seagulls. Their raucous cries formed a background to her life. The other children in her street left her out of their games. They were rough. Some went to school. Most of the older ones did odd jobs, some following their fathers around looking for work of any description. She didn't remember it as a happy street. There was an air of depression hanging around the place.

Then, magically, her life changed. One day, just after she turned six, she was bundled up in her best clothes. Her things were packed in boxes and bags. Her parents took her down to the docks, a strange, exciting place where gigantic ships moored. They led her up the gangplank to a small cabin with a tiny porthole. Pressing her nose against the glass, she watched as the grey buildings faded into the distance. The seagulls followed them for a while, but eventually they were left behind. At first the sea was choppy and the ship rode up and down the waves in a most unsettling way. Then they passed through a strait within sight of a gigantic rock into a calmer sea. The sun shone more brightly. After a longish time, she had a vague memory of the ship sailing through the desert. There were sand dunes and men on camels. Beyond that the sun was hotter than ever. The smell of the sea changed. It was a strange ocean. There were fish that flew. The various ports they called at were full of colour and bustle and odd-looking people. After a lifetime, the ship finally sailed into the port of Singapore.

Her first memories of Singapore were that it was all so bright and beautiful. There were new smells and sounds. The people were from another world, black-haired, black-eyed, with high cheekbones and tanned skins. More wonderful was the new house. Marge's father had held some position in the Harbour Board. They stayed in a gigantic bungalow with an enormous garden full of strange colourful flowers and fruit-trees. There were new fruits that she had never tasted before: a greenish-brown spiky one that stank; a hairy red one with a sweet pulp around a hard seed; a purple one the size of a small apple, with little segments you could pull apart. Behind was a green jungle-covered ridge full of squirrels and monkeys, snakes and insects. The butterflies were multi-hued and bigger than she had ever seen, not the small drab creatures she was used to. There were moths with wings as big as her face, beetles which shone a metallic green and bronze in the light. Even the ants were giants, black ones with threatening pincers and red ones whose bites really hurt. Her parents seemed happier. They smiled more and quarreled less. A year after they arrived, Tommy joined the family.

Back in England, Mummy had done everything — cooked and cleaned and mopped and shopped and washed and ironed. Here there were servants — a *kebun* to do the gardening, an *amah* to keep house, a houseboy to do the menial chores and even a cook. When Tommy came, Nenek appeared to look after him. Mummy couldn't cope with Tommy, who was a colicky baby and cried constantly. She seemed too weak to do anything; the heat was too much. Nenek lived in the kampong not far from the Barron house. She was their washerwoman but became nanny because Tommy took to her and Amah had no liking for babies. Nenek would sling up a sarong from the rafters and put him in it. Then she would rock him gently, singing to him in an unknown language until he quietened down. Nenek spoke no English, but she communicated with smiles and hugs. There was a ready supply for Marge too. Nenek stayed on as nanny even after Tommy ceased to be a baby. She continued to be their washerwoman. Marge and Tommy watched her at work. She let them play in the water, gaily splashing each other and everything else in range.

At Christmas time Father took them into town. This was a special treat. In Singapore town, they went to Robinson's, the big store on one side of the big square. There was a toy department there, with toys the like of which Marge had never seen. She got to choose her present. They had a Christmas tree, though a funny one which didn't smell right. And there was no snow, only rain. It was rain like she had never experienced in her life. It came down in buckets, in torrents, in floods, accompanied by lightning that rent the heavens and thunder that shook the house to its very foundations. It was magical.

In reality the Barrons were not exactly as rich as Marge thought. In her eyes the bungalow they lived in was a mansion. Actually, it was quite a modest house with a relatively small garden. The Harbour Board people were not at the top of the colonial social pyramid. They were engineers and workmen brought in to do technical jobs, not members of the whisky-swilling leisured class: more of the proletariat than the bourgeoisie. You didn't find Harbour Board types at the Polo Club or Tanglin Club. But to a child of six they were fabulously wealthy compared to what they left behind at home — which still meant England.

Some of the more affluent Europeans sent their children off to boarding school in England or Australia. The less affluent chose boarding schools in Malaya, like the Tanglin School in the Cameron

Highlands. Barron wasn't the sort who could afford to have his daughter attend some fancy institution in a hill station, much less England or even Australia. She went to school in Singapore with other white children of her age, a private establishment called Tomlinson House run by a retired schoolmaster and his wife. She was lucky; those who went away at a tender age came back twisted inside.

When war broke out in Europe, Aunt Dorothy came out from England to join them. Dorothy Rider was her mother's elder sister. There were only the two of them. Mrs Barron could hardly have refused to take her in. Marge's memories of England were that it was cold and grey. Dorothy Rider personified that. She had been a schoolmistress, of the most formidable sort. She found the household lax and didn't hesitate to say so. The children had been allowed to grow up wild. They had to be taken in hand. Mrs Barron hadn't the energy or inclination to fight her sister. Fortunately, the bungalow was too small to accommodate a long-term guest. Aunt Dorothy moved out to a hotel. She became a lurking menace far away. The children saw her seldom and were glad of it.

Then war came to Singapore. The first air-raid on the Harbour was frightening. There were explosions close by and the wail of the sirens terrified them. But after that, it seemed a lark to the children. Black-out curtains were procured, but they were used to build tents in the garden for camping games. There was supposed to be an air-raid shelter, which was improvised by packing gunny sacks of sweet potatoes around the large dining table. Father produced a steel helmet, which Tommy commandeered. The air-raid drills at school were a pleasant distraction from sums. At Christmas, there was still a trip to Robinson's. Mother and Father didn't seem too concerned. They talked about sending the children away, to Australia perhaps. But nothing much changed. They went swimming at the Swimming Club. Sunday tiffin was still served.

Life went on in its usual pleasant way. Until the bomb fell and blew their house down.

There was silence for a long while after that. Marge buried her face in Habibullah's chest and wept quietly. She hadn't really wept properly for her family before. He held her close, his one arm wrapped protectively around her.

22

IT took two centuries for the British to establish their empire. It took the Japanese three months to demolish it in Malaya. The onward rush of the Japanese Army did not slacken after the fall of Kuala Lumpur. There was some stiffening resistance by the Australians especially, who dealt the Japanese a sharp blow near Gemas. A well-laid ambush destroyed the Mukaide Detachment and several tanks. But this was only a minor riposte in a headlong flight. The Bhurtpores were deployed to deal with a more irritating problem, sabotage behind the lines. The lines of communication now stretched thinly practically down the whole length of the Malay Peninsula. With their customary lack of logistical organisation, the Japanese gave little thought to securing the rear areas. Their second echelon troops were spread out far and wide. It was up to the Indians to keep the peace in the occupied areas.

The Bhurtpores had lost their regimental identity upon joining the INA. They were known simply as the 2nd Provisional Battalion. Most of the officers of the 2nd Battalion were Habibullah's old comrades from the Bhurtpores. A smattering of junior subalterns from other regiments joined them. Other troops had been inducted into the 2nd Battalion from different Indian Army units. He had to work hard to win the respect of these newcomers. The Bhurtpores accepted him as their leader; there was no reason why the others should. They had no real feeling of loyalty to India, which was a political aspiration rather than a country. The only reality remained the regiment. They were orphans, shorn of their regimental allegiances and severed from their parent formations, most of which were still fighting the Japanese. Even the 1/14 Punjabis retained a shadow existence in the British forces, having been amalgamated with the remnants of the 5/14 Punjabis into a composite battalion. The Bhurtpores were the only regiment that had no rump still on the British side. How the others would perform when faced with their old regimental comrades-in-arms was a matter of grave concern.

There could no longer be any question of remaining aloof from the fighting. The INA was allied to the Japanese, not subordinate to them. This was what they had been told, and Mohan Singh tried his best to remind the Japanese of it. To many of the Japanese officers, the Indians were only good for menial tasks like road-repair. It was important that the INA should behave like an allied army and not as mere hangers-on. Mohan Singh insisted that his men be kept together as formed units and not employed as labourers. Fujiwara supported him. They got their way, but it was plain that they were not fully trusted by their new allies. Few guns were issued, despite the fact that there was *Chachiru kyoyu* aplenty after the debacle at Slim River.

The local Chinese resistance had been helping themselves to the guns and ammunition left behind by the British, even fishing weapons out of the water. The locals were untrained and inexperienced, but that didn't stop them taking to the jungle. There were a few men who had been hurriedly trained in Singapore at the 101 Special Training School and sent back to Malaya. These men, mostly Communists, formed the cadre of the Malayan Peoples' Anti-Japanese Army. They would have been formidable if there had been more time and proper instructors to teach them the niceties of irregular warfare. Their enthusiasm made up for their lack of training. Raids were made on isolated targets. But these were uncoordinated and amateurish. Even the second-line Japanese units had some battle experience and beat them off with ease. The resistance fighters suffered grievous losses and soon withdrew into their jungle fastness to lick their wounds and consolidate.

Some British stay-behind parties were active. These proved more effective, though on the strategic scale they counted for nothing. The rail line was repeatedly cut by small explosive charges near Tanjong Malim in Perak. The damage was always repaired quickly, but it happened with irritating regularity. The Japanese had little sense of rear-area security. They travelled at night in convoys with headlights blazing. A blind man could have seen them coming miles away. They were asking for trouble and soon found it. A small convoy was ambushed in a cutting outside Kuala Kubu Baru. A few nights later a staff car was shot up not far away. The locals of all races took secret pleasure at the discomfiture of the invaders. The Kempeitai, in the customary way, was let loose to find the perpetrators. They got what they needed to know using their tried and true methods. Their information was that a small party of British soldiers had made a base in the mountains around Fraser's Hill. It was impossible to track them. The Main Range stretched down the spine of Malaya for hundreds of miles, all of it covered with dense jungle. Anyway, the fighting troops were in Johore, pushing the British steadily back. The burden of dealing with these distractions fell on the second echelon units and the INA.

The task of garrisoning the line of communications around Tanjong Malim was assigned to Habibullah's battalion. Operationally, he was placed under the command of the 5th Division. His task was simple: stop the sabotage. It was no easy task for unarmed troops. The battalion was dispersed in small penny-packets at major road and rail junctions. He gave orders quietly that they should keep their heads down if there was any shooting. The Japanese may have believed in suicide charges, but that wasn't his idea of warfare. The closest his men got to real action was when a group of saboteurs blew up the rail line for the umteenth time near Kubu Road. The INA guards spotted them and alerted the Japanese. The raiders were much larger and heftier than the local Chinese. It plainly wasn't the MPAJA. The small local garrison was called out. They came rushing up the road together with the Malay police and ran straight into another ambush. The British had scattered lengths of bamboo all along the road. When the leading truck passed over one, a cord was pulled and the improvised mine went up. Grenades followed. The Japanese took casualties and the saboteurs melted back into the night. The reaction came quickly. The garrison was beefed up. They started patrolling in larger groups, in company with the INA and the local police. Kampongs and estates near the jungle were raided. Reprisals were savage if there was even a suspicion that the locals had helped the raiders. There were no more incidents for some time.

BY 31 January the Causeway had been blown and the great fortress of Singapore was invested. The talk among the *jawans* was of a long siege. Everyone believed that Singapore was invulnerable. They themselves had passed through the docks, piled high with war matériel, on their way up north. The tale of the gigantic 15-inch guns grew in the re-telling. There was no eagerness to test the defences of the island. However, no one told the Japanese that they weren't supposed to be able to storm the citadel just like that. They made plans to cross the Johore Strait. It was a gamble. Yamashita was running out of supplies. If it hadn't been for what the British left behind he would have had to stop at the border of Johore. Now was the time to push the defenders over the brink. He couldn't afford to let them catch their breath and rebuild their morale.

To Habibullah's relief, he was ordered to form a company

of able and intelligent volunteers to cross with them. Rear area security was not what he had signed up for. He wanted to march on Delhi. The road to India led through Singapore. He made a call for volunteers. There was a distinct lack of enthusiasm. The faithful Nisar Ahmad stepped up. "I go where you go, Sahib," he said simply. His example shamed others into doing the same. Soon Habibullah had his hundred men. In the normal Japanese Army fashion the detachment was called after its commander, but since the Japanese couldn't pronounce his name properly they compromised by referring to it simply as H Kikan. They were finally issued rifles for the task, but only 10 rounds of ammunition per man. There were no machineguns, mortars or any sort of support weapons. The Japanese did not wholly trust the INA. They had switched sides once; they could do so again. Habibullah knew that they were on approval.

The assault on Singapore Island was led by the veterans of the 5th and 18th Divisions while the Imperial Guards made a feint in the east around Pulau Ubin. Despite heroic resistance by the Australians and the Chinese irregulars of Dalforce, by mid-morning on 9 February the Japanese had a firm foothold. 22nd Australian Brigade ceased to exist as a fighting unit. The Australians were brave fighters but lacked discipline. Once the line broke they streamed back without orders. The gaping hole was ripe for exploitation. The INA volunteers were ferried over to start working on 44th Indian Brigade, whose right flank was exposed by the destruction of the Australians. They had discarded their Fujiwara Kikan armbands and wore their Indian Army uniform insignia on the orders of 5th Division Headquarters. It bothered Habibullah. This was a breach of the customs of war. The British would have been well within their rights to shoot anyone whom they captured as a traitor. But there was no time for expostulation. The war did not wait upon nice legal arguments about the proper interpretation of the Geneva Conventions.

They had some success with the shaken troops of 44th Indian Brigade. Some were persuaded that resistance was futile; they laid down their arms with relief and were despatched under guard to the rear. Others were tricked into withdrawing by false messages carried by the INA. Habibullah bumped into Narayanan briefly after landing on Singapore island. The man was still dressed as a civilian, but he was armed with a revolver and carried a radio transmitter. There was a brief exchange of greetings. Narayanan was in the frontline, identifying the units for the INA to target. He was the link between the various INA detachments. His stock rose in Habibullah's eyes. This was a man with the courage of his convictions, not a rear-area wallah. He did not survive to see the surrender, though. Somehow, the British located him and took him out.

After the rout of the Australians, the Malay Regiment took up the burden of defence in western Singapore. Habibullah's contact with Malays in Kelantan had been with farmers and fishermen. It was a surprise to him that the Malays were warriors too. He had met men of the Johore Military Force, who had fought to defend their state. When the British pulled back across the Straits of Johore, the Sultan had thrown in the towel. He chose to stay with his people instead of being evacuated to Singapore and thence to India. His ordered his troops to lay down their arms. Some of their officers had been trained in Dehra Dun. They had acquitted themselves well. The Malay Regiment had been recruited from all over Malaya. They fought as well as their compatriots from Johore. When 22nd Australian Brigade evaporated, the Malays held the line along Reformatory Road. They were pushed back and dug in on the high ground at Pasir Panjang, at a place called Bukit Chandu. H Kikan were called in to get them down.

Habibullah did a quick recce of the position. It wasn't going to be a cakewalk prising them from the heights. There was a problem with language. The Indian troops all understood Hindustani; the Malays didn't. That ruled out the usual ruses. A frontal assault would have been suicidal; certainly not with ten rounds each. The Japanese might have done it for their Emperor but no Indian in his right mind would have tried something so tactically idiotic. Habibullah decided that subterfuge would be necessary. He ordered his men to form ranks and sling their rifles. They would walk into the position as if they had every right to be there. The order was given. There was some hesitation, but the *havildars* and *jemadars* put paid to it in short order. They marched up the hill with weapons slung, Habibullah at the head. Nisar Ahmad insisted on marching right behind him. His mouth was dry. It was the first time he was facing the prospect of action. His stomach was in knots. He prayed fervently that his courage wouldn't fail.

It seemed to be going well at first. They got within a couple of hundred yards of the position without attracting hostile fire. He could see the Malays standing up in the trenches watching their approach. Then, suddenly, he heard someone shout that they were with the Japanese. He froze momentarily. The game was up. The next thing he knew the Malays had opened fire all along the line. He gave the order to charge. Men were falling all around him. It was an impossible task. He was blind with the rage of battle. If only they had grenades ... The men broke and fled for the rear, under the sneering eyes of the Japanese. The taste of defeat was bitter. He had failed the first challenge.

THE following day, 15 February, Lieutenant-General Percival marched up Bukit Timah Road to the Ford Factory and surrendered Singapore to Lieutenant-General Yamashita. 90,000

Empire troops were captured by a force less than half their number. Habibullah and the others could hardly believe it. All their lives they had been told over and over that the British were superior. The master race were just men after all, mastered by an Asiatic foe in a humiliatingly short time.

Most of the POWs were Indian. They were segregated from the white troops. The European officers of the Indian Army units were separated from their men and marched off to Changi. Habibullah and his men were detailed to guard the prisoners. The men looked on with mixed feelings. All had been astounded by the seeming ease with which the Imperial Japanese Army had routed the British and Australian armies. Some were openly contemptuous. A few spat at the prisoners as they walked by. Habibullah put a stop to it immediately. "Enough," he commanded. "They are not dogs to be spat at in the street."

Nisar Ahmad was at his side. He watched the procession with narrowed eyes. "They are killers of civilians, innocent men and women," he said. "Shall we find the murderers, Sahib?"

Habibullah shook his head. He had been practically consumed by hatred of the white man after Parit Batang. The rage had died down to a hot smoulder. Despite himself, he could not help feeling some admiration for the dignity with which the officers conducted themselves. Their heads were held high and they marched as smartly as their ragged state would allow. "Leave it," said Habibullah to Nisar Ahmad. "*Inshallah*, justice will find the murderers, if not now then later."

THE Indian officers, VCOs and *jawans* were paraded at Farrer Park the day after the surrender. They stood in their ranks on the field of the stadium, grouped by race rather than unit: Dogras, Sikhs, Punjabi Muslims, Baluchis, Rajputs and all the martial races of the Indian empire. There was a balcony high up in the stadium where a microphone and loudspeakers had been set up. A senior British officer appeared at the microphone and brought the parade to attention. The massed ranks obeyed with a resounding stamp of boots. The British colonel announced that they were all prisoners of war and as such they now belonged to the Japanese. From henceforth they under the orders of the Imperial Japanese Army. With that, he turned to the Japanese officer on the balcony, saluted and handed over command of the Indian regiments. Major Fujiwara, the Japanese officer, accepted the handover. The British colonel then withdrew, to join his comrades in Changi. Fujiwara turned to the Indians, still standing ramrod straight at attention on the field, maybe 40,000 of them. He made a speech in Japanese, which was translated into Hindustani. He spoke of the crusade to free Asia from the tyranny of the white man. He said with apparent sincerity that it was Japan's hope and wish to have a free India at her side in this endeavour. At the end of his short speech, he turned to General Mohan Singh and handed over command of the assembled troops to him.

Mohan Singh was a stirring speaker. There was no need for translation. He spoke directly to the troops in Hindustani, addressing each one of them directly. He proclaimed that a new dawn had broken in Asia. The moral claim of the Britishers to rule India, based on the myth of racial superiority, had been exposed as a hollow sham. A new, free India ruled by Indians for Indians was the shining goal. Come and join in this great endeavour, he invited. He spoke with conviction and a clear sense of purpose. The words found receptive ears among the troops, so recently beaten and now abandoned by their British officers. *Jai Hind! Victory to India!* cried Mohan Singh. *Azad Hindustan zindabad! Long live India!* responded the masses. If there were any voices who were less than wholly enthusiastic, they were drowned out by the din.

Habibullah was there in that balcony, wearing his best uniform with the white armband of Fujiwara Kikan. It was heady stuff.

THE Indian POWs were housed in camps all over the island, at Nee Soon, Kranji, Bidadari and Seletar, under their own Indian officers. Although the INA had recruited a large number, the majority of the 50,000 or so Indian prisoners had not yet chosen to cross over. The Japanese were treating them with kid gloves. The INA were given the trappings of an allied army. A large bungalow was put at their disposal at Mount Pleasant, grandly designated as Supreme Command, INA. As a race, the Japanese were polite. They maintained a scrupulous courtesy when dealing with their Indian counterparts, whatever their private thoughts may have been. Their major failing was a total ignorance of other cultures. They were aware only dimly of the differences between Hindu and Muslim, Sikh and Christian. These nuances were incomprehensible to them, used as they were to dealing with culturally homogenous people like the Koreans and the Chinese. There was a curious lack of inter-cultural empathy in the Japanese, almost a blindness to the fact that others were different. When coupled with their disdain for a beaten foe, this could lead to incidents of wanton cruelty, often inflicted through sheer thoughtlessness rather than actual malice. They were like schoolboys plucking wings off flies or frying ants with a magnifying glass.

Now that they were on Singapore Island, the 2nd Provisional Battalion were billeted in the former British Army barracks at Alexandra. Habibullah knew that there was a dairy herd at Bukit Timah. He put in a request for some dairy cattle so that his men might have fresh milk. The Japanese were remarkably ignorant about other people's dietary habits. They could not understand that Indian troops did not eat only rice and fish as they did. They would deal out curry powder and expect the Indians to consume it sprinkled on rice, as they did with their dried fish. They had some vague notion that some Indians didn't eat beef while others wouldn't touch pork. Milk-drinking wasn't part of their culture. A hapless young officer turned up with a herd of scrawny bulls in tow. Habibullah's quartermaster Lieutenant Chaudery took delivery.

"These are bulls," said Chaudery.

The Japanese officer looked blank.

"He-cows," repeated Chaudery slowly, "no milk from he-cows."

"No milk?" asked the Japanese.

Chaudery shook his head. "Milk come from she-cows."

"Not even little little?" he persisted, as if he might convince Chaudery of the error of his ways.

"Not even little little," answered Chaudery. "You go get us she-cows."

The young man left with his herd, looking downcast. The cows went back to their pasture. Presumably they met their fate when food shortages on the island grew more serious.

The Japanese were not so solicitous about the local Chinese. Colonel Tsuji Masanobu was a member of General Yamashita's staff. He was one of the band of militarist fanatics that had dragged Japan into the war in China. Tsuji had served in Manchuria. He knew how implacably opposed to Japan the Chinese were. The experience of the resistance upcountry confirmed his view that there was no way to reconcile the local Chinese population to Japanese overlordship. He had a cold-blooded plan to break any resistance in Singapore before it got started. Within a week of the surrender, orders went out that all Chinese males were to congregate at designated spots. There they were screened in the most arbitrary fashion. Members of the volunteer forces, Communists, gangsters, the English-educated – they were picked out almost at whim and driven away to be shot. The Sook Ching operation claimed thousands of victims. Nobody knows to this day exactly how many died, not even the Japanese themselves.

Chaudery, who was a decent man from a family of lawyers in Lahore, burst into Habibullah's office ashen-faced. "Have you heard what they are doing to the Chinese civilians?" he blurted out. "They are massacring them at the seaside."

"Who told you this?" demanded Habibullah.

"It's all over town. Everyone knows it," replied Chaudery agitatedly. "We have made a blood pact with the Devil himself."

Chaudery was not from the Bhurtpores, who had followed the Japanese Army down the length of the Peninsula. He was one of those captured after the battle at Slim River and had joined the INA in Kuala Lumpur. He hadn't seen how the Kempeitai operated. This was his first taste of their methods. By now Habibullah was inured to the tales of indiscriminate butchery. Inured did not mean indifferent. He raged, as he had raged to see the dead coolies at Parit Batang; but he knew he had to hold his peace for the sake of the dream of freedom for India. His impotence made him angry. "What do you want to do, resign your commission?" snapped Habibullah.

Chaudery looked doubtful. To quit would mean returning to the POW camp and being shipped off to God-knows-where as a labourer or worse. "Can't we do something? Talk to them?"

"You think they would listen?" asked Habibullah, a trifle shortly.

That was the end of the conversation. They never spoke of it again. The INA had thrown in its lot with the Empire of Japan. It was better not to think too deeply about what this entailed.

THE new recruits swelled the INA ranks to over 20,000. It was planned that there should be 12 battalions in three regiments, together with staff and supporting arms — a full division to start with. The regiments were named Gandhi, Azad and Nehru after the leaders of Congress. There was to be a Special Service Group for commando raids. The Hindustan Field Force would be the head of the spear when they finally debouched onto the plains of the Ganges and Brahmaputra. Planning was easy; the execution proved more challenging. Mohan Singh's position as General Officer Commanding was far from uncontested. When Singapore fell, practically all the Indian Army troops in Malaya were swept up. Included in their ranks were officers senior to Mohan Singh, including at least one lieutenant-colonel who held a King's Commission from Sandhurst. Several of these officers looked askance at General Singh. He may have been a good speaker, but physically he wasn't prepossessing. The shoes he tried to fill seemed several sizes too big for him.

There was a severe shortage of officers. Most of the Indian Army units were officered by Britishers. When the Britishers departed they left large gaps all through the chain of command. VCOs were upgraded to lieutenants, but they were not really suited by education or age for the task. The vast majority had risen from the ranks and were not trained to display initiative. There was always a white or brown sahib above them to give orders. Now they had command thrust upon them. Most coped when the crunch came; too many did not. There were about 250 KCOs and ICOs in Malaya, Indian officers who had graduated from the Royal Military Academy at Sandhurst or the Indian Military Academy at Dehra Dun; those who volunteered moved up the ranks rapidly. Mohan Singh himself had been propelled from captain to general in one giant leap.

The 2nd Provisional Battalion was dissolved and the men incorporated into the new INA battalions, numbered sequentially from 1 to 12. The Indian Army practice of keeping the men separated by class, caste, race and religion was abandoned. All the troops messed together, Hindus with Muslims, eating at the same tables though of course with different cooks. Stripped of their previous regimental affiliation, the troops had to learn a new loyalty. This was the challenge, to make a clean break with the past and build a fresh regimental spirit. The officers were encouraged to mix at all levels, irrespective of creed and race. The troops were drilled together and not in class-companies as before. They kept their khaki uniforms, with new INA armbands embroidered with the flag of the Indian Congress. This was done so as not to be assimilated into the Japanese Army like the Koreans and Formosans. They were not a subject race, not any more. Weapons were issued from the captured stocks at hand; familiar weapons that they were used to, not foreign ones from an alien army. The Japanese even allowed the INA to form an armoured unit with Bren-carriers and a handful of Marmon-Herrington armoured cars. Ironically, to the casual observer, the INA looked almost exactly like the Indian Army, down to the drill.

Habibullah was given the local rank of lieutenant-colonel and command of a unit, but not one of the 12 line battalions. He was appointed CO of the Depot Regiment, which held the troops who could not yet be assigned to the new regiments. Many of his Bhurtpores joined him, including the inseparable Nisar Ahmad. Chaudery became a captain and was appointed adjutant. On the face of it, Habibullah held a key job, training the replacements to be fed into the line. Deep inside, though, something gnawed at him. The majority of the men who joined the INA at Farrer Park had seen action, some all the way from Jitra and Kota Bahru. He hadn't. The Bhurtpores had mutinied, dispersed and surrendered without firing a shot at the enemy. His one and only taste of action at Bukit Chandu had been an unmitigated disaster. No one said anything out loud, but he felt that the veterans despised him. He had been passed over and given a second-line, second-rate unit. His rational mind told him this was nonsense; but in the still of the night, these dark thoughts haunted him. He understood now some of what Lieutenant-Colonel Holmes must have felt when he was removed from command of his regular regiment and given the Bhurtpores.

THE INA was an army without a state. With the fall of Singapore and Japanese successes in Burma, hopes were high for a quick entry into India. The local Indian associations all over Malaya had transformed themselves into branches of the Indian Independence League. Leading members of the Indian community like SC Goho and KPK Menon in Singapore and Nedyam Raghavan in Penang stepped up to head the organisation. A conference was held in Tokyo in March at the invitation of Rash Behari Bose, the old revolutionary whose main claim to fame was his attempt to assassinate the Viceroy. He had lived there in exile for decades with his Japanese wife. Fujiwara Kikan had sprung from seeds that he had planted. In April when they returned to Singapore with Bose, an All-Malayan Indian Independence League was formed in Singapore with Raghavan at its head. In June there was a conference in Bangkok, where the Indian Independence League proclaimed its right to speak for all Indians outside the motherland. A Committee of Representatives was set up, with proportional representation from Indian communities in the different territories now within the Empire of Japan. Burma had the most, followed by Malaya. The executive organ was the Council of Action of the League, to which the INA was in theory subordinate.

Meanwhile, Radio Syonan broadcast reports of an uprising in India. "Quit India" proclaimed Congress to the Britishers. They responded by rounding up the Congress leadership, including

Mahatma Gandhi and Pandit Nehru. There were riots and insurrections, at least according to the broadcast reports. Towns and garrisons in eastern India were isolated as mobs cut the roads and railway lines. Sixty battalions of troops were called in aid of the civil authority to restore order. Some people were inclined to dismiss the news as the fabrications of Japanese propaganda; but those who still had access to shortwave radios, at the peril of their lives, found confirmation from American and Australian sources, even if the British were silent. It appeared that the time was ripe. Burma had been cleared. The 15th Army stood at the gates of Assam and Manipur. Fujiwara and Mohan Singh made a tour of the POW camps upcountry. They spread the message that the Azad Hind Fauj, the Army of Free India, was a reality, not a gleam in a dreamer's eye. Mohan Singh had procured a set of resolutions, the Bidadari Resolutions, announcing that freedom was the birthright of all Indians. They stood united above caste, race and religion to achieve the independence of the motherland. The INA would be the instrument of their liberation.

All this was a matter of indifference to Habibullah. His all-consuming passion was to get his men ready for the march on Delhi. They would be drilled and trained to the highest degree of military effectiveness. He gave little thought to what the shape of an independent India might be. First thing we get rid of the Britishers, he said; the rest will follow in due course.

THE gloss came off the relationship with the Japanese quickly. Fujiwara, despite his success, was transferred. He was replaced by Colonel Iwakuro Hideo, a man whose belief in the equality of Asians was less enthusiastic than Fujiwara's. He made the right sounds, but for some reason the listener detected a certain hollowness in them. The new Iwakuro Kikan was bigger and covered more ground, having offices in Penang, Rangoon, Hong Kong and Saigon as well. It was also much more impersonal; and Colonel Iwakuro was no great enthusiast for Indian independence. Narayanan was dead. Ken Sato, their Nisei interlocutor, got snapped up by the Kempeitai as an interpreter. The Greater East Asian Co-prosperity Sphere was a reality. White rule had been overthrown in Indochina, Burma, Malaya and the East Indies. But the reality was that a new overlord had replaced the old one. True, the more obvious trappings of racist domination had gone, like whites-only clubs and beaches. Some of the civilian administrators were decent fellows, who genuinely tried to help the inhabitants of Syonan and Malai. Too many, unfortunately, had no empathy with other cultures. The inhabitants of the conquered lands should be transformed into good *Nippon-jin*, knowing their place in the new society. Those who did not accept the new order would be stamped out.

The Indian Independence League suffered from the neglect of the government in Tokyo. Above all, they wanted recognition as the legitimate representative of the millions of Indians outside India. Tokyo temporised. The matter was under "serious consideration". Those who understood the Japanese better would have known that this was tantamount to a refusal. It would have been discourteous to say "no" outright; better this way, to allow the supplicant to save face. But the leaders of the League were deaf to the nuances and waited in hope for recognition. Anticipation turned to disappointment, disappointment to disgruntlement. It seemed to the Indians that the Japanese were playing a two-faced game. For all the fine words about Pan-Asian solidarity, they were still considered an inferior race.

The Japanese saw no need for the dubious fighting qualities of the INA. These were beaten men who had let themselves be captured. Victory Disease had made the military overbearingly arrogant. Japanese carrier aircraft had bombed Vishakhapatnam and Darwin. Japanese troops were on the doorstep of Australia and India. There seemed no limit to the expansion of the Empire. The Imperial Japanese Army was more than capable of doing any fighting that needed to be done. The ease with which their conquests had been made bred a contempt for their opponents. That contempt extended to the Indian troops who had been on the wrong side of the war. Some officers, in their unguarded moments, spoke of their Indian allies as puppets. Word got back to the INA. The Indians seethed. The Japanese came to be regarded as merely fellow travellers and not real companions on the road to independence.

As the weeks lengthened into months, Mohan Singh felt more and more that the INA was not being taken seriously. He protested in vain that his units were being ordered around as if they were Japanese auxiliaries. They wanted to ship his men off to the frontline in New Guinea. He resisted. His ranks were raided for labourers. This he couldn't stop. As far as the Japanese Army was concerned, here was a ready source of men sitting idle. There were roads to repair, rubble to be cleared, ships to be unloaded, airfields to be made operational again. Let the Indians earn their keep. When it came to manual labour the Japanese made no distinction between the POWs and the INA *jawans* who were supposed to be their allies. Fujiwara had attempted, not always with success, to prevent such depredations. Iwakuro didn't even try.

General Mohan Singh dreamed of leading his army to victory on the wide plains of Bengal. Just let the Azad Hind Fauj onto the soil of India and the whole sub-continent would rise to eject the Britishers. The Japanese had cooled to the idea. They had no immediate plans to invade India. The Imperial Army had more than enough to do in China. No matter how much of that country they occupied, there was always another river to ford and another mountain to cross. The Chinese had limitless amounts of manpower and an unremitting hatred of the invader. Moving into another potentially-hostile country was the last thing on their minds. If there was to be an invasion, India would need to be softened up first. They wanted to train infiltrators who could be landed in India to perform acts of sabotage and interfere with the British war effort. Colonel Iwakuro was more interested in setting up spy schools than training a proper army. Mohan Singh resisted. The men were impatient to get on with the business of liberating India. What Iwakuro was doing would denude the INA of its best and most dynamic men, for whom the prospect of action was an irresistible lure. Mohan Singh didn't want a diversion from the primary goal. Infiltrators would inflict mosquito bites, irritating but not fatal. He pressed for the INA to be shipped to Burma in preparation for a tiger-spring into Assam and Manipur. The Iwakuro Kikan told him that the matter was receiving serious consideration.

A few volunteers were trained in Penang, despite the objections of Mohan Singh. They were sent back to India. Then the inevitable happened. Some of the infiltrators defected right back to the British and gave the game away. Most of the rest were picked up. The ones who managed to avoid arrest melted into the vastness of the sub-continent and kept their heads down. There could only be one reason for this to the Japanese mind: treachery. The Indians could not be trusted. A senior INA officer, a Sikh like Mohan Singh, was arrested on suspicion of espionage. This brought the simmering discontent to the boil. The Council of Action of the League resigned, except for Rash Behari Bose. To the others, Bose was compromised. He had lived much of his life in Tokyo. He had married a Japanese wife. He had become Japanese. Bose continued to insist on his leading role in the League. Mohan Singh thought otherwise. He had never really been keen on being supervised by

Bose or the Council. The INA was his army. They answered to him, not to Bose or any other civilian. They were under his orders. The Japanese would have to be taught not to take them for granted. He ordered his men to cease cooperation until their demands were met. He demanded that they be accorded the respect due to them as allies and equals. He demanded proper recognition of the INA as the army of free India. He demanded more and better equipment. He demanded transport, tanks, artillery.

In December, barely 10 months after the parade at Farrer Park, the Japanese arrested Mohan Singh. They packed him off to a bungalow on Pulau Ubin. He reacted by ordering the INA to disband.

23

IT'S strange how one can live on an island barely bigger than the Isle of Wight and yet be completely unaware of life-and-death dramas going on under one's nose. I well remembered those months in 1942. We knew that Indian troops in their thousands had fought and died for the Empire; my cousin May had been a nurse at an Indian Army hospital and I had tagged along as an auxiliary. We also knew of the accusations of treachery that had been hurled at the Indians, by people whose world view did not comprehend the notion that white troops could be beaten fairly in battle by buck-toothed slant-eyed orientals. Vague rumours of the Indian Independence League and the Indian National Army had reached us. We paid little attention to them. After the trauma of surrender and the nightmare of Sook Ching, we were too concerned with the mundane business of not getting our own heads lopped off. The story Habibullah unfolded was completely new to me. But I was personally a witness to the next act.

Those of us who worked for the Syonan Tokubetusi were on occasion called out to make up cheering crowds when dignitaries were in town; a sort of captive audience trotted out to demonstrate how well the Light of the South had been integrated into the Empire. In July 1943 we were told that none other than Prime Minister Tojo himself would grace Syonan with his presence. The day before there was to be a military parade. I was duly instructed to make an appearance, to cover the event for the department I worked for. My job was to write happy stories about the wonderful life we were all enjoying in the new Syonan. They needed something about the exciting preparations for the ecstatic welcome the new subjects of Nippon spontaneously accorded to the Honourable Prime Minister, General Tojo. So it was that I found myself on the fringes of the Padang, wedged between two large and sticky Tamil workers. The Padang was covered with ranks of troops in what I took to be Indian Army uniforms. It was raining hard. Water was diluting the ink in my fountain pen. Slipping away was not an option; my departmental supervisor expected a report from beginning to end of the proceedings. I tried to get a little shelter under one of the shady rain trees at the edge of the Padang, but the water just cascaded through the leaves. I let my mind wander far away from the damp and the noise.

Suddenly I was hauled back to reality by a command that brought the assembled troops to attention. A man appeared on the steps of the Municipal Building. He was dressed in a rather theatrical khaki uniform with gold aiguilettes, riding breeches and shiny jackboots. He looked the most unlikely military leader with his glasses and paunch. The rain didn't seem to bother him. Then he spoke. I didn't understand the words, but the effect on the crowd was electrifying. It was as if someone had thrown the off-switch; the noise and babble ceased completely as they strained to hear his every word. The man had the gift of oratory. He exuded magnetism. He worked up that crowd to a pitch of excitement that I have never seen again. There was something hypnotic about him, a force of personality that enmeshed the listener. Habibullah was there too, utterly transfixed. He recounted to me what the speaker had said: "Our task will not end until our surviving heroes hold the victory parade on the graveyard of the British Empire — the Lal Qila, the Red Fort of Delhi! *Chalo Delhi!* On to Delhi!" he cried. The crowd responded rapturously. "*Azad Hind zindabad!* Long live Free India!" they yelled. By the time he finished, they would have flung themselves off a cliff if he had ordered them to. That man was Subash Chandra Bose. The Indians called him Netaji, the beloved leader.

I LET Habibullah take up his story again. After the shattering events of December, he had almost lost faith in the cause. Rash Behari Bose tried to salvage something from the wreck, but too many of the men who had volunteered so eagerly in Farrer Park felt completely betrayed. They dropped away and returned to the POW cage. Habibullah stayed. He felt he owed it to his troops, the ones who remained. Their motives were mixed. Some, a small minority, still believed in the promises that had been made that the Japanese would help them liberate the motherland. For the majority, it was a matter of cold calculation. To return to their units as POWs would not only mean privation, it would have been a massive humiliation. Sincere or not, the Japanese were in charge and there were advantages to being on the winning side. For Habibullah there was no choice. He had pledged his honour to the cause of Indian independence; there could be no turning back.

Training continued in a desultory and half-hearted fashion. The INA was leaderless, decapitated by the removal of Mohan Singh. None of the remaining senior officers even tried to fill the gap. It wasn't because Mohan Singh was such a towering figure that no one could replace him. The fact is, there were no takers for the hot seat. Responsibility without power, with the certainty of blame if things went badly wrong; this was hardly an alluring proposition. Recruitment fell to practically nothing. The idealists had been disillusioned; only the crass opportunists now came forward, and precious few of those. It was soul-destroying. Habibullah toyed with the idea of resigning his commission and volunteering as a private soldier to be trained as an infiltrator at one of the spy schools set up by Iwakuro. Then came Netaji.

Subhas Chandra Bose was a man with stature. He had been a personage of substance in India: mayor of Calcutta, president of the Congress Party, rebel against the Raj. When the War started in Europe, he had been arrested by the British. He went on a hunger strike. Not wanting to make him a martyr, they put him under house arrest instead. He gave them the slip and made his way across India, then through Afghanistan and on to Germany. In Berlin he met Foreign Minister von Ribbentrop and other Nazi Party grandees. He even had a short audience with the Führer himself. He talked them into allowing him to form a Free India Legion from Indian prisoners taken in the Middle East. The Germans thought that at some point they might be useful to stir up the tribes on the Northwest Frontier. In the meantime, they could make themselves useful in the Mediterranean. Bose felt that Europe was too far from the centre of action; he had absolutely no interest in the acquisition of *Lebensraum* in the vastness of Russia for the greater glory of the Reich. He needed to be near India. The outbreak of the Pacific War gave him his chance. With his characteristic dynamism and persuasiveness he obtained passage on a U-boot to the Indian Ocean, where he was transferred to a Japanese submarine off Madagascar. They landed him on the north coast of Sumatra, where he caught a flight to Tokyo. He was met by his old friend Colonel Yamamoto, who had been military attaché at the Japanese Embassy in Berlin. There, at the heart of the Japanese Empire, he managed through a mixture of charm, bluster and sheer force of will to get an audience with Prime Minister Tojo.

Tojo was convinced that he could do business with Bose. Here was a man with big dreams and the will to realise them. India freed from the British Empire might be a useful ally someday.

India in turmoil within the Empire would be better still. Tojo ordered that arrangements be made for him to be transported to Singapore, where he was met by the leaders of the League. Within days, he had mesmerised everyone who was anyone and a good many nobodies besides. He put new life into the League. Rash Behari was sidelined. Netaji was the man in the centre. With his tireless energy he galvanised the movement. The dispirited INA found new hope. Netaji went all over Malaya making speeches. He demanded three lakhs of soldiers. Recruitment soared. They were no longer taking in former Indian Army sepoys; that well was dry. The new volunteers came from the domiciled Indian communities in Malaya and the Straits Settlements. Most were Tamils, a race considered by the British fit only to be sappers and miners. Habibullah's Depot Regiment found itself with more men than they could cope with. To the existing three regiments of the Azad Hind Fauj was added a fourth: the Subhas Brigade it was called, after the Netaji himself. It ranked first in the line of battle, ahead of the Gandhi, Azad and Nehru Regiments.

By October Netaji was ready for his greatest political *coup de théâtre*. He addressed a crowd which filled the Cathay Cinema and overflowed into the street. The Provisional Government of Free India, Azri Hukumat-e-Azad Hind, was proclaimed. "Give me your blood, and I will give you freedom!" thundered Netaji. The assembled multitude responded with thunderous applause and shouts of acclamation. The governments of Japan, Germany and their allies recognised the Provisional Government within days. Free India in turn declared war on Great Britain and the United States. At last the INA had a government to which it could pledge allegiance, not just to an ideal. "Free India" had no territory. Netaji got the Japanese to transport him to Port Blair in the Andaman Islands, the only bit of India under Japanese occupation. Symbolically, he raised the green-white-orange tricolour of Free

India; this was the flag of Congress, with a springing tiger in the centre. There were speeches and ceremonies and photographs for the newspapers. After everyone had gone home, the Japanese garrison commander had the Indian flag lowered again. The *Hinomaru* hoisted back up. They weren't about to concede any actual territory to the Azri Hukumat-e-Azad Hind.

Bose knew that the Provisional Government could not stay in Singapore. Singapore was a dead end. Inactivity would kill the independence movement. It was a movement almost in the literal sense; if they stopped men would drop away. He badgered Iwakuro to have them moved to Rangoon. This was the closest he could get to India. He threatened and cajoled. He went over Iwakuro's head to his superiors, reminding them that he had the ear of General Tojo. They gave in. It was too much trouble to argue with this demanding and imperious Indian. Let the Burma Army deal with him. Tokyo concurred. The whole apparatus of the provisional government was duly moved to Rangoon. With it went the fighting units of the INA, including the newly-formed Rani of Jhansi Regiment consisting entirely of women.

Rangoon was the seat of the government of Burma. President Ba Maw welcomed Netaji as a fellow head of state. Burma was independent in theory. It even had its own army. The Burma Independence Army under Aung San had marched with the Japanese when they drove out the British. But it got too big and popular. Once the British were gone, the BIA was reduced to a more manageable size and given garrison duties. Its soldiers wore Japanese uniforms and were drilled by Japanese instructors. The best officers were sent to Japan for training. Bose was determined that the INA should not suffer that fate. He insisted that the units be kept together under their own officers. They reported to INA Headquarters, not to the Imperial Japanese Army. Netaji was Supreme Commander; there were to be no more ersatz generals like Mohan Singh. When the Japanese planned their thrust at Manipur, Netaji insisted that the INA should be part of the offensive. This was the way to India. Imphal and Kohima were the keys to Manipur. Beyond Kohima was Dimapur, the railhead and main British logistics base in Assam. Take Kohima and the road to Dimapur would be open. And beyond that lay Bengal, his own homeland.

Habibullah had only met Netaji in person once, when the senior officers of the INA had been presented to him. It was enough. He fell immediately under Bose's spell. Here was a real leader, not a long-winded head-in-the-clouds politician. This was the man to lead them to the promised land. The INA would be the instrument of liberation. Re-energised, Habibullah threw himself into the task of turning the motley crew of coolies, peons and *babus* into real soldiers. The Depot Regiment was transferred to Taiping, where the 29th Army had its headquarters. Singapore was getting too crowded and the food situation was deteriorating. Unemployed Indian soliders were just useless mouths to the Japanese. The transfer suited Habibullah fine. He got permission to set up a training camp on the road to Grik. The men could be properly trained in jungle warfare there. The distractions of the city were far away. There were Chinese guerillas active in the jungles around. He had no quarrel with them. Indeed, they were fighting for the same thing as he was, freedom from colonial rule; except that the ironies of war had placed them on opposite sides. Habibullah gave instructions that the guerillas were not to be molested. When his troops bumped into them in the jungle, they pretended that they weren't there. The guerillas soon got the idea. They too pretended that the Indians were part of the local fauna. Habibullah had his men out in the jungle every day and most nights. He drilled them with a ferocity that would have impressed even Lieutenant-Colonel Holmes. When the news came that the 1st INA Division was being shipped to Burma his spirits soared. This was it, the time had come.

He was in for a disappointment. Orders came from Headquarters that the Depot Regiment would remain in Malaya to continue processing the stream of recruits. He would remain with them as their commanding officer. His superiors told him that he had a vital task. Keep the pipeline filled, they said. No one can do a better job than you, they said. He resented their transparent lies. They obviously didn't trust him. He hadn't fought the Japanese. His regiment had surrendered without firing a shot. The Bhurtpores had forfeited all honour. They were mutineers, and he was their leader.

The humiliation could not be borne. He marched right up to the staff colonel in charge and requested to be relieved of his command. He wanted to be in the fight. He demanded to be at the front. The colonel commiserated. He tried to placate Habibullah. No need for precipitate action, he counselled. Perhaps in the next draft of replacements, he said soothingly. Habibullah would not be fobbed off. Back in his quarters, he dashed off a letter to Netaji. He offered his services in any capacity. He would fight in the ranks as an ordinary *jawan* if necessary. The reply came a fortnight later, signed by Netaji's military secretary. Netaji understood Lieutenant-Colonel Habibullah's feelings. He had decided to accede to his request for a posting. The Lieutenant-Colonel would reliquish his local rank and revert to his substantive rank of major. He would be given command of the a company in one of the line regiments. Posting orders would follow forthwith. Never had demotion been so sweet.

"I envy you," said Chaudery while Habibullah packed.

"They also serve who only stand and wait," replied Habibullah, surprised at himself for recovering the dimly-remembered quotation from his school days. He clapped his hand on Chaudery's shoulder. "I've put in a word for you to take my place. It's practically in the bag. It'll mean promotion."

"Thanks for that," responded Chaudery. "Take care. Don't go charging tanks or any such tomfoolery." They shook hands and parted with an almost English reserve.

Habibullah climbed into the staff car that was to take him to the docks. Three Bedford three-tonners followed. Nisar Ahmad of course insisted on coming with him. So had a handful of his men, mostly old Bhurtpores. He had handpicked the others, men he felt could be trusted to buy into the regimental tradition. These men were meant as replacements to be distributed among the units of the INA. Habibullah had other plans. He meant to keep them together as his own Praetorian Guard. He would show them all — British, Indian and Japanese — what stuff the Bhurtpores were made of.

24

GENERAL MUTAGUCHI RENYA'S 15th Army was responsible for the Imphal-Kohima campaign. Mutaguchi was a veteran of Malaya, having commanded the 18th Division there. It was his men who had attacked and taken Kota Bahru. He had no great regard for British troops, or for Indian ones for that matter. The Japanese 33rd Division was tasked with taking Imphal. On the headquarters staff of 33rd Division was Lieutenant-Colonel Fujiwara Iwaichi of the now-superseded Fujiwara Kikan. He met his Indian friends with delight. The delight was mutual. Over a glass of sake, Fujiwara explained that they were on trial. Not everyone was so pleased to see them. They were considered by many to be a drain on resources. Fujiwara, who was Intelligence Officer for the division, appreciated the value that INA troops might have in weakening the resolve of their opposite numbers in the Indian Army. If they could replicate the tactics that had served them so well in Malaya, they could achieve outstanding results. But his was very much a minority view. The prevailing opinion was that Indian troops were only good as labourers. At a pinch they could be deployed to secure the rear areas in order to relieve Japanese units from the menial task. As fighting troops, they had a dismal reputation. They would have to prove themselves.

The battle was in full swing when Habibullah's men disembarked at Rangoon. He had gotten his way as far as his unit was concerned. Normally, replacement drafts would be fed piecemeal to whichever units needed them. Habibullah tried to convince Headquarters that he had a functioning company, drilled to a high standard and ready to fight as a unit. They were sceptical. He persisted, threatening to take his case to Netaji himself. At length they consented to consider the matter. He mounted a demonstration for the brass-hats. In an open field outside Rangoon his men were deployed to take a position defended by a platoon of the Azad Regiment. The defenders were old hands, blooded in battle and disdainful of the newcomers. They didn't take his motley crew seriously. The hours of unrelenting drill paid off. While one platoon fixed the attention of the defenders with a feint, the rest of the company crept along a neglected nullah to take them in the rear. The Azads didn't know what hit them. The position was overrun quickly and with professional flair. Habibullah was pleased; the men had not let him down. They had performed like veterans. The headquarters staff saw the advantages of keeping the unit together rather than breaking it up. The 6th Guerilla Company was activated and officially designated a supernumerary unit of the Subash Brigade. It went into the line at Tamu, southeast of Imphal.

The INA troops around Tamu were in a wretched state. Half of them were sick with malaria. Supplies arrived intermittently. They made do with biscuits and tea. The Japanese were never much good at logistics even at the best of times. Under the stress of operations, the supply system fell to pieces. If it hadn't been for food and ammunition captured from the British, the INA would have been in a very bad way indeed. The tactics that had served them so well in Malaya did not work in Burma. Apart from anything else, the INA was trained as a regular force, to fight face-to-face rather than subvert the enemy. This was the dream of the Provisional Government: that Free Indian troops would march victorious over the border, not sneak in behind the invading Japanese like jackals following a tiger.

But even if they had tried to seduce their opponents with the siren song of Indian independence rather than attack them openly, success would not have been assured. In Malaya, the Indian troops had been shaken by the speed of the Japanese advance and the rapid disintegration of the British. Their morale had been undermined by the suspicions of their erstwhile comrades-in-arms and the open racism of the white civilian population. The 14th Army in Burma was a different proposition. Lieutenant-General William Slim had been an officer in the 6th Gurkha Rifles. He was a much better fighting leader than Lieutenant-General Percival, a staff-wallah whose rabbit-toothed visage did not inspire his men with confidence. Slim knew how to handle Indian troops. He treated them with respect and cared for their welfare. They responded with loyalty and fortitude in adversity. In Burma, Slim's Indian regiments redeemed the honour of the Indian Army that had been lost in the disastrous campaign in Malaya.

Habibullah's company were light infantry, without support weapons. The other INA battalions went into battle as regular infantry in set-piece assaults on prepared positions. Ironically, they were using the same tactics that had so signally failed against the Japanese in Malaya. They were beaten back with heavy losses. Habibullah had no intention of making that mistake. His long odyssey with the Japanese Army had taught him that a frontal attack in the jungle was futile. The Japanese had won by exploiting their mobility. "Around, not through," he exhorted his men. They did as they had been trained. The tactics worked. First one, then another and then a third position fell to the 6th Guerilla Company. The bottleneck at Tamu was uncorked. The British fell back towards Imphal.

The success of Habibullah's men was gratifying. 6th Guerilla Company unofficially adopted the name of the Bhurtpores. The stigma of surrender had been expunged. Brigade HQ was impressed. They were even more impressed when the Bhurtpores stormed an impregnable position at Klang Klang. This was a fortified hilltop which the British used as an observation post. It was surrounded on three sides by sheer cliffs. The fourth side was strung with barbed wire and sown with mines. The Japanese themselves had failed to take it. Habibullah scanned the position. His men were from the foothills of the Himalayas. They weren't intimidated by heights. Picking the most agile of his troops, Habibullah led the way up what seemed to be an unscalable precipice. The defenders were taken completely by surprise. A couple of well-placed grenades knocked out the machine-gun nests covering the approaches. The Bhurtpores were at the summit before the British could react. INA Headquarters heard of the feat. Habibullah was summoned by the divisional commander. He was promoted once again, to a substantive and not a local rank. Lieutenant-Colonel Habibullah was tasked with training more troops like his Bhurtpores.

Meanwile, the campaign proved much tougher than the Japanese had anticipated. In Malaya three divisions had sufficed to rout the British and Indian Armies. They thought that three divisions would be enough to do the same to the 14th Army. They were mistaken. The British and Indians held on with an unexpected tenacity. They were resupplied from the air when the Imphal-Kohima Road was cut. The RAF had air superiority and exploited it to deliver food and ammunition to their troops in the Imphal pocket. Kohima obstinately refused to fall even though it was defended initially only by the 161st Indian Brigade against the weight of a full Japanese division. INA reconnaissance patrols probed the defences looking for weak spots. They were beaten back. The stubborness of the Indian defence surprised the Japanese. This wasn't the sepoy rabble that they had beaten so easily two years before. But the Japanese equally refused to give up. They kept hammering away at the British and Indian positions. When all else failed, in a frenzy of frustration they would make a banzai charge. Sometimes it worked; most of the time it didn't.

As the monsoon approached, the morale of the INA troops plummeted. When the rains came all fighting would stop. There would be no chance of breaking through to Dimapur, not to speak of Bengal. Netaji had announced back in March that a detachment of the Azad Hind Fauj had penetrated into Manipur and planted the flag of Free India at a place called Moirang. It was, he said, the beginning of the liberation. Yet the months went by and the siege of Imphal still continued. At Kohima, the Indian Army stubbornly declined to collapse or defect, despite all that the Japanese could throw against it. Ugly rumours began to spread that the Japanese were deliberately sacrificing the INA. A couple of men decided to pack it in. They had had enough. It was time to go home. They left their posts and surrendered to the Indian troops in front of them. Soon there was a steady trickle of desertions. It was Malaya all over again, only in reverse. Then came a military embarrasment. The Subhas Brigade blundered into an ambush and was severely handled by the Gurkhas at a place called Palel. They lost two hundred men, wounded and killed. More men deserted. The Subhas Brigade was pulled back from the front to lick its wounds. The Japanese did not bother to conceal their disdain under any veneer of courtesy.

The end came with unexpected swiftness. Habibullah was at the HQ of the Gandhi Regiment conferring with the regimental staff about forming a guerilla company on the same lines as the Bhurtpores when all hell broke loose. They were holding a position on the Tamu Road. This was supposed to be a quiet sector; all the fighting had moved northwest towards Imphal. Suddenly, they found their positions shelled without warning. A wave of Mahrattas broke over the frontline units, many of which were battalions only in name, having been reduced to company size by sickness and casualties. The INA men broke and fled for the rear. They were followed by the victorious Mahrattas, who gave no quarter to the traitors and renegades. Mass surrenders took place. The Gandhi Regiment dissolved completely under the tidal wave. The first reports of the rout started coming in while Habibullah was still talking to the staff officers of the regiment. The next thing they knew, panicked men were running through the camp. The sound of small arms fire at a disturbingly close range was clearly heard. Habibullah rushed out of the tent revolver in hand. He caught the full blast of a mortar bomb.

That was the end of Habibullah's war. How he ended up in the field hospital he did not know. All he knew was that his arm was missing. His faithful Nisar Ahmad was at his side, patiently sponging his fevered brow. The journey from Tamu to Rangoon was a jumble of hazy images. In Rangoon he was put on a freighter back to Malaya. This was a journey fraught with peril, for Allied submarines roamed freely in the Bay of Bengal. They made it back to Penang despite having been torpedoed; by the greatest of good luck the torpedo failed to detonate. From Penang he was sent by rail to Singapore. His convalescence took months. Drugs and bandages were in short supply. The INA was not anywhere near the top of the priority list for anything. He was saved by the dedication of the civilian Indian doctors, who conjured miracles from thin air. Chaudery came to see him once, but he had no heart to meet his old comrades. When the doctors decided that his body was sufficiently healed, they bundled him out to make room for other casualties. He was sent by truck to Taiping. There he was put out to pasture, with the rump of the Depot Regiment. Their task now was to provide rear-area security against the MPAJA. His journey had come full circle.

"There you have it," said Habibullah, "my life story. When the Japs surrendered, the Britishers picked me up. The End."

"Not quite the end," I reminded him. "You've still got a fighting chance, with d'Almeida defending. He's never let a client hang."

"Always a first time," responded Habibullah insouciantly. "But it doesn't matter. What happens to me isn't important. It's only a matter of time before we kick the Britishers out. Netaji will keep on fighting, wherever he is."

I was taken aback. "You didn't know?" I blurted out.

"Know what?" he asked perplexed.

"Subhas Chandra Bose is dead," I replied. "He was killed in a plane crash just after the Japs surrendered."

25

I DON'T know what I would have done without Marge. The news of Subhas Chandra Bose's death completely devastated Habibullah. He put his head between knees. I thought he was going to break down and cry. It made me feel uncomfortable to see him like this. Emotion of that sort always unsettles me. All throughout he had maintained a steady calm, as if there was nothing that the world could do to him. If there was anything he had learnt from his school days in England, it was how to keep the upper lip stiff. The loss of his arm, of his unit, of the war — all could be borne because the cause was still alive. To be told that the dream was over and that Netaji was dead ... The dam that held back his feelings seemed to be cracking and was on the verge of breaking. "I'm pleading guilty," he said in a choked voice, "it's all over for me."

Then Marge put her hand on his shoulder. "Don't," she said softly, "Don't give up. You mustn't. You can't."

He gave her a wan smile and put his hand on hers. "Why, child?" he asked. "All is finished now. Let the Britishers hang me and have done with it."

"No!" she responded with sudden vehemence. "After all you've said, after all you've been through, how can you think of dying? Think of your men, what they did. If you give up now, it will have all been for nothing."

It was like a douche of ice water. He shook himself once and regained his composure. "You want me to fight your people for my people's freedom?"

"Not ... not my people," she replied hesitantly. "I'm not one of them any more. I don't know how the *Orang Puteh* can have been so mean. I can't imagine ..." Her voice trailed off.

He looked very tired and shrunken. His empty sleeve hung loosely. "Read to me," he said. "Please."

She hesitated a moment. "What would you like me to read?" she asked quietly.

"Anything. Anything to take me away from here."

She took up the book that she had borrowed from d'Almeida's library. "It's the *Wind in the Willows,*" she said. "I'm afraid it's all I have. Will that do?"

He nodded. She looked at me. I signalled my assent. Slowly she began. I left them quietly in the world of Toad and Mole and Rat and Badger by that sunny riverbank far away; two wounded souls alone as the dark closed in.

CHRISTMAS of 1945 was cheerless. True, we had been freed of the incubus that had oppressed us for the last three Christmases. But the empty chair at the dinner table where Julie used to sit painfully reminded us every night of our loss. I remember that my uncle used to celebrate Christmas in a big way, even though he was pagan to the roots. We had fake holly and fake ivy, cotton-wool snow and a small casuarina tree decked with fairy lights. There were crackers and paper-hats and presents and a perspiring Santa Claus, whom I presume promptly expired in the kitchen once he was done distributing the goodies to the children. Mak kept up the tradition even after Pa died, though on a smaller, more intimate scale. Even during the straitened war years, we had made do. This year no one had any heart to celebrate. Ralph missed his family, far away in Australia. They were alone and so was he. Augusta missed Julie and refused to be coaxed out of her room. I missed my dinner, having been dragooned into working over the holidays to prepare for the impending trial.

To top it all, there came news from Colonel Newman that Miss Rider had finally managed to get to the Head of the Legal Department at ALFSEA HQ. Miss Rider was not the sort of person who would be gainsaid. She started small, meeting a junior legal officer at the bottom of the totem pole. She insisted on her right as a subject of the King to have justice. Justice in her view meant reclaiming her niece from the clutches of the natives. The legal officer wavered. He promised to refer her request to higher authority. Miss Rider would not be put off; she badgered him ceaselessly. The hapless officer sent her up to his superior, the Deputy Head of the Legal Department. From him she extracted a promise that Marge would be taken into British custody while waiting for the necessary court order. She demanded that Lord Mountbatten be told, and if they wouldn't do it she would see him herself. The Deputy Head capitulated. The necessary papers were prepared the same day and forwarded to the Head of Department, who passed the application on to the Supreme Commander for his instructions. Newman was gravely concerned. He knew the repercussions of taking Marge against her will. He tipped us off to be ready for trouble.

June was worried about Marge. The improvement we had seen during her time with Habibullah had vanished. Marge had sunk back into a gloom of the darkest hue upon hearing the news that her aunt wanted to have her put in the custody of the British. June was concerned. She locked up all the knives, hid all the poisons in the medicine chest and made sure that all spare ropes were taken out of the house. I was more worried about Karim. We kept the news from him for fear of his reaction. Marge had confided to

Habibullah that Karim wasn't just another warm body press-ganged into working for the Japanese. He had signed up willingly for the *Giyu-gun*, the volunteer army that the Japanese had formed to defend Malaya. The volunteers, or *giyu-hei* as they were called, were given military training and uniformed like the Imperial Army. Their officers even carried a *shin gunto* sword and strutted around in imitation of their masters. Karim would definitely fight if the British came to take Marge. He wouldn't be alone. They would proclaim a jihad and raise all the kampongs on the island.

The problem was intractable. Marge was fifteen, not of age to decide anything for herself. She had no parents. Normally, the court would appoint a guardian, but there were no courts for the time being; at least, no courts that dealt with civil matters. Strictly speaking Miss Rider had no business trying to take Marge. She wasn't her legal guardian, not until she could get a court order. Technically, Pak Chik Ahmad had a better claim, having brought Marge up and protected her all those years. But the British would never consent to letting her stay with the natives in defiance of the wishes of her only living relative. Karim and his people would never allow them to take her. Both Miss Rider and Karim were immovable. A clash was inevitable. No matter who won, Marge would be the loser.

"Can't we send her away somewhere to hide?" asked June.

"Where to?" I responded. "Singapore island's far too small. Sooner or later they'll catch up with her."

"But she hid from the *Jepun* during the War," countered June.

"Yes," I replied, "but the Japs weren't looking for her. They didn't know she existed. Miss Rider knows and Miss Rider has the instincts of a terrier cross-bred with a bloodhound. She's not going to give up."

"Maybe upcountry?" suggested June.

I snorted. "I tried that, for two years. It's no joke living among strangers trying not to be noticed. Besides, who'd take care of her? Where could a young white girl hide? She'd be spotted right away in any kampong in the Peninsula."

June lapsed into silence. There was no way out, literally. I noted as I arrived that there were now two stalled jeeps outside d'Almeida's gate. Either the British were having great problems maintaining their vehicles or Major Ridley was taking no chances on Marge making a break for it. Nor had Karim been idle. His sharp eyes had spotted the increase in activity around d'Almeida's house. There were now groups of idle Malay youths hanging around the gate. Some had a distinctly military bearing. I had no doubt that they were *giyu-hei* like Karim. He intended to make good on his promise to fight. The thunder rumbled ominously overhead.

I WAS immured with George and d'Almeida putting the last touches to Habibullah's defence. We worked on the Saturday and Sunday and carried on till the wee hours of Monday, Christmas Eve. With a Scrooge-like indifference to the season, d'Almeida had us back in the office after dinner. We ploughed on through the night. Uncharacteristically, Habibullah's trial had been set for the Thursday after Boxing Day. In normal times, that whole week would have been off-limits for anything resembling real work. Evidently the British wanted to get it over with as soon as possible, holiday or no holiday. There was some urgency to it. The Red Fort trials of the INA senior officers in Delhi were coming to a close. If the judges were to return a verdict of "guilty" and sentence the defendants to death as expected, there would be mass insurrection throughout the subcontinent. Things could get very ugly very quickly in volatile Singapore. The last thing that the BMA wanted was to have to hang Habibullah after the Red Fort defendants.

The court-martial was held in the Police Courts right next

to where Nakamura had been tried. As before, access to the courtroom was restricted. The trial had attracted a great deal of attention among the Indian community. Every seat in the gallery was taken. People were practically sitting on one another. Outside the crowd pressed up against the barbed wire which surrounded the building. The monsoon had arrived with a vengence and the rain poured down in torrents of Biblical proportions. That didn't deter the onlookers. They stood there stoically staring at the blank walls of the granite building as if they would suddenly part to give a view of the drama within. British troops ringed the courts. The guards were from the Parachute Regiment, tough men with stern faces, distinctive in their maroon berets. The Gurkhas were on standby just in case. The authorities were taking no chances.

Prosecuting counsel was Lieutenant-Colonel Selwyn-Jones, the Deputy Judge-Advocate General at HQ ALFSEA. Selwyn-Jones was a guardsman, from the Coldstreams. He had a thin military moustache which ran straight under his aristocratic nose, as straight as his back. He was assisted by my friend Major Beatty, who didn't appear to bear us any ill-will after the Nakamura affair. He waved pleasantly at me and I acknowledged the greeting. Beatty's harrassed young assistant Second-Lieutenant Ward was there too, nervously shuffling papers. He half-smiled uncertainly at me. D'Almeida sat impassively in his seat, his fingers touching under his chin as if in prayer. He hadn't confided in us. I had no idea what his line would be. This was the most infuriating thing I found about working with d'Almeida. He never tipped his hand, not even to his own assistants. He would sit there, inscrutable, thinking deep thoughts. I thought at one time that it was because he enjoyed pulling rabbits out of hats like a conjurer in a music hall, basking in the surprised admiration of the audience. As I got to know him better, I began to suspect that perhaps his reticence was a reflection of caution; he was not a man to propound a theory half-baked. He was too fastidious for that. Only when the product was fully ready would he reveal it. Whatever the reason may have been, he was the most frustrating man to assist in a case.

There was a ripple of excitement when Habibullah was brought into the dock. The cells were directly below and he ascended through a trapdoor in the floor. I looked at him. His face betrayed no emotion. It had taken a lot of patience to persuade him not to throw in the towel after the crushing news of Netaji's death. Neither George nor I could make him change his mind. Even d'Almeida had not made any impression on his rock-hard determination to make no defence. Marge had been wonderful despite her own troubles. It was she who talked him round. The days she spent reading to him distracted him from the impending trial. It was not so much the trial that troubled him, I suspect. It was the death of his hope for Indian independence. Netaji was dead. India would never be free, certainly not in his lifetime. Marge comforted him, talked to him, read to him. She kept at him until at length he gave in. She made him promise firmly not to plead guilty and just let d'Almeida work his magic. Of her own worries she said not a word. It seemed that having someone else to worry about took her mind off them, at least for a while.

I turned and scanned the crowd. Most of them were dark-skinned, Tamils and Malayalees from south India. There were a few faces of a lighter tone, men from the northern provinces: a scattering of full-bearded Sikhs, a few Chettiars and Sindhi merchants. Occasionally I spotted a visage that might have belonged to a Pathan or one of the other martial races. Habibullah had turned to the crowd too, as if looking for someone. I fancied that some of them acknowledged him with a nod or knowing glance. It was hard to be sure.

The members of the Court Martial filed into the room.

Silence descended. Presiding was a full colonel of the Gordon Highlanders, the rows of medal ribbons on his chest indicating service in the Great War as well as the Northwest Frontier. His regiment had been in Singapore when it fell. I wondered whether he might have been one of the lucky ones who had gotten away. He was flanked by an Australian major on one side. The Australians did not wear regimental titles on their uniforms so it was impossible to speculate on his experience. On the other side sat an Indian lieutenant-colonel from the Queen's Own Corps of Guides. I eyed him curiously. He was comparatively young, evidently one of the breed who had proven himself in battle with the Japanese. He was a man of a frontier race like Habibullah. I wasn't quite sure whether this was a good thing. On one hand, it did give the court a bit of racial balance; on the other hand, how would a member of the Indian Army view a renegade who had turned his coat and gone over to the other side? My faith in British justice had increased a little after Nakamura's trial, but this was different. Could they let a man like Habibullah off? He had challenged the legitimacy of the Raj. To acquit him would be tantamount to conceding the point.

There was always a whiff of victors' justice about courts like this, so soon after the end of hostilities. In early December we had gotten news that an American military tribunal in Manila had convicted General Yamashita, the Tiger of Malaya, of war crimes and sentenced him to death. No one shed any tears for him, but the information we received about the trial was disquieting. Even his American counsel had doubts about its fairness. It was said that General MacArthur needed a human sacrifice to wipe out the humiliation of having been defeated in the Philippines. How many professional and political reputations had to be salvaged from the wreck of the Malayan Campaign? There had been no parliamentary inquiry into the fall of Singapore, nor was there likely to be one. Those of us who had been left behind knew all about the arrogance and incompetence of the colonial and military leadership. That version of the truth would have caused too much damage to too many important people, all the way to the very top. How much more convenient it would be if it could be proven that responsibility for the debacle lay at the feet of the Indian troops and their traitorous leaders.

AS a prosecutor Selwyn-Jones was quite different from Beatty. He made it quite clear from the start that he was going for the maximum penalty the law would allow. His opening address was liberally peppered with references to ingratitude, disloyalty, treachery, treason, breach of faith, snakes in the grass and stabs in the back. He got quite passionate about it; at least, as passionate as an Englishman of his class could get. It was quite a theatrical performance. No one could accuse him of playing to the gallery though; the gallery groaned, grumbled and growled as he unfolded the catalogue of sins that Habibullah was accused of. The President had to bang his gavel more than once to restore an atmosphere of proper legal decorum.

The main problem that the prosecution faced was that they had no one who had actually been there to see what Habibullah did or did not do. Their case was entirely circumstantial. Selwyn-Jones admitted as much in his opening address. The first charge was murder, or alternatively, abetment of murder. Either he had shot Lieutenant-Colonel Holmes or he had instigated his men to do so. The second charge was waging war against the King-Emperor. Here they were on surer ground, for Habibullah had been captured wearing the uniform of the Indian National Army. He had demanded to be treated with the courtesies due to a lieutenant-colonel in an enemy army. Though the British had not taken him fighting, it was a much easier case to make unless he chose to deny all involvement in hostilities against the British Empire and its allies. This he steadfastly refused to do. It seemed to me that all my recent clients harboured a secret death wish.

The first few witnesses were dealt with efficiently by Selwyn-Jones and Beatty, who took turns to lead the evidence. The witnesses were ground staff at RAF Batu Sembilan and testified to the mutiny of the Bhurtpores. Their evidence was uncontroverted; d'Almeida let George do the cross-examination. Most of what came out we already knew. A pretty convincing case was built up that Habibullah was at the centre of the storm. The most damaging evidence came from Wing-Commander Jackson, the Station Commander. Jackson testified that it had been reported to him that Habibullah had threatened Holmes's life when taken to the station lock-up. This had been duly recorded and a report made to 8th Indian Brigade HQ. Jackson had been one of the last to leave the station after the mutiny had broken out. He heard that Habibullah had been freed by the mutineers and was leading them. There was no question about Jackson's honesty. He was a genuine war hero, a decorated veteran of the Battle of Britain. He had spent the last three and a half years in Changi. His testimony clearly made an impact on the judges. Yet d'Almeida held fire. He contented himself with a couple of mild questions to establish that Jackson had seen nothing himself, only heard the news from his subordinates.

Trials are a lot less exciting than most people think. The proceedings were dull. The witnesses were boring. The rain was still coming down hard, but not in as large buckets as before. The raindrops made a steady monotonous drumming on the roof. It was hot and sticky; the ceiling fans only spread the warm air around. I began to feel drowsy, especially after lunch. I was jerked awake when I heard the prosecution call their last witness for the day: Lieutenant Bhajan Singh.

Bhajan Singh's appearance provoked a rumble of disapproval from the crowd. He appeared in the jungle green uniform of the victorious Indian Army, in contrast to Habibullah's worn and faded khaki of the defeated INA. On his shoulder was the regimental title of the 1/16 Punjab Regiment. Selwyn-Jones took him through his evidence-in-chief. According to him, he had pretended to join the INA in order to find a means to escape from captivity. Although he had been a major in the INA, his loyalty had always been to the King-Emperor. He took the first opportunity to desert when his battalion had been sent to fight in the Arakan. He brought with him his whole platoon and intelligence about the dispositions of the Japanese. After debriefing, he had been reinstated in his old rank and posted to the 1/16 Punjabis. Bhajan described his dealings with Habibullah in detail, painting him as the moving spirit behind the collaborators. It was well known among the captured Indian Army troops that Habibullah had instigated his men to mutiny against the British and murder his commanding officer, he said. In fact, said Bhajan, Habibullah had boasted of it. Habibullah was most active in recruiting among the Indian POWs after Jitra, while he, Bhajan Singh, had hung back. As a reward the Japanese made him a major and entrusted him with command of a full battalion based on the treacherous Bhurtpore Regiment. He was in charge of hunting down stragglers in the rear areas around Tanjong Malim. Any British prisoners were handed over to the tender mercies of the Japanese. Saboteurs were summarily executed.

Bhajan was looking rather smug when d'Almeida rose to cross-examine. "Lieutenant Bhajan Singh," began d'Almeida softly, "isn't it true that you became a member of the Indian National Army long before Lieutenant Habibullah Khan?"

Bhajan's self-satisfied smirk vanished. He hesitated. He hadn't expected that the defence would have known anything about him. "What do you mean, long before?" he temporised.

"The 1/14 Punjabis were overrun at Jitra," continued d'Almeida calmly. "That was what, in the second week of December 1941?"

Bhajan nodded reluctantly.

"I didn't quite hear your answer, Lieutenant Bhajan," d'Almeida pressed. He picked up a piece of paper from his folder and looked at it. I knew for a fact that the folder contained scrap paper on which he doodled during trials. "You joined the INA around 14 December, after your battalion was overrun at Jitra, am I correct?" he asked, waving the paper at Bhajan.

Bhajan swallowed hard. You could almost see the gears turning in his head. What did d'Almeida know? What was on that piece of paper? He was obviously weighing up the pros and cons of lying. Discretion got the better of him. "Yes," he said, "I joined in December of 1941, after the Battle of Jitra."

"And Lieutenant Habibullah joined the INA when?" He picked up another paper from the folder and scrutinized it. I had a peek. It was an old bill from his *dhobi*. "Just before the battle at Slim River at the beginning of January 1942, was it not?" he asked, peering intently at his *dhobi* list.

The flapping piece of paper seemed to mesmerise Bhajan. "Yes, yes, correct, in January 1942."

"In fact, it was you who persuaded him to join the INA?" d'Almeida went on relentlessly.

"Not persuaded," answered Bhajan, squirming, "he did not need to be persuaded. He was anti-British already."

"Did you not take him in early January 1942 to a rubber estate at Parit Batang?"

Bhajan started to look distinctly uncomfortable. Selwyn-Jones was frowning. His eyebrows almost touched. "Yes," answered Bhajan nervously.

"Why did you take him there? What was it you wanted him to see?"

"There were ... there were dead rubber tappers," replied Bhajan.

"Dead rubber tappers," repeated d'Almeida. "Around, what, 50 of them?"

Selwyn-Jones's brow was dark as thunder. He rose to object. "Mr President," he rumbled, "this evidence is wholly irrelevant to the charge."

"On the contrary," responded d'Almeida calmly, "Lieutentant Habibullah is on trial for his life for waging war against his sovereign. The circumstances under which he joined the Indian National Army are highly relevant."

Colonel Huntly, the President, conferred with his colleagues on the bench. "We'll allow it," he said shortly.

"Much obliged," responded d'Almeida with a slight bow. He turned back to the witness. "Lieutenant Bhajan Singh, you showed this massacre to Habibullah in order to induce him to join you in the INA, is that not correct?

"I cannot ... I cannot say for certain," replied Bhajan Singh with obvious discomfort. He looked around the court, as if for support.

"Lieutenant Bhajan Singh, I remind you that you are on oath," said d'Almeida quietly, looking him straight in the eyes. "Who killed those rubber tappers? Was it the Japanese?"

Bhajan was silent. D'Almeida stared directly at him in a contest of wills. "Was it the Japanese who massacred them?" repeated d'Almeida.

"No," said Bhajan after an eternity. There was a sharp intake of breathe from the gallery. The members of the court looked disturbed.

"Who, then?" pressed d'Almeida remorselessly.

"It was the North Anglian Yeomanry," replied Bhajan in a strangled voice, "that is why I brought him there. To show him what the Britishers had done. He was very, very angry. He joined up immediately after he saw the bodies at Parit Batang. He wanted revenge on the Britishers."

The gallery erupted. It was with great difficulty and much pounding of the gavel that Colonel Huntly restored order. Beatty was dumbfounded. Young Second-Lieutenant Ward looked as if he was going to be sick. It was clear that Bhajan had not told them any of this beforehand. Selwyn-Jones looked murderous. He had blundered into an ambush and didn't enjoy the experience.

THE rain was still heavy when we emerged from the court. After his exchange with d'Almeida Bhajan had completely collapsed as a witness. The re-examination didn't do anything to restore his credibility. If he had thought that he could get back into the good books of the British by his testimony, his gambit had backfired spectacularly. We saw him scuttle off escorted by a couple of redcaps. Damage control parties were doubtless going around fixing the press coverage. The six of us were huddled under the porch, prosecution and defence, bunched together waiting for our cars. Major Beatty was still quite affable despite the shellacking that d'Almeida had subjected Bhajan Singh to. He made polite conversation with George about the atrocious weather we were having. Lieutenant-Colonel Selwyn-Jones stood next to d'Almeida, having acknowledged him with a stiff nod. He maintained a cold silence, his military moustache stiff under his nose. Second-Lieutenant Ward shuffled uneasily at my side, not quite sure whether to fraternise with the enemy. I encouraged him with a smile.

"No sign of it clearing up, I'm afraid," I remarked conversationally.

"No," he replied, "doesn't look like it." After a slight pause, he continued, "I heard that you're an old Fentonian."

I was surprised. Hardly anyone had heard of my old school. "Yes, as a matter of fact," I said. "Are you?"

"No, not at all," he answered. "But I live nearby, at Walsingham in fact. I often used to cycle past Fenton Abbey."

I warmed to him. Though I hated the place when I was there, in a strange way the fact that he came from that part of the world was a bond. I was about to make another trite remark about how small the world was when there was a pop, like a cork coming out of a champagne bottle.

"Down!" yelled Beatty, "Someone's firing at us."

There was no time for thought. Everyone hit the ground instinctively; everyone except young Ward, whose brand-new uniform had yet to fade in the sun. The next thing I knew his blood and brains were all over my coat.

26

MY knees were still weak when we got back to the office. I thought that I was inured to death, but at such close quarters the shock was considerable.

"Damned close call," said George. "If your reflexes weren't so quick ..." He let the sentence trail off. "Bad luck about poor Ward, though. The boy can't have been more than 20, if that. What a way to go, after all the shooting's stopped."

"Things are really getting out of hand if someone's actually out to kill the prosecutors," I replied. "I know there've been riots in India over these Red Fort trials, but I didn't think matters had gotten so bad here."

George was about to answer when d'Almeida summoned us to his office.

"Are you all right?" he asked me solicitously.

I nodded. "I've been worse," I answered shortly.

"This incident has put a new dimension on the case," said d'Almeida. "I must consider it carefully." I waited for him to vouchsafe to us some gem of insight, but he didn't say more.

"Well," remarked George, "we've got them on the run after your demolition of Bhajan Singh."

D'Almeida's eyebrows arched. "Indeed?" he said. "All we have established is that Bhajan Singh is a rank opportunist and not to be trusted. But his evidence is that Habibullah Khan did join the

INA willingly and did so because of his revulsion at the atrocity perpetrated by the North Anglians. On the charge of waging war, this evidence supports the prosecution."

George deflated. I was downcast. It had felt like a victory at the time, but now it seemed that we had scored an own goal. "So where do we stand?" I asked.

"We stand where we have always stood," replied d'Almeida cryptically, "but with a surer foothold than before." He got up and paced. This was his habit when he was thinking. He removed his glasses and started polishing them. This meant that the thoughts were really deep. We watched him in silence.

Suddenly he rounded on George. "Is there any word of Flight-Sergeant Dave Blake?"

"You mean the Australian airman who was at Batu Sembilan when Holmes was killed?" responded George calmly. He was used to d'Almeida's sudden changes of course. "No, not a word. We know he was in Singapore at the Fall. Dennis saw him on the last day when all the Aussie brass-hats were getting out. After that, there were some reports that he'd made it to Sumatra on a small boat. One of my contacts picked up the scent in Medan. But that's as far as it goes. The RAAF has no records of any Flight-Sergeant Blake among the men who got away. Either he's dead or hiding somewhere in the wilds of Sumatra. If he's still alive and in the jungle he may not even know that the war's over."

D'Almeida started polishing his spectacles again. "Without Blake, we have no eyewitness to the killing of Holmes," he said, speaking more to himself than to us. "We need to do more than rely entrirely on the prosecution's burden to prove the murder beyond reasonable doubt."

Abruptly, he turned to me. "Habibullah mentioned in his statement his contact with Chinese guerillas at Batu Sembilan. We should follow this up. I know that it is very late in the day, but we must do what we can. Will you see to this matter?"

I was unsure. "Where do I start? They're upcountry in Kelantan. We don't even know who they are."

D'Almeida nodded. In the old days he would have been impatient. The War had one good side-effect; it had mellowed him, at least as far as I was concerned. "We have one contact point: that young lady Madam — or I should properly say Miss — Ah Moy."

"Ah Moy? The one who claimed to be Gim Huat's mother?" I asked, surprised. "What's she got to do with it?"

"She is Kuomintang," replied d'Almeida patiently. "The guerilla band around Kota Bahru is Nationalist Chinese, not Communist; one of the few. The American OSS has been supplying them and her. That is the connection. She may be able to give us a name and a means of contacting them."

"Where do I find her?" I asked uncertainly.

George intervened. "Her real name's Sim Moy Yin, but she goes by the monicker of Helen Sim. She works with a *getai* troupe in Great World, the Fenghuang. We found that out when digging into the Lao Leong Ann case. They're playing at the Chien-tien Nightclub and Cabaret. She's their star attraction, believe it or not."

"Helen Sim at the Chien-tien Cabaret in Great World. Right, got it. I'll go straightaway." I rose to leave and so did George.

As we reached the door d'Almeida spoke again. "Dennis, take care," he said simply. I was shocked. He never used my Christian name. What had I let myself in for, I wondered. When we were outside, I turned to George. "What did the old man mean by that? Is there something you're not telling me?"

George was serious for a change. He clapped his hand on my shoulder. "Nothing certain, just a feeling. You don't seriously think that they were gunning for the prosecutors do you?"

"What do you mean?"

"Think about it," responded George, "If they wanted to kill

the prosecutors, why pick on the youngest and least valuable one? No, my bet is that they were aiming at someone else."

"Not the prosecutors? Then who? D'Almeida?" I asked astounded.

"I think that the bullets were meant for you," replied George seriously. "I think someone's out to get you."

MY first instinct was to head back home, lock myself in and hide under the bed. After the initial irrational fear had passed, I knew that it couldn't be done. If anyone wanted to get me, the old house in Cavanagh Road wouldn't have stopped them. Anyway, I had a job to do. I couldn't very well slink off and crawl under a rock until everything was over. Before the War I'd done exactly that; gone into hiding to avoid being killed by a thug. It was the most miserable time of my life. I had become fatalistic with age. If whoever was trying to get me got me, then so be it; I wasn't going through all that again. The world's not big enough to hide from all your fears. I tried to think of possible suspects. There might have been any number of people who were upset that 'Nakamura' had gotten off, ostensibly because of what I did. But I knew it was no use worrying about anonymous homicidal nuts. It's like lightning; you can be struck anywhere, so there's no point brooding about it. The only one I could think of who had a personal grude was Eng Tong. He might possibly be angry about the rejection of his suit for June or the exposure of his plot to have Lim Tay Lin hang for Warrant Officer Nakamura's crimes. But why try to kill me?

It wasn't in a very comfortable frame of mind that I reached Great World. Being fatalistic didn't stop me from being jumpy. I wished I had a gun with me. I felt very exposed. Great World was one of the few places of amusement that had stayed open during the War. With the return of peace, the lights were blazing and the place was packed. People came to forget their cares. There were cinemas and cabarets, gambling dens and opium dens. Cantonese and Hokkien opera were performed alongside American-style girlie revues. Food was still officially rationed, but the denizens of the dark corners of Great World knew where to find what they wanted. Among the hawkers, the street entertainers, the sideshows, the fortune-tellers, the quacks and the freaks lurked another world, murky and dim in the shadows. You could get anything you wanted at the Great World, from bootleg liquor to narcotics and, for the right price, information of any sort. I threaded my way cautiously through the crowd, looking for the Chien-tien Nightclub and Cabaret.

The cabaret was a garish structure tucked between the merry-go-round and the dodgems. Having paid the extortionate entrance fee, I bought a grossly-overpriced and over-watered whiskey and plunked myself down at a free table. The patrons were a mixed lot. There were a number of people in evening dress, carefully conserved during the hard days of the Occupation. Uniforms there were in abundance, all officers. The bouncers at the door no doubt had orders to keep the riff-raff out, and that meant all Other Ranks. There were less exclusive joints for them. The civilians were mostly Chinese, the military men white. I saw no Indians among them.

I didn't have long to wait for Ah Moy — or more properly Helen Sim — to make her appearance. She was greeted with enthusiatic applause and wolf-whistles. I must say that she really looked dazzling, in a pink silk cheongsam that clung closely to her curves. She looked like she had been poured into it. Her voice was seductive and though I couldn't understand the words, the meaning was plain. She had a way of singing at the patrons, singling out some lucky fellow for her attention. Then, suddenly, her eyes lighted on me. They widened for an instant. She aimed her charms at me, the notes cascading in my direction. Then she passed on to a new target, bewitching one poor soul after another in turn.

When the act ended, Helen came down to mix with the audience. She was in great demand and had to fend off the attentions of some of the more uninhibited customers. One whose hands wandered too far south was unceremoniously hauled off by the bouncers and cast into outer darkness. I was wondering how I could possibly make contact when she sidled over to my table and sat down.

"Well, if it ain't Dennis Chiang," she said in her sultry voice.

"Hello, Miss Sim," I ventured haltingly. I didn't quite know how to start.

"Helen," she said. "Buy me a drink."

A waiter materialised at her side with a fancy cocktail before I could agree. He presented the bill to me. I gagged a bit, but paid up.

"Surprised to see you here," she continued, sipping her cocktail. "Enjoying the show?" Her vocabulary was Hollywoodish and her accent American, but clearly not native. It had a strange though not unpleasing Chinese-Japanese lilt which gave it an exotic undertone.

"Yes, quite," I answered fatuously. "As a matter of fact, I came to see you."

Her eyes widened again. "Me? Really? I didn't think you were the type."

I reddened a little. "No, I mean, I came to see you on business."

"On business? What kind of business?" The way she said the word "business" imbued it with all sorts of unspoken promises.

"Actually, it's a case I'm working on." My heart was pounding. I don't know why I felt so unsettled. She must have been at least half a decade younger than me, and here I was as nervous as an adolescent on a first date. I took a deep breath and pressed on. "We need to contact the Nationalist guerillas upcountry around Kota Bahru. Can you help us?"

"Ah, that sort of business," she said, with what I thought

might have been a tinge of regret. "Okay, later. I'll be done in an hour. Come on backstage to my dressing room." She withdrew something from her stocking-top and handed it to me. It was a card tied with a silk ribbon, on which were written characters that I couldn't understand. "Give this to the guy at the door. He'll let you in." Then she left to continue her rounds. I watched her go and settled down to enjoy the rest of the Fenghuang *getai* troupe's repetoire.

THE guy at the door proved to be large and hairy and obviously directly descended from Peking Man. I wouldn't have wanted to tangle with him on a dark night — or on any night for that matter, dark or bright. The magic pass that I handed to him gave me entry to the inner sanctum without trouble. He had a cursory look at it and grunted. Evidently, he'd seen it before. He pointed me in the right direction. Helen's dressing room was large and well-lit. The door was ajar. I knocked. "Come on in," she called.

She hadn't changed out of her cheongsam. At close quarters she was more stunning than ever. I would never have connected her with the fresh-faced pig-tailed girl I knew as Ah Moy. She indicated that I should sit on the settee that took up one wall. She set herself down close to me, with a whiff of perfume and a rustle of silk on nylon. I cleared my throat.

"It's like this," I began. "My client's being charged with treason against the British Crown. He was upcountry at RAF Batu Sembilan when the War started. That's up north in Kelantan, right by the Siamese border near Kota Bahru. The airfield was abandoned before the Japs could take it, but some Chinese guerillas came and emptied the armoury. Habibullah — that's the client — let them have all the guns and ammunition they could carry. We know that they're Nationalists, like you. We need to get in touch with them if we can. It could save his neck, literally."

"Yeah, I heard about that when I was upcountry," she said. "I might have met one of the guys involved." My surprise must have shown, because she laughed and continued, "I'm not what I seem, you know. You wanna hear my story?" I nodded, fascinated. "Okay, you got it," she said, leaning forward, "here goes."

27

SHE was Japanese. At least, she had been born a Japanese subject in Formosa, or Takasago Koku to give it its proper Japanese name. Her father was an official in the colonial government in Taihoku, though his family had been Formosan for generations. Her mother came from Shanghai. They had met when he worked in the Japanese Consulate there. After the Great War, more and more Japanese flocked to Shanghai. The whole area around Hongkew became completely Japanese; Little Tokyo they called it. They married there and set up house. After a couple of years, he got promoted and they moved back to Taihoku. Helen was their only child.

The marriage didn't last. Her mother missed the bright lights and international flavour of Shanghai. Taihoku was straitlaced and stifling. The Japanese were stifling and straitlaced. She felt herself to be Chinese. The colonial authorities wanted everyone to become Japanese. Takasago Koku was Japan's first colony. The natives were to be assimilated. During the Great War, Japan had tried to take advantage by pressing the infamous Twenty-One Demands on China. A wave of nationalism erupted and Japan backed down. But the resentment lingered among all Chinese. Helen's mother felt alien and alone. She couldn't assimilate; she wouldn't assimilate. When Helen was six, she left and returned to Shanghai.

Helen's father had no time for a little girl. His own parents were dead. The girl was left in the care of an *amah*. There were lots of luxuries of course, a big house, servants at her beck and call. She went to school like any other little Japanese girl, learning to be loyal to the Showa Emperor, being prepared for a glittering marriage, preferably to some aristocrat. She would have none of it. Secretly, she rebelled against her destiny. Her Chinese *amah* fed her tales of Japanese atrocities in China. She listened to the radio clandestinely and read about the humiliations China had endured at the hands of the European and Japanese imperialists. In 1931, the Japanese provoked an incident in Manchuria and marched in. The Chinese reacted by boycotting all Japanese trade. At the end of January 1932 the Japanese landed naval troops to break the boycott in Shanghai, the centre of Chinese resistance. They expected a cakewalk. Instead, General Tsai Ting-kai's small 19th Route Army held them off for more than a month, fighting against stupendous odds. This was stirring stuff. Helen determined that she would go to Shanghai, where her mother was. She plotted for months, gathering information. She took to writing to her mother's sisters, who were pleasantly surprised to hear from little Moy Yin. She preferred the Chinese version of her name to the official Japanese one. Her aunts were gratified. They described life in Shanghai and encouraged her to come. When she was ready, she raided the locked chest where she knew her father kept his money. Taking only what she needed, she bought a ticket on a steamer to Shanghai. When the clerk at the shipping line looked dubious, she pouted. "Do you know who my father is?" she demanded. "He is Councillor Shin Takamori." At the mention of his name, the clerk gave in. She was 13.

Her mother wasn't overjoyed to see her at first. She had made a career for herself as a singer in the International Settlement, where she was known as Madam Shin, using her husband's Japanese surname. The last thing she needed was a young girl. But the girl was there. On further reflection, Madam Shin concluded that there could be some advantages to the arrangement. Councillor Shin Takamori was cabled and told of the situation. He demanded that Helen return at first, but her mother was adamant. Helen herself refused to go back. Councillor Shin capitulated. He hadn't time to deal with this sort of thing. He agreed that she should stay with her mother. He would wire money every month, a promise that he kept until the day he died. He did insist on one thing, however: that she should have her status regularised by registering with the Japanese Consulate. This was a small price to pay for freedom. The papers were duly obtained. She later found that her status as a subject of the Emperor of Japan conferred many benefits. Ordinary Chinese could not move freely in Shanghai, even though it was a Chinese city. The International Settlement was run practically as a British colony, with a Municipal Council headed by a Briton. It was defended by British soldiers and American marines and had its own Municipal Police Force, complete with a Sikh contingent in their red turbans. The French had their own Concession outside the International Settlement, which they ran with Gallic flair. Avenue Joffre was the most glamorous boulevard in the city. Chinese were not welcome in the European areas. They had to have permission to enter the Settlement and the Concession. As a Japanese subject, Helen was free to cross the boundaries at will. She became familiar with all three areas, moving between Little Tokyo, the International Settlement and the French Concession. But the Chinese city was closed to her. It would have been too dangerous to wander there unescorted.

Helen and her mother lived in a spacious airy apartment with a view of the Whangpoo River. They were well-off. Her father's allowance was ample. Her mother's friends were generous. She brought them often to the apartment, a different one every week.

Madam Shin was popular as a nightclub singer. She appeared every night at the Metropole. Her daughter was blossoming; the girl had promise. Madam Shin decided that it was worth investing in her. Helen was sent to a local academy run by a Swiss woman, to be polished like a rare jade. At night, she would accompany her mother to the Metropole and learn the trade. Then came the Marco Polo Bridge Incident. The Japanese trumped up another excuse for aggression. The whole of Chinese Shanghai was in uproar. The Japanese landed troops again. Chiang Kai-shek committed the best of the Nationalist Army to the defence of Shanghai. It took two months of bitter fighting before the Chinese were defeated. After the fall of Shanghai came the Rape of Nanking. Like everyone else of her age, Helen was instantly politicised. She would have rushed out to volunteer immediately had her mother not locked her in the apartment. After that, she wasn't allowed out anywhere except under escort by one of Madam Shin's nightclub bouncers.

Her father died in 1938 and the allowance stopped. It didn't affect her. She had disclaimed any relationship to him, a lackey and running-dog of the hated invaders. They could have gotten by with her mother's earnings, but she too died within a couple of months. Helen was 18, alone and destitute. The apartment didn't belong to them. Her mother's sisters had moved away after the Japanese took Shanghai. They left no forwarding address. Helen got the landlord to allow her to stay for a couple of months while she looked for a new place. To keep body and soul together, she took to the only trade she knew: singing in a nightclub. That was how she met Harry Wilson. Harry Wilson was in his forties, chubby and practically bald. He also was a shrewd judge of character. He saw great potential in this young nightingale. When he first asked to meet her, she thought that he was going to propose that she should be his mistress. Harry did make her a proposal, but not the one she was expecting. For Harry worked for the American

Office of Strategic Services; in a word, he was a spy. He proposed that she be trained as an agent. She agreed immediately. It was all very exciting.

FOR the next three years after her training Helen worked as an OSS agent in Shanghai. Wilson got her a job at the Cathay Hotel, the swankiest address in town. She took the name of Helen Sim then. Her mother had taught her well. She attracted the attention of many men, Europeans, Japanese and Chinese. Eventually, she became the mistress of a high official in the Wang Ching-wei government, which claimed to rule China in rivalry to the Kuomintang. He set her up in an apartment overlooking the Bund. Most of the time he was in Nanking. It was a valuable connection. He had a leaky mouth, especially in bed. She fed a steady stream of intelligence to the OSS, who in turn passed on useful titbits to the local Chinese resistance. They had no idea who she was. Harry made quite sure that he was the only contact. When the Japanese attacked Pearl Harbour, the International Settlement was finally occupied. Harry disappeared, leaving her an address where she could drop messages. But her position became increasingly precarious. The International Settlement was infested with agents of the *Tokoka*, the political police branch of the Kempeitai. The Wang Ching-wei regime had its own intelligence service, which fought a vicious shadow war with the resistance. It was only a matter of time before she was caught. Late in 1942, she got a message from Harry: get out quick.

It was easy to arrange for her lover to be caught in a compromising position with another woman. That sort of man poses no challenge to ensnare. The breakup was public and messy. All their friends were on her side. The man was quite obviously scum. She was the wronged party. She let it be known that she was retiring, going back to Taihoku to live quietly. They saw her off at the docks. In the ladies' room she wiped off her make-up, plaited her hair and got rid of her fancy clothes. Dressed as a simple proletarian worker she caught the train to Nanking. From there she made her way across occupied China, always wary of the *Tokoka*. Often she had to sleep in the open or in farmhouses, trusting to the hospitality of strangers. After nearly six months, she reached Chungking. There she was debriefed by the Nationalists, who viewed her with some suspicion. For all they knew, she might be a Japanese plant. They kept her under surveillance. The Americans vouched for her. Chiang Kai-shek had a difficult relationship with the Americans. He needed their help, but he didn't trust them fully. They wanted him to cooperate with the Communists, whom he knew would turn on him the moment they could. His Chief of Staff was an American, Lieutenant-General Joseph Stilwell, known to all as "Vinegar Joe". Vinegar Joe didn't get along with Generalissimo Chiang, whom he despised and referred to disparagingly as "Peanut". Chiang's people didn't know what the Americans might be plotting behind their backs. Helen was caught in the middle. She was an OSS agent. Where did her loyaties lie? She found herself in limbo, unable to move. It was in Chungking that she met a young overseas Chinese who had escaped from Singapore before it fell. His name was Lim Bo Seng.

Lim Bo Seng had been active in the anti-Japanese movement in Malaya. He knew that there was a price on his head, whether on or off his shoulders. When it became clear that Singapore could not be held, he was forced to leave his family behind and get out. He went first to India and then to Chungking. When the British Special Operations Executive conceived the idea of infiltrating agents into occupied Malaya, they recruited Lim. He was their prize catch. He joined Force 136, which the SOE had set up for the operation, with the rank of major. Chinese from China and

Malaya were trained in guerilla tactics and the art of sabotage at Sinhgarh Fort near Poona. Lim Bo Seng was considered to be the leader on the Chinese side. He spoke fluent English and was the liaison between the Chinese-speaking recruits and their British instructors.

There were two camps among the Chinese: those who had come directly from Malaya and those who had been sent over from Chungking. The latter had no loyalty to the British, even though some of them had been born in Malaya. They considered themselves to be Chinese first and last. Relations between the British and the Nationalist Chinese recruits were not good. Many of the instructors were former members of the colonial civil service or police force. They hadn't shaken off their colonial attitudes towards the natives. There was always a tinge of racial arrogance in the British; it was felt more keenly by the Chungking faction. Things came to a head when Lim Bo Seng was away from the camp. The Nationalist Chinese recruits went on strike, disgruntled at their treatment. They felt that the British were taking them for granted. The OC, Captain Daniels, threatened to court-martial them for mutiny. Daniels was not well liked. He was arrogant and abrasive. His actions did little to endear him to the Nationalists. Lim Bo Seng rushed back from Chungking. It took all of his tact and diplomacy to smoothen things out.

The Nationalist recruits confided their fears to Lim. They had volunteered to fight the Japanese in order to liberate China, not to restore British rule in Malaya. They suspected that the British were merely using them. The main resistance groups in Malaya were Communist. As long as the war lasted, the Communists would keep their politics submerged; but they were biding their time in Malaya as in China. The British were being very naïve in believing that the Communists were trustworthy allies. The moment the Japanese were defeated they would turn Malaya into a People's

Republic. Chungking could not sit idly by and let this happen. The Nationalists had no faith that the British would take care of their interests. Lim knew the truth of this. The British cooperated with him because they needed him; but at the end of the day, they were working to restore their colonial rule in Malaya. China's interests were very much secondary. The Americans were on the Chinese side. President Roosevelt wasn't sacrificing American lives and money to keep the British Empire alive. Vinegar Joe Stilwell had as much respect for the British as he did for the Chinese. He and the OSS saw eye to eye on the need to keep watch on what was going on in Malaya. Harry Wilson, who had resurfaced in Chungking, had the perfect candidate.

He brought Helen to meet Lim Bo Seng. They hit it off from the start. She was impressed with his sincerity and courage. He didn't have to go back into occupied Malaya at the risk of his life. He could have stayed in Chungking or Calcutta like so many other overseas Chinese to wait out the war. But he felt that had a duty to lead his men. They were to set up an intelligence network in Malaya, against the day when the Allies should invade the country and drive the Japanese out. The network was to consist of Chinese radio operators and specialists supplied by Chungking, with agents trained in sabotage and intelligence-gathering recruited from the Malayan Chinese. They would cooperate with the local Communist guerillas. The whole network would be under the control of the SOE. Chungking thought it best to hedge their bets. With OSS help, they planned to set up a parallel network with the Nationalist guerillas. They needed someone to do it. Lim Bo Seng asked Helen if she was willing. She asked for time to think about the matter. The following day, she volunteered to go to Malaya, a country that she had never seen in her life.

THE plan was hatched in secrecy. The British were not to know. Helen was briefed about the country and its customs. She had the advantage of having real papers identifying her as a Japanese subject. Of course she could not just turn up as if by magic. They would land her on the coast of Malaya near Pulau Pangkor, accompanied by a Malayan Chinese. There she would be met by the local Kuomintang agent. She was to make contact with the Nationalist guerilla band in northern Perak. They would put her in touch with the Kelantan group around Kuala Krai. When she had established contact with the guerillas in northern Malaya, she would catch a train to Singapore. She would report to the Kuomintang Central Secretariat in Malaya. Her reports would be forwarded to Chungking, as a check on the intelligence that the British provided. When the time of liberation came, Chinese troops would be part of the Allied invasion force. Chungking didn't intend to let Malaya slip into the hands of the Communists through British negligence.

In October 1943 Helen was sent to India. With all China's ports in Japanese hands and the Burma Road closed, the Allies kept China supplied by air over the Hump, flying over the tallest mountains in the world. Supply planes went to Yunnan loaded with ammunition, fuel and spares; they came back to Assam filled with Chinese troops, to join the veteran Chinese divisions in northern Burma. It was in one of these unpressurised Dakotas that Helen made the trip, bundled up against the cold, her face swathed in scarves. No one could tell that she was a woman. As far as everyone was concerned, she was just another fresh-faced farm boy to be fed into the meat-grinder in Burma. From the airhead in Assam she was conveyed in secret to Calcutta and thence to Trincomalee in Ceylon. SOE had commandeered the single submarine available to land their agents. The only transport for Helen was an ancient Catalina flying-boat, which had the range to reach Malaya but was a sitting duck for enemy fighters. She was joined by a taciturn young Malayan Chinese called Choo Kee. This wasn't his real name, which he didn't reveal to her. The Catalina took off at the dead of night, striking straight across the Bay of Bengal. The gunners in the waist kept a constant watch for enemy aircraft. Helen dozed for most of the flight. After an interminable time, the Catalina suddenly lost altitude. To the passengers, it looked like they were crashing. The great bird hit the sea in a spray of white water. The hatch opened and a rubber dinghy was inflated. Choo Kee and Helen bundled themselves into it. The new moon was still barely visible in the dawn light. They waved to the crew as the Catalina took off again. Before them lay a long ribbon of golden sand. They were in Malaya.

28

IT was only when they reached the beach that the enormity of the task that faced them hit Helen. She was in a strange country of which she knew practically nothing. Their instructions were sketchy. Lim Bo Seng had told them that the Force 136 operatives had established a base at Lumut, which was a small port on the mainland facing Pulau Pangkor. After hiding the dinghy, Choo and Helen began the long trek to the other side of the island. They had no papers. If caught, they would have been shot out of hand. To make contact with Force 136, they were to hang a white cloth at a designated beach. In retrospect it was a foolish way to proceed. Any passing Japanese patrol boat would have spotted it and come to investigate.

They were in luck. After only a day, a junk did appear at the beach. The sampan it towed was cast off. They identified themselves to the occupant, who introduced himself simply as Ah Chong. He asked no more questions, simply loading them and their belongings onto the sampan. Money changed hands; they had brought thousands of Straits dollars to finance the network. Ah Chong seemed very eager to be off. They didn't dawdle.

Lumut had seen better times. Before the War it had been a British naval base. The base was destroyed in the retreat. The Japanese didn't bother to have it repaired. All that was left was the jetty. On disembarking, they passed a couple of Malay policemen who eyed them suspiciously. Ah Chong slipped them an envelope. They had a peek inside and lost interest in the new arrivals. Following Ah Chong's directions, they made their way to a shophouse just off the main street. They were received by a lean Chinese man, who did not bother with introductions. The town was considered to be safe, but there were still informers of all sorts. Choo Kee was to pose as a businessman from Syonan while Helen played the part of his wife. Again money changed hands. Their host produced food and clothing for them. They spent the night there in separate rooms.

The following day, a new contact appeared. His name was Goh Beng Chye and he was the proprietor of Chop Wan Seng, a prosperous business in town. Chop Wan Seng had just been established in Lumut. Its main office was located in Ipoh. Goh knew why they had come. He was one of the men sent out from Chungking to be trained at Sinhgarh Fort. Choo Kee had met him before. In fact, he was their Kuomintang contact. He gave them details of how to get information to the Central Secretariat. He also cautioned them that the Communists had no idea of their presence. If they were found out, they were as good as dead. The MPAJA fought a little side war with the independent resistance groups that they termed as bandits. The main bands of Nationalist guerillas had formed the Overseas Chinese Anti-Japanese Army up north in Perak at Grik and in Kelantan around the railhead at Kuala Krai. Getting there would be next to impossible, given the current Japanese activity in the area. Goh himself hadn't yet gotten in touch with them. There was one band of non-communist guerillas active in the Dindings, across the mouth of the Perak River not far away. Force 136 had little to do with them. Choo thought that they should try to make contact. Goh promised to do so as soon as practicable.

He was as good as his word, though the process took far longer than Helen had hoped. They spent nearly a month in

Lumut posing as Goh's business associates from Syonan. He got them residency papers and ration cards from the local office of the Overseas Chinese Association. As an upstanding citizen and businessman, the OCA took his word for it when he vouched for them. Any lingering doubts were cleared with an envelope under the table. During that month Helen learnt a lot about the country and its customs. She had never dealt with Malays before. Her only experience of Indians was with the Sikhs of the Shanghai Municipal Police. The racial differences bewildered her. Choo Kee tried his best to point out the defining characteristics of each race, but there was too much to absorb in too little time. She resolved to keep to herself. Two minutes' conversation with a native would have blown her cover. She pretended to have come down with malaria and took to her bed. Finally, Goh Beng Chye announced that he had managed to arrange a rendezvous with the Dindings guerillas.

The guerillas were in truth a band of bandits, dominated by the triads. The headman was a man called Wong, who lived in a hut in a little fishing village with his three mistresses. They were armed with an assortment of British weapons salvaged from the Slim River. Most of these were practically useless for want of maintenance, but they seemed to have a lot of ammunition. The Dindings were not strategically important. As long as the triads didn't interfere with seaborne traffic, the local police were content to leave them alone. Wong had an understanding with the local Malay constabulary; occasionally, they would make a sweep through the area when pressed to do so by the Japanese, blundering around making noise that a deaf man could hear from a mile away. The band would slip away until the disturbance was over.

The triads gave protection to the nearby villages. The villagers paid up in cash and kind to avoid trouble from the police and the Communist hill-rats. When MPAJA cadres tried to muscle in on his territory there was a shootout. They wanted to take over the area; Wong's band resisted. There was an ideological element to the rivalry. Wong was a capitalist freebooter and didn't hold with communism. The MPAJA wasn't welcome. He made it quite plain with bullets. The MPAJA retreated back to their jungle fastness at Bukit Segari. The little scrap of land wasn't worth any blood to them.

Choo and Helen spent a week with the bandits. The gang members lived in huts with their mistresses and wives. They wore wide-brimmed hats and were festooned with bandoliers when they sortied out to collect their protection money. Many were opium addicts. Discipline was relaxed, though there was a clear hierarchy. Wong was quite taken by Helen and wanted to add her to his harem. It didn't fit in with her plans. Rather than rebuff him openly, she led him on with smiles full of promise, spiked his drink and made off in the night back to Lumut together with Choo.

Goh Beng Chye wasn't happy to see them. For some reason anti-guerilla activity had intensified. Japanese troops and their locally-recruited Malay and Indian auxiliaries were pressing the MPAJA patrol based around Sitiawan. Lumut was full of informers. Every town had a *Jikeidan* or Home Guard which was meant to keep an eye out for strangers. Normally, they suffered from myopia when given coffee money. Of late, they had become more vigilant. A Japanese concern had set up the Syonan Shipbuilding Company in the nearby coastal village of Keling Wang. The staff spoke Hokkien with a Formosan accent. Goh suspected that this was a front for counter-insurgent activities. The *Tokoka* from nearby Sitiawan paid visits more frequently. Sometimes they were accompanied by Hojo Kempeitai troops, recruited from the Japanese colonies. The worst ones were the Hokkien-speaking *kempei* from Formosa. They outdid their masters in cruelty. Many of the atrocities attributed to the Japanese could be laid at their doorstep.

The atmosphere was tense. It wasn't safe for them to stay much longer. There was to be a meeting of Force 136 and the guerillas in December at their camp at Blantan, in the foothills of the Main Range near Bidor. Goh had been instructed to attend in order to bring supplies and money. He told Choo and Helen to come with him. It was risky. If the MPAJA suspected that they were Nationalist agents their lives would be forfeit and so would his. They were to pose as local recruits for Force 136. The cover story that they were from Syonan would be maintained. They would travel openly together by taxi to the designated rendezvous. The presence of a woman would help allay the suspicions of the security forces. They were always on the lookout for groups of young males heading into the *ulu*.

THE journey to Bidor was tense. The three of them took the bus to Sitiawan and caught a taxi outside town. The driver was friendly and not inclined to ask too many questions. Guerilla activity meant heightened security along the road. There were checkpoints at Kampar, Tapah and Bidor. Goh was nervous. They negotiated the first checkpoint at Kampar without difficulty, the Malay policemen waving them through. At Tapah it was a different story. There was a line of vehicles at the roadblock. The guards were checking people's papers more thoroughly. There were *kempei* lurking sinisterly in the background. Goh began to sweat. But with Helen in the car, they didn't fit the usual profile of subversives. They were allowed to pass with only a cursory glance by the soldiers on duty. Goh breathed a little easier. The rest of the journey passed uneventfully. The taxi driver let them out by the side of the road on the outskirts of Bidor and made himself scarce. They trekked through the rubber estate to a small hut, where they waited patiently. At dusk, a guide appeared. He led them uphill along the jungle paths. They camped overnight in the jungle. The next day a new guide appeared, a Sakai. He was naked except for a loincloth and parang. The Sakai took them to the camp, which was on a plateau overlooking the plains. In the distance they could see Pulau Pangkor.

The camp was laid out neatly, with communal barracks for all. The new arrivals were shown to one of the long huts and assigned a sleeping area. In contrast to the haphazard situation of the guerillas in the Dindings, the MPAJA were well organised and disciplined. They had vegetable gardens as well as a small parade square. The mornings were given over to military exercises and the evenings to political education. There were a dozen young girls, some barely out of their teens. These did the household chores, cleaning and mending. They also did their fair share of guard duty out in the jungle. There were no ranks. Everyone was addressed as "comrade". The Communists were very puritanical. There was no mixing of the sexes. Everyone was very earnest and serious on the surface. Beneath the surface they were like a bunch of school kids. Helen was an object of curiousity. Her accent was strange. They asked her about herself when the Commissar was out of earshot. She told them that she was from Shanghai and had been stranded in Singapore with the outbreak of war. There she had met Choo, who had recruited her for Force 136. Her young interlocutors seemed satisfied. They were surprisingly trusting, given their situation.

There were three British officers resident in the camp. They were Captains Broome and Davis of Force 136 and Major Spencer Chapman, who had commanded a stay-behind party during the retreat to Singapore. Chapman had been active in sabotage activities around Tanjong Malim back in January 1942. Since then, he had been moving around organising the various resistance groups. Broome and Davis were former Malaya hands who had joined Force 136 in India after escaping through Sumatra. They had been at the training camp at Sinhgarh Fort. Choo Kee had heard of them, but they had never met. Lim Bo Seng turned up a few days later in the company of Chin Peng, the Party Secretary of the Perak Branch of the Malayan Communist Party, and Colonel Itu, the commander of the MPAJA's 5th Independent Regiment. With Lim came two men whom he introduced as Koh Kim Seng and Leong Yeok. From their pallor it was clear that they had been in the jungle for some time. Lim pretended not to recognise Helen or Choo Kee. Goh Beng Chye introduced them and he shook hands gravely. As he did so, he whispered in her ear that they should meet quietly.

It wasn't easy to meet privately in the camp. All activities were communal. Solitary pursuits were frowned upon. The Communists had a fondness for singing and other group activities. The British officers kept to themselves of course, but what could be expected of the red-haired devils? Lim managed to get them some time together on the pretext of debriefing Choo Kee and Helen on the situation in Singapore. Leong Yeok and Koh Kim Seng came along too. It was only then that it was revealed that these men were Nationalist guerillas, members of the Overseas Chinese Anti-Japanese Army. They had managed to make contact with one of the Force 136 parties around Taiping and had been brought along to meet Lim Bo Seng. The Communists had granted them safe passage for the duration of the meeting.

The news from Grik was encouraging. It transpired that the area around Grik was now being patrolled by Indian troops. They were training in the jungles. An informal truce had been agreed. The Indians had no quarrel with the guerillas. In turn, the guerillas saw no need to interfere with the Indians. In fact, said Koh, he had a similar experience near Kota Bahru at the very start of the War. He and his men were allowed to take all the arms and ammunition from the RAF airfield at Batu Sembilan by an Indian officer who had remained there after all the British and Australian personnel had decamped. Some of these arms found their way to the Grik group. Without them, they would have been totally toothless. Lim instructed that Choo Kee should return with them to Grik and from there make contact with the Kelantan group. The OSS would arrange to supply them from the east coast. It was too dangerous to do it from the west, as that meant crossing the width of the Malay Peninsula. Helen would go on south to Singapore, where she would make contact with the local Nationalist cell.

The main participant in the meeting had yet to arrive. The MPAJA was to be represented by the Secretary-General of the Malayan Communist Party. There was nothing to do but wait. Finally, on the last day of December he turned up. He was a youngish man who called himself Chang Hong. The British officers referred to him as "The Plen", short for plenipotentiary. The guerillas spoke in hushed tones of his uncanny ability to evade the Japanese and traverse the length of Malaya. He had escaped by the skin of his teeth when Japanese troops had cornered the leadership of the MPAJA at the Batu Caves the previous year. The Selangor MPAJA had been decapitated at one fell swoop; Chang Hong was the only one who got away.

The Bidor meeting was by all accounts a success. On behalf of Southeast Asia Command Captain Broome signed a formal alliance with the Malayan Communist Party. The British would supply arms, ammunition, food and money in return for cooperation against the Japanese. Politics would be forgotten for the duration of the War. They stood arm in arm against a common enemy. The MPAJA regiments would receive Force 136 advisers. Command and control would remain with the MCP. Working together, they would create a formidable guerilla army, ready to strike when the Allies landed once more in Malaya. Toasts were drunk and promises of friendship made. The British officers were well-satisfied with what had been accomplished. Things were looking up.

Within three months the whole network of agents in Perak had unravelled.

AFTER the Bidor meeting Choo Kee, Leong Yeok and Koh Kim Seng went north to rejoin the OCAJA patrol at Grik. Goh Beng Chye and Helen made their way to Ipoh, where the main branch of Goh's business Chop Wan Seng was located. Helen stayed with him, posing as his niece. She needed the time to learn more about living in Malaya. As it was, some of the older Communists were becoming suspicious of her. A stranger from Shanghai was suspect, especially since Shanghai had been controlled by the Japanese for nearly six years. She hadn't been entirely comfortable in Bidor. It seemed to her that Chang Hong, for all his protestations of comradeship, looked askance at Lim Bo Seng. He knew that when Malaya was liberated, there would be a reckoning between the Kuomintang and the MCP. Lim, with his dynamism, courage and status as a war hero, would be a rival for leadership among the Chinese. It didn't take a genius to see that. She was relieved to leave the camp and get away from the guerillas.

In February 1944 Lim Bo Seng emerged from the jungle to expand the network of agents and make contact with the submarine sent from Ceylon. Force 136 had brought transmitters with them, but unfortunately they didn't work in the damp climate of Malaya. The Nationalist radio operators found themselves out of a job. The only way to get information back to Ceylon was to physically send it out by submarine. They were also running out of money to finance the intelligence network. The MCP had no leverage with any of the *towkays*. Lim decided that he had to go himself. He made it to Ipoh, where he stayed in one of the safe houses while waiting for the rendezvous with the submarine. On March 21 the Kempeitai struck. They blockaded Pulau Pangkor and picked up the local agents. Within days they had rounded up practically the whole network. Lim Bo Seng tried to escape. He was stopped at a roadblock driving out of Ipoh. Even though he gave a false name, the Kempeitai arrested him. They obviously knew exactly who they were looking for. He didn't survive the interrogation.

Helen was lucky to escape the disaster. When the Kempeitai came to pick up Goh Beng Chye she had been in the back room of Chop Wan Seng. She heard their chatter before she saw them and understood immediately what they had come for. Fortunately, she had taken the precaution of preparing for precisely this contingency. Rushing back to her bedroom, she scooped up her small suitcase and made her way to the top floor. Already, she could hear the sounds of scuffling as the Japanese subdued Goh and his assistants downstairs. The noise of their boots could be heard on the steps. She pulled the cord that lowered the ladder to the attic. Scampering up quickly, she retracted the ladder. It would take some time for them to find it, hidden as it was in the ceiling. Chop Wan Seng was in a terrace house. The attics of the adjoining terraces abutted one another. A hole had been made in the wall separating the shop from the next building. She wriggled through it, then through another similar passage into the building beyond. She lowered the ladder from the attic carefully and went downstairs. Pausing only to ensure that she had not been pursued, she made her way out the front door. The road was swarming with troops. Fortunately, their attention was focussed on Chop Wan Seng. She slipped away unnoticed.

Ipoh Railway Station was only a few minutes' walk away. She had her ticket, a forged one showing her point of departure as Bangkok. A quick visit to a public convenience allowed her to transform herself. Gone were the *samfoo* and the pigtails. She hurriedly applied her makeup and slipped on a floral frock. When she reached the guard at the platform, she presented her papers with regal condescension. He stared at them for a long moment. She put him in his place with exquisite courtesy, in perfect Japanese. The soldier, a peasant from Korea, clicked to attention and bowed. She swept past him into the first class carriage.

The trip to Singapore took the whole day. The train stopped at every station along the way. There were few passengers in first class. She had a bit of luck. A couple of Japanese officers boarded at Kuala Lumpur and asked to share her compartment. She agreed readily. They were pleased to be in the company of a pretty girl, and a Japanese-speaking one at that. They were so tired of the peasant women of the country. Her companions proved good company on the 17-hour journey from KL to Singapore. They were cultured and entertaining. It was obvious to them that she was not Japanese; they were all the more delighted to discover that she had been in cosmopolitan Shanghai. There was no talk of politics and the war. Instead, they bantered and spoke of music and art. Best of all, they kept others away. A civilian tried to enter the compartment but retreated hurriedly when he saw the uniforms. When night fell, the officers gallantly allowed her to have the whole compartment to herself. They stood guard outside to make sure that she was not molested. It was not an unpleasant journey.

At Keppel Road Station she managed to hail one of the few taxis. The driver took her straight to the address that she gave. It was Lao Leong Ann's shop in Jim Chuan Place.

"And that's how I came to be with him," she said. "He set me up in the house next door with the comfort women."

I was astounded. "You were a comfort woman?"

"No," she said with a wicked smile, "I was the *mama-san*. Lao ran the comfort house for the Japs and the locals who could pay. Having a *Nippon-jin mama-san* was good for business. It was really a great place to hear things. Men can't keep their mouths shut in bed. They're always bragging about how important they are, what great things they've done — even when they're paying for the girl. I got a lot of info from the girls. I passed it on to Chungking and the Americans."

"And the singing?"

"Nope, got that job myself after the Liberation. A girl's gotta eat. But it's a good place too. Lots of folks with big mouths and money to burn. I even saw that Commie bastard from Bidor once, that Chang Hong. He had some tart on his arm and was shooting his mouth off about having got rid of all his rivals."

This was interesting information, but a question burned in my mind. I had to ask. "Were you Lao's mistress?"

She laughed, an incongruously girlish laugh. "Hell, no. Not that he didn't try, though. I told him, nothing doing buster, this is strictly business. Though it might have made getting my hands on the property easier if I had agreed."

I was shocked. "You'd have become his mistress for the property?"

"Gimme a break, he wasn't my type. You can take that look off your face now," she said, with her eyes twinking mischievously, "I'm just yanking your chain."

"So he was working for the resistance all along," I mused. "I've misjudged him."

"Nope, don't think so. Old Lao was working for number one," she replied. "He needed us to protect himself. Yeah, I know, he was a bastard; but he was our bastard, and that's what counts, right?"

I realised with a start that it was getting light. There was a moment of panic before I remembered that we were no longer on Tokyo time and that sunrise was at six o'clock and not seven-thirty. "I've taken up enough of your time, Miss … er … Helen," I said awkwardly.

She laughed again. "Yeah, you sure got me going there. What was it you wanted? It wasn't to hear the story of my life for sure."

In my fascination I'd completely forgotten the purpose of my visit. "Oh, right. We wanted to get in touch with your friends from Kelantan. They might be able to say something helpful for Habibullah. If there's some way … I'd appreciate it."

"Okay, I'll give it a go, but no promises," she replied. "It's not like I can just get them on the phone, if you know what I mean. It may take time."

"Thanks," I answered. "It was … interesting." I backed out the door.

"Come anytime," she called after me coquettishly. "You're real cute. Gimme a call, Dennis Chiang." Her teasing discomfited me for some reason I could not fathom. I retired, trying hard not to show it.

29

I WENT straight back to the office from Great World. It was a long walk, but the morning was cool, with a little mist left over from the rains. My path took me along the banks of the Singapore River, where the godowns were already bustling even at that early hour. *Tongkangs* were chugging up and down, laden with cargo. In the last year of the War trade had practically stopped. Most of the Japanese merchant marine was at the bottom of the sea, sunk by Allied submarines. The Allies practised unrestricted submarine warfare and didn't give any warning before sinking freighters. They roamed the seas at will like wolves, singly rather than in packs. With peace came trade. The Inner and Outer Roads were full of shipping again. The port of Singapore was the lifeline of Malaya.

George was already in when I reached the office. He had sharp eyes. "That must have been some night out," he remarked, scanning my rumpled suit. "I thought you just went to have a quick word with Ah Moy."

"Turned out to be more interesting than I thought," I replied. "She's had some real adventures."

"And the contact?"

"She'll let us know."

"She'd better. I've drawn a complete blank with the Bhurtpores. The only INA men still around are fellows recruited from around here. We've got no witnesses who can testify to the shooting of Holmes."

"I don't understand what the old man wants with the guerillas," I said. "They won't have been there when Holmes was killed either."

"The old man thinks that the guerillas may have some knowledge of the incident," said a voice from behind me. "One never knows."

I spun around, cursing d'Almeida's cat-like tread. "Mr d'Almeida," I sputtered, "I didn't know you were in."

"Evidently not," he said drily. "What news did you get from Miss Ah Moy?"

I gave him the highlights of her story, summarising the night's narrative in ten minutes. "Interesting, very interesting," he mused, rubbing his spectacles. He turned to go. "Please have her come to see me this morning before tiffin."

"Before tiffin?" I queried. "Aren't we going to be in court?"

"No, I fancy not," he replied. "After last evening's tragic turn of events I am certain that the courthouse will need to be properly secured. They will have to screen all visitors to the building. I do not anticipate having to resume until the afternoon at the earliest."

I had forgotten all about poor Ward. Death had become so commonplace in the last few years that it could be erased from memory in an instant. The lack of sleep and the fascination of Helen's story had driven it from my mind. "Get some rest," d'Almeida called out to me as he left.

IT seemed like I had only put my head down on the cushions of the settee when I was woken by a commotion. I looked at the wall clock; it was nearly eleven. I roused myself quickly and went out to have a look. A dishevelled Indian man was in the foyer, being bundled into Simon's room by two rough coolies. George was directing operations. "What's going on?" I asked.

"Got one," answered George, "a Bhurtpore, alive and kicking."

"How ever did you manage that?" I asked with admiration. George was getting to be like his Uncle Clarence when it came to pulling rabbits out of hats.

"I had my friends in the League look out at the courthouse for anyone who might have been in the INA," he answered. "We picked him up this morning when he came back to watch the proceedings."

"I thought that you and the League had parted company long ago," I commented.

"Parted company, yes. Lost contact, no. They still owe me for services rendered and favours done. I called in the markers." We were in Simon's room now. Our unwilling guest was seated in front of his desk, staring at us truculently. He was wearing a stained civilian shirt and what appeared to be khaki army trousers, tattered at the cuffs. Round his throat a dirty towel was wound. With the air of a conjurer George introduced us. "May I present to you Lance-Naik Nisar Ahmad, late of the 1st Battalion, Bhurtpore Regiment."

I was elated. We had our witness at last. But Nisar Ahmad didn't appear in the mood to cooperate. He said not a word. "Will you testify for Habibullah?" asked George. "He needs you."

Nisar Ahmad shook his head. He unwrapped the towel from his throat. An ugly scar disfigured it. He grunted and motioned for pencil and paper. George handed them to him. He wrote on the paper in indecipherable scratches and handed it to George, who squinted at it for a minute. "Damn!" exclaimed George, "the man's lost the power of speech. Took a bullet through the throat."

"So you mean he can't testify?"

"Not orally," responded George.

"But he can write, can't he?" I suggested hopefully.

"Barely," answered George bitterly. "Those squiggles are about as much as he can manage. It's kindergarten stuff. I could just about make them out. But how he's going to give evidence is beyond me." George turned to Nisar Ahmad and fired a series of questions at him in Hindustani. He nodded repeatedly after each one. "Just as I suspected," said George, "he's practically illiterate. He can write his name and a few military terms in Urdu, but that's it."

"We could put questions to him and he could nod," I ventured. "He seems to understand English well enough."

"Hah! I can just see Selwyn-Jones on his feet like a jack-in-the-box. Literally putting words in the mouth of the witness he'll say, and he'd be right." George slumped back into Simon's chair and swivelled, his fingers touching under his chin. Strange how he had adopted d'Almeida's habits.

Singh the *jaga* entered. "Tuan," he said to me, "there is a woman to see you."

I left George and Nisar Ahmad and went back to my little broom-closet of an office. It was Helen. She was dressed simply, without the full warpaint of the previous night but still fetching. The last time she had been in our office she looked like a proletarian worker. The transformation was unbelievable.

"Hi, Dennis," she said brightly, "got word that your boss wanted to see me. I brought you a present." She tossed a cloth bag onto my desk. It made a metallic sound and an oval object rolled out. I sprang forward to catch the grenade before it hit the floor. She laughed her little laugh again.

"Take it easy," she said, "they're duds. Least, I think so. We steamed the TNT out of them to make bombs, but we might have left some in. I heard that the Limeys are paying good money for ammo and guns to be handed in. You could make a couple of bucks."

I put the wretched thing back into the bag and gingerly lifted it up. Half-filled grenades are not my favourite playthings. After showing her to d'Almeida's room, I returned to George. Simon had just arrived and wasn't amused to find George, two burly coolies and what appeared to be a tramp in possession of his room. I was the last straw. "What do you want?" he demanded, losing his customary suaveness. "What have you got there?"

"Just grenades," I answered, putting the bag down on his desk.

He shrank back alarmed. "What in heaven's name … take them away immediately. Don't just leave them there!"

"There's nowhere else to leave them. You've got a filing cabinet. Put them in there," I replied, indicating the old-fashioned cabinet in the corner.

"There's no lock," he protested.

"No one's going to steal them," I responded as we hurried Nisar Ahmad out of the room. "Just hold onto them for me, there's a good fellow."

WE confronted Habibullah within the hour. "Why didn't you tell us that Nisar Ahmad was in Singapore?" demanded George.

Habibullah looked tired, much more tired than I'd seen him before. "What good would it have done? He can't speak. His windpipe is shot through. He's no use to you. If the Britishers had known they'd have arrested him too. He's gone through enough. Leave him in peace. What have you done with him?"

"Nothing," answered George, "he's out there in the car. He can't take the stand. You realise that you've no witnesses at all."

"Yes, I realise that," he replied, "I've realised that from the start. My men are all dead somewhere in Burma, or in a cage in India. I have no illusions. Let me be."

D'Almeida had joined us. "Are you instructing us to change

your plea to guilty?" he queried. "Before you do, remember your promise to Miss Barron. The last thing she needs now is to hear that you have surrendered."

"What do you mean, the last thing she needs now?" asked Habibullah, looking up abruptly. "What's happened to her?"

"Nothing yet," responded d'Almeida. "Colonel Newman just informed me not an hour ago that the Supreme Commander has agreed to a recommendation to take her into protective custody until the matter of her guardianship is resolved. Major Ridley is just waiting for the official order."

"They can't do that!" said Habibullah with some heat. "She doesn't want to go back to England. There's nothing for her there. She said she'd rather die."

"Be that as it may," responded d'Almeida calmly, "the matter is now with the British authorities. Newman will do what he can. We are more concerned at the moment with your case. Are you going to give up?" He looked Habibullah directly in the eyes.

Habibullah met his gaze and then lowered his head. "No," he said, "I promised Marge I would fight on. I surrendered once in my life; that was one time too much. Do what you can, Mr d'Almeida." He paused. "You say that you have Nisar Ahmad in the car outside?"

"Yes," said George, "he wanted to see you in court."

"Can I talk to him one last time?"

"It can be arranged," said George, "but not now. We'll get him a court orderly's uniform and tidy him up a bit. He'll come with me on my next visit this afternoon. I don't think the guards will notice anything amiss. You can have a few minutes, no more. Then we'll let him get lost. If he wants to stick around in the gallery, I don't want to know about it."

Habibullah nodded in appreciation.

As we were gathering our things before proceeding upstairs to the court, d'Almeida put his hand on my arm. "I have something to ask of you, my boy," he said. Drawing me out of earshot of Habibullah, he said softly, "I need you to go back to my house and keep watch on Miss Barron. She is not to leave the compound under any circumstances."

I was astounded. "Is it that serious? Would they take her just like that?"

"It is not just Miss Rider and Major Ridley I fear," he replied. "Karim has been very restless. He is impetuous and has no love for the British. He might take it into his head to spirit her away."

It was a bit of a disappointment to be left out of the show that afternoon, but I knew I had to do it. June wouldn't have been able to cope alone. I indicated my assent. D'Almeida put his hand on my shoulder. "Good," he said, "I count on you. And take care; we cannot afford to lose you." With that he vanished up the stairs, leaving me to wonder what exactly he meant.

30

CONTRARY to all precedent Colonel Huntly had ordained that the court would sit not only on Saturday but also for the whole day on Sunday. He was determined to have everything all tied up neatly on Monday, New Year's Eve. The Red Fort trials in Delhi were drawing to a close. The Advocate-General of India would deliver his closing speech that very Saturday. Habibullah's trial had to be over by Monday, come hell or high water.

I was out of the action completely. I didn't relish my job as guard dog, but someone had to do it. Marge couldn't bring herself to come to the courthouse. It would have be inadvisable in any case, with Ridley just waiting to pounce. She retreated to the little bower at the bottom of d'Almeida's garden. It was a pleasant little thatched structure with a couple of rattan chairs and a table, surrounded with flowers. The perfume of the frangipani trees suffused the atmosphere. All the flowering shrubs were in bloom, the red and orange hibiscus complementing the pink and yellow oleaders. She took her favourite book from d'Almeida's library, a collection of Tennyson's poetry. June and I left her alone.

"How's your matter with Simon coming?" I asked her.

She shook her head morosely. "We have solved it. The marriage is void. The girl had no capacity to marry. She was too young."

"You're awfully down for someone who's won the client's case," I commented.

"It is very sad," she responded. "I met the man, Mr Augustine.

He was not as bad as I thought. He said that his wife does not love him. She complained all the time, nag, nag, nag, this not right, that not right. That young girl Dorothea treated him nicely. She has no family. He needed someone to look after him. She needed someone to protect her. So he divorced the old wife and married the girl. But the marriage is void because she was under sixteen. If she was a Muslim, she would have been old enough. He said to me, 'I am old, I don't have much longer. Why won't they let me be happy?' I felt so sad for him."

"How did he get divorced in the first place?" I asked curiously. "Marriage isn't like a jail sentence. You don't get time off for good behaviour — or in this case, bad behaviour. He can't just opt out just like that."

"The wife divorced him for adultery," replied June. "He did not contest."

"And now that's he's remarried she's changed her mind, I suppose."

"No, it is the children," said June, "they do not want Dorothea to be their step-mother, especially when she is half their age. Also I learned something from Gim Huat's case. If he dies intestate, half his money goes to her if she is his wife."

"Well," I commented, "the divorce is valid, so at least he's got rid of the old witch. He's a free man. There's nothing to stop him carrying on living with the girl and marrying her properly when she's of age. Or he can get a special licence when she's 18, if memory serves me correctly."

June brightened up. "Yes, you are right. He can marry her with special permission. I will look up the details."

"You realise of course that you can't tell him any of this," I warned. "His children are our clients and they've retained the firm to set aside the marriage with the girl. You can't go around advising the other party what to do."

"I know that, we will get the marriage set aside as instructed. But," she said decidedly, "there are many people with *mulot bochor** who may talk about such things. I cannot help it if Mr Augustine gets the idea from someone else."

I heaved a big sigh. That was June's way. She was great at fixing other people's matrimonial problems. If only she could fix her own.

GEORGE reported that there were no surprises in the rest of the prosecution's case. Our friend Major Beatty took over from Selwyn-Jones. The remaining witnesses were mainly formal ones, testifying to the accuracy of documents and to the investigation process. A new young assistant had replaced the luckless Ward. The MPs were scrutinising everyone coming into the courthouse. Outside, the Paras had moved the perimeter outwards. The crowd no longer pressed up to the building. "And they're holding a requiem mass for Ward on New Year's Day," said George.

"I suppose we should go," I said. I felt a twinge of guilt. He had been standing right next to me and that bullet was probably aimed at me. "Where's it to be?"

"At the Chapel of Our Lady in Changi. That's the one the Roman Catholic POWs put up during the War. There's a memorial mass for the Norfolks and the North Anglians too. You'd think they'd have a little more sensitivity, after what came out in court about Parit Batang," remarked George acerbically.

"Let bygones be bygones," I responded. "A lot of horrible things happened, on all sides. I'll be there."

"So will Uncle Clarence, and Huntly and Selwyn-Jones and Beatty. The whole lot will be there to pay respects to Ward. But

---

* *Literally, leaky mouths.*

you can be sure there aren't going to be any masses for the poor sods who died at Parit Batang," said George darkly.

IT was on Sunday night that d'Almeida broke the news to me. "I shall put you on the stand tomorrow," he said, "as the first witness for the defence."

I was completely astounded. "You can't do that," I expostulated, "I'm part of the defence team. Selwyn-Jones will go beserk."

"Leave Lieutenant-Colonel Selwyn-Jones to me," replied d'Almeida evenly. "The President, Colonel Huntly, is a fair man. He has been scrupulously allowing as much leeway to the defence as he can."

"But what could I possibly say?" I persisted.

"You are the only one we have who has any personal knowledge of the circumstances leading up to the death of Holmes at Batu Sembilan. Nisar Ahmad cannot testify, and even if he could his testimony would be discounted because of his personal loyalty to Habibullah."

"That would mean revealing our activities there and subsequently," I replied. "I thought we were still meant to keep those secret."

D'Almeida looked grave. "What Miss Ah Moy has told me has changed the game. The secret we are protecting no longer needs protection. It will all come out in due course, maybe not immediately but certainly some time in the near future. I have kept Mr Newman informed. SOE and Special Branch will have to work out between themselves how they wish to handle this. You are released from the bonds of secrecy."

To tell the truth, I was absolutely relieved to hear it. All throughout the war years I had kept silent about my activities. Even my family didn't know the full details. I had suffered under the burden of collaboration with the occupiers. Our neighbours and acquaintainces thought that I was a Japanese running-dog. To be allowed finally to explain, that was true liberation.

AS I anticipated, Selwyn-Jones put up enormous difficulties about my testimony. He had closed his case on Sunday and did not anticipate that the defence would have much to say. It was a surprise to be told on Monday that one of the junior counsel for the defence would be testifying for the defence.

"This is most irregular," he protested to the Court. "I must register my strenuous opposition to this."

D'Almeida countered, "Are we here to see justice done to the accused or to play a party game by the rules? Mr Chiang was there at Batu Sembilan at the time the events in question took place. He can provide an eyewitness account."

"Preposterous!" blustered Selwyn-Jones. "This is far too convenient. Are we to believe that this young man was based at RAF Batu Sembilan in December 1941, at exactly the time when Lieutenant-Colonel Holmes was murdered? The whole story beggars belief."

"I am prepared to call Colonel Fredrick Newman, late of the Singapore Special Branch, to confirm this," replied d'Almeida.

That deflated Selwyn-Jones. As d'Almeida expected, Colonel Huntly ruled in favour of allowing me to testify, after consultation with his colleagues. The court-martial was evidently determined to let justice be seen to be done.

I explained to the court that I had been placed at Batu Sembilan as an agent by Newman to find out who was subverting the Bhurtpores. Upon d'Almeida's instructions I omitted any mention of his role; he still did not want his cover blown. I narrated the course of events that led up to the mutiny. There was a buzz in the courtroom when I told of Holmes's maltreatment of his men.

The members of the court-martial frowned. When it came to the fateful day, I stated exactly what Corporal Dave Blake had told me of the shooting.

Selwyn-Jones was on his feet in an instant. "This is complete hearsay and inadmissible," he objected.

D'Almeida didn't miss a beat. "If my learned friend would care to consult the Evidence Ordinance, he will find that hearsay is admissible if the maker of the statement is dead or cannot be found. Mr Chiang's evidence is based on what was told to him by Corporal Dave Blake of the RAAF. We have been unable to locate Corporal Blake. There is no record of him rejoining the RAAF after the fall of Singapore. We can only presume that he is dead."

Colonel Huntly intervened, posing a question directly to me. "Did this Corporal Blake actually see the shooting?"

"Yes, Sir," I replied. "He was taken prisoner by the mutineers and was there when Lieutenant-Colonel Holmes was shot."

"And he was positive that it was not the accused who fired the fatal shot?"

"He was absolutely positive, Sir," I replied. "Blake told me that the accused wasn't happy about it at all."

Huntly conferred with his colleagues on the bench, then indicated that we should carry on. D'Almeida finished the examination-in-chief. Selwyn-Jones tried his best to shake me on cross-examination, but I knew what I saw and held up well, if I do say so myself.

D'Almeida had one final question in re-examination. "Why have you kept silent all these years?"

This was the one I was waiting for. "Because I was instructed to do so by Special Branch. They didn't want it known what we were doing upcountry. During the War, I became involved with the resistance in Singapore. It was necessary not to reveal to the Japanese my connection with Special Branch in order to preserve my value to the resistance." I felt the load lift off my shoulders.

D'Almeida's next witness caused a real stir. It was Ah Moy, alias Helen Sim. She had toned down the Shanghainese songbird look and was dressed in a frock with minimal makeup, her hair slightly waved. To the casual observer she appeared to be a young middle-class working girl, though with an indefinable touch of glamour. One would have guessed her to have been a secretary or typist with some big European company. It was amazing to me how much of a chameleon she could be. In grubby post-war Singapore she stood out like a bird-of-paradise among the pigeons. Selwyn-Jones eyed her suspiciously.

Her narrative of her intelligence work in Malaya clearly created a sensation. Most of the onlookers had been completely unaware of the activities of Force 136. Though much of the detail was still classified, Helen revealed enough to establish her credentials. D'Almeida took her through the meeting she had with Koh Kim Seng and Leong Yeok at Bukit Bidor, studiously avoiding any mention of Lim Bo Seng or the Plen. I could see Selwyn-Jones teetering on the verge of objection. However, having once been mauled on the point of law, he decided to hold back. Helen recounted what Koh had told her of the events at Batu Sembilan, how the Indian officer there had allowed them to take the weapons and ammunition. She mentioned the de facto truces with the Indian troops. At the end of her testimony, d'Almeida asked: "You were born a subject of the Emperor of Japan. What made you renounce that allegiance?"

"My parents were Chinese. I was born in an occupied country," she replied. "We didn't ask to be Japanese. Formosa was taken from China in an unjust imperialist war. I was brought up Chinese. I sure didn't feel Japanese."

"Yet you continued to hold papers identifying yourself as a Japanese subject."

"I worked for the resistance. It was useful for my work. The Americans provided training and support. But we Chinese had to free ourselves from the foreigners. Kids of my age felt it strongly. I mean, we had to do something even if it meant dying. Some of the older folks made their peace, but we couldn't."

"There was a Chinese government in Nanking recognised by the Japanese, headed by Wang Ching-wei. Did you feel no obligation towards the legal government of China?" asked d'Almeida.

"Legal government?" scoffed Helen. "Not on your life. They're nothing but a bunch of rats. They'll get what's coming to them now the war's over."

"And how were you rewarded for your services, for fighting against the Japanese in China and Malaya?" concluded d'Almeida.

"I got a medal from the Chinese government in Chungking," said Helen. "The Americans gave me a medal too, for passing on stuff to them."

There were a few perfunctory questions from the prosecution and then Helen was excused. Court proceedings went into temporary suspension as she glided out of the room.

HABIBULLAH'S testimony was awaited with great anticipation, not least by Selwyn-Jones, who was itching to get stuck into him. It was with a great sense of anticlimax therefore that d'Almeida announced that he would not be taking the stand but would instead make an unsworn statement from the dock. I had questioned this strategy the night before. "Won't the judges take it amiss if he doesn't offer himself up for cross-examination?" I had asked.

"The key facts are not in dispute," d'Almeida had answered. "There is nothing to gain and much to lose by allowing Lieutenant-Colonel Selwyn-Jones to attack Habibullah in the witness box."

So there it was. I had my reservations, but he was the boss.

Colonel Huntly did in fact appear to take it amiss. He pointed out that the members of the court would discount any unsworn testimony. D'Almeida met the objections with equanimity. Habibullah would not be testifying on oath. Selwyn-Jones was disgruntled, but he could do nothing about it. It was the privilege of the accused to decide whether or not to testify.

Habibullah's statement took a long time. He told the story from the time he arrived in Malaya until his capture by the British in simple, short sentences devoid of rhetorical flourishes. He was a good speaker and did not falter. I thought that he made a favourable impression. At the conclusion of his statement he said:

"I am not an enemy of Great Britain by choice. My country has been occupied and kept in servitude by force of arms. I am ashamed to have been part of the apparatus of occupation. What I did during the War, I did out of loyalty to my country, India. That was the guiding principle of our training at Dehra Dun — the safety, honour and welfare of my country come first each and every time. Great Britain forfeited all moral right to rule India after the massacre at Jallianwala Bagh. What I saw at Parit Batang only confirmed what I already felt in my heart, that I had a duty to fight for the freedom of India. We allied with Japan not because of any desire to support Japan's war aims. They provided only the opportunity for us to proclaim the Provisional Government of Free India in exile, right here in Singapore. I am not a traitor. I am a soldier of the Azad Hind Fauj, the army of Free India. Though the War may be lost, the struggle goes on."

Then, unexpectedly, he raised his good arm, punched his fist in the air and yelled, "*Jai Hind!*" The onlookers responded enthusiastically with calls of "*Jai Hind!*" and "*Azad Hindustan zindabad!*". The redcaps bundled the more vociferous ones out of the building. It was only with much pounding of the gavel that Colonel Huntly managed to restore order in the court.

SELWYN-JONES summed up the case against Habibullah, meticulously going over every scrap of evidence and pointing out every inconsistency in the defence's case. He went on and on, interminably. Then it was d'Almeida's turn. He kept it short and sharp.

"The golden thread of English justice is the presumption of innocence. It is for the prosecution to prove the case against the accused beyond reasonable doubt. On the charge of murder, the prosecution's evidence is entirely circumstantial and open to reasonable doubt. For this reason alone, the charge must fail. But we do not rely upon this negative lack of proof. We rely on the positive evidence that this honourable court has heard, that Lieutenant Habibullah did not fire the shot that killed Lieutenant-Colonel Holmes, that he did not encourage his men to do so and that, far from rejoicing in the deed, he was forced to assume command by the exigencies of war and the pressure of events. Lieutenant Habibullah cannot be convicted of murder merely because he was there. On the charge of murder, he is factually as well as legally innocent.

"On the charge of waging war against the King-Emperor, may I direct this court's attention to another man who was a soldier in the service of the Crown. He campaigned with the British Army against the King's enemies. But when Great Britain's rule over his country became oppressive, his people rose against the colonial power. This man joined the revolution and rose to lead it. His name was George Washington.

"The custom of nations recognises the right of a colonised people to fight for their freedom. The custom of nations also allows soldiers to struggle against an occupying power, as General Washington did. Great Britain has indeed confirmed that custom during the War. General de Gaulle refused to lay down his arms despite the orders of his government. He created a government-in-exile and a Free French army. That government and army were recognised, hosted and supported by Great Britain, as were so many other governments-in-exile of countries under occupation by hostile powers.

"We have also heard the testimony of Miss Sim Moy Yin. She is a Japanese subject. But she took up arms against the power that occupied and colonised her country. She fought for her country, side-by-side with the patriots who came back to Malaya at the behest of the British, and who gave their lives in the cause. Miss Sim is not a traitor. She is a freedom fighter and has been recognised as such by the allies of Great Britain, China and America.

"Lieutenant Habibullah Khan is not a traitor to the Crown. He was a member of an army that fought against Great Britain, that is true. But that army owed allegiance to the Azri Hukumat-e-Azad Hind, the Provisional Government of Free India, a government properly constituted by the law of nations, albeit in opposition to Great Britain. That government and that army were allied to the Empire of Japan, but this fact alone does not make them illegal. The Azri Hukumat-e-Azad Hind was as much a legitimate government-in-exile as that of General de Gaulle. The Azad Hind Fauj was the army of that government. Lieutenant Habibullah Khan was a member of that army. He fought honourably as a soldier in a proper uniform, in a regular unit, in open battle with the forces of Great Britain. We may decry his choice of allies, but this alone does not make him a traitor. He is a prisoner of war. He should be treated as such."

There was an attempt at applause from the gallery at the conclusion of d'Almeida's speech, but that was suppressed instantly. The judges rose and left the courtroom. There was nothing to do but wait. And wait we did for most of the afternoon. By 4 o'clock my stomach was growling for tea and I had given up hope of a verdict that day. Then came the news that the judges were ready. We hurriedly resumed our seats. Outside, the rain came down in torrents and the thunder shook the building.

Colonel Huntly's face was set in granite as he took his place. Habibullah was instructed to stand. He rose and stood stiffly to attention, his empty sleeve flapping slightly under the fan.

"Lieutenant Habibullah Khan," intoned Colonel Huntly solemnly, " you have been charged with the wilful murder of your commanding officer Lieutenant-Colonel Reginald Holmes. This court has considered the evidence tendered both for and against you very carefully. It is our unanimous opinion that you are not guilty of the charge."

There was a hubbub of approval, quickly suppressed.

"On the second charge of waging war against the King-Emperor, we have also considered the evidence on both sides. It is accepted that you took up arms against the Crown in an attempt to rid India of its current sovereign. Your counsel has eloquently put the case on your behalf in terms of a struggle for independence. However, these fine words cannot change the fact that you have betrayed the trust placed in you as an officer of the Indian Army in time of war. Whatever your motives may have been, it is clear beyond doubt that you have waged war against His Majesty the King-Emperor. The penalty for this is death ..."

The watching crowd erupted in total pandemonium.

31

IT took the combined efforts of the redcaps and the Paras to restore order. For a moment I thought there would be a riot. Out of the corner of my eye I saw Nisar Ahmad exit the courtroom along with a dozen others before the doors were shut. Habibullah remained totally calm throughout. He had been expecting this. Selwyn-Jones looked triumphant. D'Almeida was inscrutable. As far as I knew, this was the first time that a client of his had been sentenced to death. He betrayed no reaction. He was practically the only one.

When things had settled down somewhat, Colonel Huntly resumed. "As I was saying before I was so rudely interrupted," he continued, glaring severely at the spectators in the gallery, "this court finds Lieutenant Habibullah Khan guilty of the charge of waging war against the King-Emperor. The penalty for this is death. But we are fully cognizant of the circumstances under which Lieutenant Habibullah Khan joined the Indian National Army. We have heard of the assistance that he provided to the anti-Japanese resistance in Malaya. We are satisfied that he has spoken the truth when he said that he did not share the war aims of the Japanese. It is reprehensible that he should have turned his back on his former comrades and fought against them. We understand why he did so, but we cannot condone it. Nonetheless, in view of the extenuating circumstances so forcefully urged upon this court by counsel for the defence, it is our unanimous verdict that the sentence of death shall be suspended ..."

There was a collective gasp from the gallery. Colonel Huntly stopped and stared around the room. A hush descended.

"The sentence of death shall be suspended and the accused shall be banished from India. As long as he does not set foot within the bounds of India and the Crown Colony of Ceylon, the sentence shall remain suspended. Should he be apprehended within those limits, the full sentence will be carried out. He is to be dishonourably discharged from the service of His Majesty the King-Emperor and forfeit all pay, privileges and honours."

"In view of the sensitivity of this trial, we have taken the unusual step of informing the Supreme Allied Commander, Southeast Asia of our verdict before announcing it in open court. We trust that counsel will not think us lacking in courtesy in so doing." Here Colonel Huntly paused to look at d'Almeida, who stood and responded, "We are very much obliged to your Honours."

Huntly nodded in acknowledgment and continued, "We were informed by the Supreme Allied Commander that a letter has been received from His Highness the Rajah of Bhurtpore, asking that the life of the prisoner be spared on condition that he remain in exile. It is with satisfaction that we note that our verdict accords with the wishes of His Highness. The Supreme Allied Commander has indicated his concurrence. The prisoner is hereby discharged."

The court rose. This time there was no containing the outpouring of elation. The crowd surged forward towards Habibullah, who had descended from the dock. Hands were patting him on the shoulder, on the back, shaking his good hand. We fought our way through the scrum towards the door, the MPs pushing the mass of humanity aside. The torrent of rain hadn't dampened the spirits of the crowd, who were chanting in Hindustani. That and the din of the rain and thunder made conversation impossible. At last we reached the Registry and practically fell through the door. "Congratulations," I said breathlessly to Habibullah, having had the wind squeezed out of me by the press of humanity. He sat in a chair with d'Almeida, almost in a daze. "Am I free to go?" he asked unbelievingly.

"Yes," replied d'Almeida, "as soon as the paperwork is done. It should not take more than an hour or so."

"Mr d'Almeida," said Habibullah quietly, "I owe my life to you. What can I do to repay you?" Beneath the exterior calm I could see that his emotions were boiling.

"There is nothing that I wish for myself," replied d'Almeida, "but you can be of great service to a certain young person."

JUNE was already at the steps of d'Almeida's house when we got back, waiting in anticipation. Her eyes widened in surprise when she saw Habibullah with us. No one had any real hope that he would cheat the gallows, even with d'Almeida defending. "Where is Miss Barron?" d'Almeida asked her immediately as we got out of the car.

"In the garden," replied June, "Some wild man with red eyes who could not speak came to the gate just before you arrived. He gave me a note for her. She cried and went off to the bower with her favourite Tennyson book."

"That must have been Nisar Ahmad," said Habibullah. "When you brought him to me I gave him a farewell note to pass to her. Forgive me Mr d'Almeida, I thought there was no hope at the time."

"That Tennyson book," d'Almeida asked June with a look of grave concern, "is it the *The Lady of Shallot*?"

"Yes it is, why?" she replied.

"I trust we are not too late," he said in a voice tinged with alarm, "we must hurry. You have secured all the poisons and ropes?"

"Yes, as you instructed, but why? What is going on?" asked June plaintively as we rushed out into the garden.

"Do you know the poem?" responded d'Almeida. June shook her head. He quoted,

"For ere she reached upon the tide
The first house by the water-side
Singing in her song she died,
The Lady of Shalott.

"The bower is surrounded by oleander shrubs. The leaves are poisonous. I fear the worst."

D'Almeida had four acres of garden. The bower was as far from the house as it was possible to get. The path to it was deliberately winding, edged with bamboo and shrubs to give it privacy. It seemed an eternity before we got there. She was sitting with her back to us. In her hand was a mug. She lifted it up.

"Stop!" yelled Habibullah. "For God's sake, don't drink that!"

It was too late. She had swallowed the contents of the mug. She turned in wide-eyed surprise as Habibullah bounded into the bower.

"You're alive!" she exclaimed. She buried her head in his chest. "I'm so glad. When the note came … I thought … I thought it was all over."

"Oh Marge, Marge," he cried, holding her tightly, "why did you have to do it? Why did you drink that infernal brew?"

She raised her head in astonishment. "That infernal brew? Horlicks? I always drink Horlicks when I'm upset."

We practically collapsed with relief.

WE were all gathered in the library, Ahmad included. D'Almeida was speaking.

"Miss Barron, I know that this is very sudden, but we could not put it to you before this afternoon. In the eyes of the common law you are still a minor. But as far as Shariah law is concerned, you achieved your majority with puberty. By Shariah law you have capacity to marry. Enchik Ahmad, your *wali*, has indicated his consent. If you choose to marry, there will be no question of your aunt Miss Rider taking you into her guardianship."

Habibullah spoke. "Marge, my dear," he said, "it did not cross my mind to ask you before, with the sentence of death hanging over my head. Now that that threat is gone, there is nothing I would desire more than for you to accept me as your husband."

Marge hesitated. "You're just asking because he told you to," she answered in a soft voice.

"No," replied Habibullah with emotion, "not just because Mr d'Almeida asked. It is true that it did not occur to me until he suggested it. But now that it has been suggested, I ask you sincerely to be my wife."

"But I don't ... I don't love you," she said in an even softer voice.

"Could you learn to do so?" he asked earnestly. "That is all that is necessary. I promise to protect and take care of you. It would kill me to see you taken back to England against your will."

"Take your time, Miss Barron," said d'Almeida. "A decision like this should not be rushed. But please remember that the sands are slipping through the hourglass. Your aunt Miss Rider has applied to have you taken into custody as soon as possible. My information is that the application has already been approved."

Marge looked up suddenly. "I'll do it," she said.

"Are you sure?" asked June gently. "No need to decide just like that."

"Yes," she said determinedly, "I ... I'm sure." She turned to

Habibullah. "I know that we haven't known each other long, but I feel that you're a good man. I don't love you, but I could learn. Is that enough for you?"

He took her hands in his. "It is enough for me, my dear," he said tenderly. "You will be the flower of my life from henceforward." There was something of the Persian poet in his soul, which I had not seen before.

She turned to Ahmad and asked in Malay, "*Ayah*, do I have your blessing?"

Ahmad's eyes were moist. "You have my blessings, my child. Go in the hands of God. May his peace be upon you."

It was all very touching. D'Almeida broke the spell. "Now," he said decisively, "we must act. The wedding cannot take place in this house. Indeed, it would be hard to hold it anywhere in the Colony. We must get you both out." He turned to me. "Come," he said, "we have much to do and little time to do it."

WITH the rain dusk had come early that day. We belted out the gate of d'Almeida's house without headlights and without looking out for traffic. We barrelled past the two jeeps before they could react. The old Morris was straining. Ahmad had done wonders over the months, carefully rebuilding the engine. Now we would see what the old girl could do.

The jeeps were on tail soon enough. If the weather had been clear we would have had no chance at all. But the canvas covers on the jeeps hardly kept the rain out. The drivers were deluged and blinded. The windscreen wipers on the Morris were working at full blast but I still could hardly see the way ahead. Bukit Timah Road was under six inches of water in some places. At one point the water extended for a couple of hundred yards on either side of the road, like a great marsh. It was difficult to determine where the road ended and the canal began. Fortunately, there were street lamps on one side. I kept as close to the centre as I dared, hoping that the engine wouldn't stall. We ploughed through the flood in a wave of white water.

At the junction with Holland Road another jeep joined our little procession. This one was better weatherproofed but we had a head start and maintained our lead. We were heading due north towards the Causeway and Johore. Johore was legally a sovereign state, not British territory. All we had to do was make it over the halfway point on the Causeway. We would then be in the Sultan's dominions. The British wouldn't dare try anything there, given the delicate state of relations after the furore over the Malayan Union proposals.

The road was in almost total darkness. The only light was provided by our anaemic headlamps. We passed the occasional cluster of houses, which allowed us to see the road better. Beyond Bukit Panjang, the houses disappeared. There were rubber plantations to either side of us. It was impossible to see anything except the thin sliver of road illuminated by the weak light of the headlamps. The darkness was our ally; I knew the road well enough, but our pursuers had to be careful not to stray onto the soft clay on the verges. That kept their speed down. The road was slick with rain and potholes appeared out of the night with alarming suddenness. We rounded a bend and there in the distance was the bright ribbon of the Causeway ahead of us, lighted along its length in a way that had not been seen for many years. My worry was the petrol gauge; the needle moved inexorably towards "empty". The rain had ceased. I coaxed the engine into one last heroic spurt.

There were no checkpoints or guards on the Causeway. Both ends were in friendly territory. No artificial frontier separated Singapore Island from its hinterland. On either side of the road was the sea. The railroad and water pipes ran alongside into the gloom at the farther end. We reached the marker in the centre and I eased off the accelerator, not wanting to burn up what little remained of our fuel. It was a mistake. The lead jeep roared past us and pulled up ahead, blocking our way. I jammed on the brakes. The two other jeeps screeched to a halt just behind, disgorging half a dozen soliders with sten guns at the ready. A figure emerged from the front jeep, revolver in hand.

"Out!" he commanded. I recognised him. It was Major Ridley. When I showed no signs of moving, he pointed his gun at me and repeated, "Get out now!"

I got out of the car slowly, my hands in the air. "You've no right to do this," I said heatedly, "we're not in the Colony anymore."

Without a word Ridley went over and wrenched open the passenger door. "Get out!" he commanded again.

My passenger emerged, her *tudung* clapsed around her face like a veil. I protested once more, "You're overstepping your authority, Ridley. You can't arrest us here. We're in Johore. The Sultan will have your guts."

"Don't try any of your lawyer's tricks," he addressed me belligerently. "I know exactly where we are. The moment my lads told me that you and the girl had taken off I knew where you were going. I don't give a hoot whether we're still in the Colony or not. It's all British territory. Now Miss Barron, we're going to take you home where you belong, with your people and not with this sorry lot."

At that moment, the wind caught the *tudung* and blew it wide. Ridley recoiled. "Why do you stop us?" demanded June. "We have done nothing wrong."

THE rain had died down to a light drizzle. Ridley had slunk off with his tail between his legs, still snapping though. "You think you've been very clever," he growled between clenched teeth. "Next time this happens, we'll put the girl in a convent first."

I riposted by complaining loudly about brazen interference with private rights and threatened to sue for false imprisonment. He didn't apologise, but he didn't make any more trouble either. I drove into Johore Bahru and did a quick U-turn on the deserted road. We retraced our path slowly, avoiding the worst of the potholes. The flood had receded somewhat so the going was better. By the time we got back to the house it was past nine o'clock.

It was only when I pulled up under the porch that I realised that all the lights were blazing. The lights were never all on at the same time, not unless something had happened. Fearing the worst, June skipped out the moment the car stopped. She bounded up the stairs two at a time and through the open front door into the hall. Mak, Ah Sum, Gek Neo and Augusta fell on her immediately. I joined them as soon as I had parked the car. There were floods of tears to match the floodwaters we had just been through. "What's going on?" I demanded perplexed.

June was crying too. She gestured at the hall table. A telegram lay there. "Telegram," she sobbed, "from Japan."

My heart sank. As long as we had no news, there was still hope that Julie was alive. "It's Julie isn't it," I said, my throat constricting with emotion. "Hell and damnation! Of all things, to get the bad news on New Year's Eve like this."

"No, you *gobblock*," said June, laughing through her tears. "Julie is safe. The telegram from Japan says it. They were not in Nagasaki when the bomb fell. They are safe!" The five of them surrounded and inundated me with tears and hugs.

32

WE had a celebratory feast that New Year's Day, rationing or no rationing. Mak and Gek Neo performed culinary miracles with what we had. D'Almeida, Cuthbert and Simon were there, together with George and Ralph. We ate and drank as if we had no cares in the world; which was entirely true, at least for the moment.

"So, did Marge and Habibullah get off all right?" I asked George after we had both stuffed ourselves sufficiently.

"Like a charm," replied George, wiping the crumbs off his shirt. "The moment the Britishers saw your car zoom past, both jeeps took off after you. We got Habibullah and Marge out in the Humber under a couple of blankets. Karim was waiting with his *prahu* at Pasir Panjang. Ahmad said that there was no problem pushing off despite the swell."

"Our minders must have called Ridley on their walkie-talkies," I contributed, "he turned up after Holland Road, mad as hell. I don't think it ever crossed his mind that Marge might be heading south and not north."

"They're in Tanjong Pinang, right?" asked Ralph.

"Right," answered George. "Karim's half-brothers are there. They'll arrange the *akad nikah* and *bersanding* ceremony and do everything right and proper. Ahmad and the rest of his family will join them shortly. Once Marge is legally married there's no way Miss Rider can get her hot little paws on her."

"Will it stick?" asked Ralph doubtfully. "After all, she was baptised a Christian."

"She's been brought up as a Muslim," said George. "Uncle Clarence says that it's fine. Anyway, it counts as a valid Muslim marriage even if she's a Christian. There's a word that Uncle Clarence used … *kitabiyyah*, people of the book. A Muslim man can validly marry a *kitabiyyah.*"

"Still, I can't help feeling sorry for Marge," said Ralph reflectively. "She hardly knows him. It's a big step to take. And she'll be living in a foreign land."

"He's a good man," I assured him. "He'll take proper care of her. She could do much worse."

Ralph cleared his throat. "I've got some news too."

We looked at him expectantly. "Well, spit it out!"

"I've signed on," he said simply.

"Signed on!" exclaimed George. "What did you go and do that for?"

"Well," replied Ralph, "they offered me a job after my mob was demobbed. At the legal department of ALFSEA HQ here in Singapore. It's court work and it means an extra pip. I'll have to leave the firm though."

"Leave the firm!" said George. "Give up your career! You must be barmy."

Ralph glanced at me. He knew I understood. "It was too good a chance to miss," he said without elaboration. "And it means I can bring May and Grace home. They'll be giving me a house and a car."

I grasped his hand and shook it warmly. "That's marvellous! Have you told Mak and the girls? May and Baby Grace coming home. And Julie safe. Our little circle's whole again."

Mak and the girls were ecstatic at the news. Gek Neo went off to tell all the neighbours. Augusta snapped completely out of the depression that had gripped her. June was positively bubbling.

I gazed around contentedly. The new year was starting well. Then I saw a figure under a tree in the garden, staring in through the open windows. It was Eng Tong.

"YOU'VE got some nerve coming here after trying to kill me!" I said heatedly, confronting Eng Tong.

"I try to kill you? Where got?" he responded.

"Don't you play dumb with me," I answered with passion, "you took a pot shot at me outside the courthouse. Poor Ward took the bullet instead."

"I want to kill you for what?" he retorted, his brow furrowed. "I only want to talk to June."

D'Almeida had joined me on the verandah. "You swear you did not shoot at Mr Chiang here?"

"Towkay," replied Eng Tong, "I promise I never shoot at anybody. What for I want to kill him?"

"Where have you been these past weeks then? Why did you run off?"

"Towkay, sorry-lah," he said with apparent contrition, "I scared you angry because I lie about that bastard Lim Tay Lin. I know you find out after you talk to him. Then I also go and look for work so I can marry June."

"You were looking for a job!" I exclaimed. "You had a job and ran out on it. You left me high and dry."

"I need a better job," he replied. "Now I work for *ang-moh*. I am chief clerk at a company. I will ask June to marry me."

"It was a wicked thing that you did, trying to get Lim hanged as Nakamura," said d'Almeida severely.

Eng Tong hung his head. D'Almeida stroked his chin. "It seems that he speaks the truth," he said. "This eliminates one of the two possibilities. I trust we are not too late."

"Too late?" I exclaimed. "Too late for what?"

"Too late to stop another killing," he replied shortly and strode off. I knew better than to press for an immediate explanation. Collecting George on the way, we piled into the Humber and sped off.

THE Chapel of Our Lady was a simple wooden structure, built somewhat like a barn. It was one of several chapels that the European POWs had been allowed by the Japanese to put up during their captivity. This one was fairly elaborate, with the framework of a belfry and a series of hand-painted stations of the cross. D'Almeida had explained his conjectures on the drive out to Changi.

"So no one was really after me?" I asked, just to be sure.

"No, I am fairly sure that the target was not you," explained d'Almeida. "When Yeo said that he did not shoot at you, there were only two other reasonable possibilities: firstly, that it was some anonymous person who had some unknown reason to want you dead; or secondly, that the assailant wanted to kill Second-Lieutenant Ward. I eliminate the first as unlikely. This leaves us the second possibility."

"Why Ward?" asked George. "What harm did he do?"

"None, personally," replied d'Almeida, "unless again there is an unknown killer with a grudge. But young Lieutenant Ward was a member of the regiment that perpetrated the massacre at Parit Batang. I surmise that the killer is out for revenge for that event. This seems to be the only plausible explanation."

"Poor Ward," I said with feeling. "He wasn't even there. He must still have been in school when it happened."

"People who seek vengence of this sort rarely think of such things," said d'Almeida. "It is enough that he was associated with the regiment. And now we must try to stop the killer striking again."

"How can you be sure that he will strike again?" queried George.

"I cannot be absolutely sure," answered d'Almeida, "but if I am correct, the memorial mass will be the ideal place. All the survivors of the North Anglians will be there. Perhaps even some of those responsible for the massacre."

By the time we got there the mass had already commenced. The interior was packed. The large windows were shut on account of the rain, which was coming down in a steady curtain. It was stifling inside. D'Almeida moved to the front pew, instructing me and George to take our places at the side. I looked around as I sat. There was a sea of khaki and jungle green. All the faces were white. As far as I could see, no one there stood out as a possible assassin.

Church services have a soporific effect on me. This one was no exception. With the windows closed the heat was intense. There were no fans. Everyone was sweating buckets. The chanting and the incense made things worse. I could stand it no longer. I bolted for the door before I fainted.

The drizzle outside was a welcome relief. There was a breeze too. I lifted up my face to catch the raindrops. Looking up at the roof of the chapel, I spotted a dark figure hunched in the makeshift belfry. He was poised right above the entrance. Soon the coffin would be brought out. That would be the ideal time to strike. There would be no escape for him, but he could cause mayhem below.

I looked around for help. There was no one in sight. A ladder stood against the wall. That was the only way up. I clambered up as fast as I dared, trying to make no noise. There was a ledge that ran around the roof of the building. Gingerly, I crept forward, praying that he would not turn around. From below came the sounds of the mass sonorously intoned by the priest.

"*Agnus dei, qui tollis peccata mundi, dona eis requiem*."

The wind was strong and I nearly lost my footing. The sound of the rain on the wooden roof hid my approach.

"*Agnus dei, qui tollis peccata mundi, dona eis requiem*."

I was upon him before he realised that I was there. He had a hand grenade. The pin was out. We struggled. It was wet underfoot.

"*Agnus dei, qui tollis peccata mundi, dona eis requiem sempiternem*."

We slipped. The next thing I knew, the ground was hurtling towards me.

"WHAT is this strange affinity that you have for hand grenades?" asked George. "You seem to be attracted to them constantly."

I was lying on my hospital bed. I grimaced at him.

"Does it hurt much?" asked Ralph.

"Only when I laugh," I replied.

"Don't laugh then," said George unsympathetically. "You'll be all right. It's only a couple of cracked ribs. Which is a damned sight better than what happened to Nisar Ahmad when you fell on top of him."

I wasn't in the mood to be concerned about Nisar Ahmad. "He's dead, I suppose?"

"As a doornail," replied George. "So would you be, if the grenade hadn't been a dud. Seems he got it from the little store you left with Simon."

"How'd he manage that?" I asked. My ribcage was itchy. I shifted to a more comfortable position.

"As far as we've been able to make out, after Huntly pronounced sentence he delivered Habibullah's note to June, then went right back to our office, sneaked past Singh the *jaga*, got into Simon's filing cabinet and swiped the whole lot. We found the sack in the belfry. There were at least a dozen of the things. He intended to go out in a blaze of glory, literally."

"That seems a bit extreme," commented Ralph, "seeing as he wasn't directly affected by what the North Anglians did."

"It was more than that," interrupted a voice from the door. D'Almeida had made his usual unexpected entrance. "Nisar Ahmad had left immediately when Colonel Huntly pronounced the death sentence on Habibullah. He did not wait to hear the conclusion, which was suspension of the sentence. This attack was meant to be revenge for the sentence of death pronounced on his master. He confided in one of the men who left with him that he did not intend to survive. I am sure that he meant to kill all the officers who participated in the court-martial, along with all the survivors of the North Anglians and any other British officers who happened to be there for good measure."

"He wouldn't have succeeded," I replied, "not with the dud grenades Helen gave me. If I'd known I wouldn't have risked my neck."

"He did not know that and neither did you," said d'Almeida. "It was a brave thing that you did. I have spoken with Cuthbert and Simon da Silva. We are agreed. When you come back, it will be as a junior partner."

I was overwhelmed. "Mr d'Almeida," I exclaimed, "what can I say?"

"Say nothing, my boy," he replied, "just get well. I'll not trouble you now. Come in next Monday and we can discuss the details. I must take my leave now. A little matter of a sack of hand grenades, you understand. And there is Mr Yeo Eng Tong to settle with."

"He's not given June any trouble?" I asked anxiously.

"No, I think not," replied d'Almeida. "I understand that she made her position quite clear and he has accepted the rebuff as a gentleman should. But he has performed services for the firm. For this he should be paid."

After he left, George and Ralph started pumping my arms. My chest hurt but I felt good. A sudden thought struck me. "What am I going to call him now? I can't keep on calling him Mr d'Almeida. Can I?"

"You could call him Clarence. Or Uncle Clarence, if that makes it any better," suggested George helpfully.

I turned it over in my mind. Clarence … Uncle Clarence … it just didn't seem right. "I suppose I'll figure it out. Eventually. In the meantime, I'll just follow your lead," I said to George.

"Ah …" responded George, going uncharacteristically solemn all of a sudden, "I wouldn't count on that. I'm going."

"Going? What do you mean you're going? Going where?" I exclaimed.

"To Delhi," he answered. "Clarence was good enough to write me a letter of introduction to a friend of his."

I was stunned. "To Delhi! Why in the name of heaven do you want to leave now? We're just getting back on our feet. We need you here. There's so much to do in the firm … here in the Colony."

"What would I do here in the Colony except get thrown into the clanger for trying to overthrow the Raj?" asked George. "I can do that better in Delhi. There's a brave new world out there and the wind is changing. I want to be where the action is."

I said nothing, just sat there and clasped his hand. He was right. The wind was changing. Thunder rumbled in the distance. Outside the window the watery evening sun broke through the rainclouds.

GLOSSARY

Adek	Younger brother or sister. Generally, any younger person.
ALFSEA	Allied Land Forces South East Asia.
Akad nikah	Solemnisation ceremony of a Malay wedding.
Ang-moh	European, in the local slang.
Anjung	Covered porch at the front of a Malay house.
Apa khabar?	Literally, "what news?": the normal Malay greeting.
Ashigaru	The lowest class of men-at-arms in feudal Japan.
Azad Hind	Free India.
Azad Hind Fauj	The Indian National Army.
Azri Hukumat-e-Azad Hind	The Provisional Government of Free India.
Baba	Straits-born Chinese.
Babu	Derogatory term for an English-speaking Indian.
Baju kurung	Malay dress consisting of a sarong and loose blouse.
BEF	British Expeditionary Force.
Belukar	Secondary forest.
Bersanding	Malay customary marriage ceremony.
BIA	Burma Independence Army
BMA	British Military Administration, the military government of Malaya.

Bunkentai	A unit of roughly 20 men led by a lieutenant or warrant-officer.
Bushido	Literally, "the way of the warrior"; the code of the samurai.
Chachiru kyoyu	"Churchill rations", the Japanese term for the supplies left behind by the retreating British forces.
Changkul	A mattock used for tilling the soil.
CO	Commanding Officer.
Dhobi	Laundryman
DUKW	US-made amphibious truck.
Getai	Chinese song and dance troupe
Giyu-gun	Volunteer Army formed by the Japanese to defend Malaya.
Giyu-hei	Member of the *Giyu-gun*.
Gobblock	Idiot in the local *Baba* patois.
Hantu	Ghosts, spirits.
Hara-kiri	Ritual suicide, traditionally by disembowelment.
Hari Raya Puasa	The feast of Eid, celebrated at the end of the fasting month of Ramadan.
Havildar	Indian Army NCO equivalent to a sergeant.
Heiho	Auxiliary service set up by the Japanese as a labour corps.
Hinomaru	The rising sun flag of Japan.
Hojo Kempeitai	Kempeitai auxiliaries, recruited from Formosa and Korea.
Ikan bilis	Local anchovies, used extensively in Malay and Nonya cuisine.
ICO	Indian Commisioned Officer, a graduate of Dehra Dun.

INA	Indian National Army.
Jaga	Watchman, very often a Sikh.
Jawan	Private soldier in the Indian Army, formerly known as a sepoy.
Jemadar	Lowest commissioned rank in the Indian Army, a Viceroy's Commissioned Officer.
Jepun	Japan, Japanese.
Jif	British term for INA troops, from the designation "Japanese-Indian fifth columnist".
Jikeidan	Home guard formed by the Japanese in each town.
Kak	Short for *kakak*, elder sister. A polite term of address.
Kati	Measure of weight, equivalent to approximately 600 grams.
KC	King's Counsel.
KCO	King's Commissioned Officer, Indian graduate of Sandhurst.
Kebun	Gardener, usually Malay.
Kelong	Fishing trap built on stilts in the sea.
Kempei	Member of the Kempeitai.
Kempeitai	Japanese security police, officially part of the armed forces
Ketua Kampong	Village headman.
Kitabiyyah	Literally, "people of the book", viz, Christians and Jews.
Kueh	Malay or Nonya sweetmeats.
Lakh	One hundred thousand.
Lallang	Razor grass.
Lathi	Stout stick used as a weapon.
MCP	Malayan Communist Party

MP	Military Police.
MPAJA	Malayan Peoples' Anti-Japanese Army – the Chinese Communist-dominated resistance movement in Malaya.
NCO	Non-commissioned officer.
Nippon-jin	Japanese person or subject.
Nisei	Second-generation American-born Japanese.
Nonya	A female *Baba*.
OBI	Order of British India. The award of the OBI First Class carried with it the title of Sardar Bahadur.
OC	Officer commanding.
OCAJA	Overseas Chinese Anti-Japanese Army, the non-communist resistance.
Orang Puteh	Literally, "white man". All Europeans were *Orang Puteh*.
OSS	Office of Strategic Services, the predecessor of the Central Intelligence Agency.
Pak Chik	"Uncle" in Malay. General polite term of address for any older male person, whether or not a relative.
Parang	Machete.
Pasal	Business, affair.
Penghulu	District headman, above the *ketua kampong*.
Potong jalan	Literally, "cut into the path".
Prahu	Malay wooden fishing boat.
Purna swaraj	Full independence, in particular for India.
RAF	Royal Air Force.
RAAF	Royal Australian Air Force.
Redcap	Slang for a British military policeman.
SACSEA	Supreme Allied Commander, Southeast Asia.

Samseng	A bad character.
See-hum	Cockles.
Sepoy	Private soldier in the Indian Army, later known as a *jawan*.
Sepukku	Hara-kiri, ritual suicide by disembowelment.
Shin gunto	Military sword, generally of indifferent quality, as contrasted to a true samurai's *katana* or *tachi*.
Sinkhek	China-born Chinese, as compared to the Straits-born *Babas*.
SOE	Special Operations Executive, the British department that coordinated resistance movements in occupied territories.
Sook Ching	The operation in February 1942 to purge Singapore of anti-Japanese Chinese.
STC	Singapore Traction Company, the major public bus company.
Subedar	In the Indian Army, a Viceroy's Commissioned Officer one rank higher than a *jemadar*.
Subedar-major	The most senior subedar in a battalion.
Surau	A prayer house, smaller than a mosque.
Syonan Tokubetusi	Singapore municipal government during the Japanese Occupation.
Tokoka	Japanese political police. A branch of the Kempeitai originally.
Towkay	Boss or rich businessman.
Tudung	Malay woman's headscarf.
ulu	Literally, the headwaters of a river. Figuratively, an out-of-the-way place.
VCO	Viceroy's Commissioned Officer, viz., a *jemadar*, subedar or subedar-major.
Wazir	Chief minister of a princely state.
Yukata	Informal kimono, worn by men or women.

ABOUT THE AUTHOR

Walter Woon was educated at the National University of Singapore and St John's College. Cambridge. He has been at various times the Sub-Dean and Vice-Dean of the NUS Law Faculty, a nominated Member of Parliament, a director of two listed companies, legal adviser to the President, ambassador to several European countries, Solicitor-General and Attorney-General. He is presently a Senior Counsel, David Marshall Professor of Law at the NUS Law Faculty and Dean of the Singapore Institute of Legal Education.

He is married with two sons.

The Devil's Circle is the latest installment of *The Advocate's Devil* Trilogy.

OTHER BOOKS BY WALTER WOON

The Advocate's Devil

Dennis Chiang is a stranger in his homeland. Just returned to the Straits Settlements after spending half his life in England, the young lawyer is thrown into the swirling brew that is colonial society in 1930s Singapore. It is a society of *tuans* and *towkays*, of *Babas* and *babus*, where race is everything and even love cannot be wholly colour-blind.

As he juggles his career and personal responsibilities, Chiang encounters a life full of courtroom dramas, cultural prejudices and even communist intrigue. And never far away is his mentor, the unflappable d'Almeida. In public d'Almeida is a calm, efficient lawyer, but he possesses a shrewd investigative streak and uses unorthodox methos that result in his young protégé being caught up in a succession of captivating adventures.

Welcome to the world of The Advocate's Devil, a humourous, fast-moving tale set against the backdrop of colonial Singapore and the Straits Settlements — a world that Dennis Chiang soon finds is full of excitement, disillusionment and danger.

The Devil to Pay

Set in the period just before the Fall of Singapore, this story —the second in the trilogy — unfolds in a time of great uncertainty as news of an impending Japanese invasion looms. Dennis Chiang returns as the young and eager lawyer at d'Almeida's law firm. But little does he know that his life would soon become a lot more exciting — and dangerous.

Roped in by the British Special Branch as an undercover operative to weed out Japanese agents subverting and undermining the morale of an Indian Army garrison sent to defend Malaya, CHiang finds himself going from criminal lawyer in a courtroom to an adept and rugged spy in the jungles of Malaya. This fast-paced and absorbing tale of adventure and espionage will get you hooked from the get-go.